The Long Count

A John Q Mystery

JM GULVIN

FABER & FABER

First published in 2016
by Faber & Faber Ltd
Bloomsbury House
74–77 Great Russell Street
London WC1B 3DA

Typeset by Faber & Faber Ltd
Printed and bound by CPI Group (UK) Ltd, Croydon CR0 4YY

A CIP record for this book
is available from the British Library

ISBN 978–0–571–32378–4

FSC
www.fsc.org
MIX
Paper from
responsible sources
FSC® C101712

2 4 6 8 10 9 7 5 3 1

Born in the UK, JM Gulvin divides his time between Wales and the western United States. He is the author of many previous novels, as well as Ewan McGregor and Charley Boorman's bestselling travel book *Long Way Down*. *The Long Count* is his first John Q mystery and he is currently at work on the follow up. He is married and has two daughters.

WITHDRAWN

Sandy, this is for John.
1948–2014

I'd like to say a big thank you to Robert Kirby and Ben Camardi
who helped develop this every step of the way.

Also,

Angus Cargill, Katherine Armstrong and everyone at Faber &
Faber.

Matthew & Pamela White for all their support.

My daughters Amy & Chloe for the Father's Day cards
and the map of San Saba County.

And,

A very special thanks to my wife Kim,
who continues to back me come what may.

One

Leaving the door wide open he stepped out into the night. A brief glance left and right, he walked the shadows to the wheat fields and disappeared into the crop. No wind, no stars in the sky, just cloud the color of smoke.

Beyond the fields he crossed the railroad tracks, heading for the depot lights. Sleeveless Levi soaked in sweat; he made the platform where his gaze fixed on a Coca-Cola machine. Nobody following, nobody heading this way, there was no one in the waiting room. All he could see was a wooden bench, a clock on the wall above the door; no water fountain to quench his thirst.

Searching his pockets he found no nickel, no dime. He studied that Coke machine as if debating whether to give it a thump, then his attention was diverted to the end of the platform where a set of headlights spilled across the rails.

Inside the waiting room he sat on the bench. He did not move. He listened to the sound of footfall as, slowly, someone approached. He watched the glow of a flashlight before it was echoed by the shadow of a man. Moments later the door swung open and his gaze fastened on a holstered gun.

Still he sat there. He could see the cop's shoes, dust on the toes, the hem of his trouser leg. Finally he lifted his head. Dark hair curled from under his cap, He was broad in the chest and heavy in the arms where they bulged from the sleeves of his pale blue shirt. A badge above his left breast, cap peak high. They considered one another and neither of them spoke. The cop's right hand hung loose at his thigh, and he studied that hand, long fingers, dirt under the nails, where it hung just ahead of the gun.

Working his jaws across a piece of gum the cop looked him up and down. 'What're you doing here, boy?'

From where he sat he could see the clock fixed on the wall. 'I'm waiting on the four-oh-five.'

'You seem a little sweaty, like you been running or something. Who are you? What's your name?'

'My name isn't anybody's business but mine.'

The cop expelled a breath. 'Two in the morning at the railroad depot and he's waiting on the four-oh-five. Are you kidding me, boy? All soaked in sweat and you ain't giving up your name?'

'Mister, I'm just set here waiting on a train.'

The cop stared at him with his fingers twitching at his thigh. 'I'll ask you again: what's your name?'

He said nothing. He stared at the floor and the cop took a pace into the room.

'Boy,' he said, 'best you answer my questions. What're you doing here? What's your name?'

He was looking at the floor then he closed his eyes. 'I told you. I'm waiting on the four-oh-five.'

'So you must have a ticket then. Guess you can show it to me, huh?'

He shook his head. 'Going to buy me one from the conductor just as soon as I get on the train.'

'Is that a fact? So where is it you're headed then?'

'Houston, like it says on the board.'

'So what's in Houston? That where you're from?'

He looked at him. He nodded. He shook his head.

The cop furrowed his brow. 'Yes and no,' he said. 'That what you're telling me, huh?' He took a pace backwards again, occupying the gap where the door hung open and a little night air filtered in. Right hand at his side he made a beckoning motion with his left. 'I don't know who you are and I don't like the answers you're giving to my questions, so I'm going to have you come down to the station house where we can ask you a couple more.' He jerked his head. 'Come ahead now, on your feet.'

Still he sat there and still the cop looked on. 'I won't tell you a second time.' Reaching for his billy club the cop slid it loose of its sleeve.

He sat there a moment longer. Then he got to his feet. The cop held the door open and he stepped out onto the platform where, apart from a couple of lamps, the darkness was complete.

They paced the length of the platform with nobody else around and no sound save the pinging of railroad steel. They were almost at the car, a blue Plymouth with four doors and a metal grille separating the front from the back. A single red light on the roof, he looked at the car and then he looked back. The cop had his holstered gun almost proffered as he reached for the door.

In the blink of an eye he had that gun out of the holster and clattered the cop over the head. On his knees, blood spilling where his skull was split, the cop tried to get up, tried to bring the Billy around but he hit him again and again. He stood above him, one leg either side, he was straddling the officer now. Stuffing the gun in the waistband of his jeans, he picked up the fallen billy club and started pounding him with it.

Finally he stopped. Soaked in sweat, hair flopping in front of his eyes, he stood straight with the club held loose at his side. There was no one around, not a sound from the sleepy little town. He looked down at the cop as blood spread the dirt in a thickening pool. He looked at the cruiser where the back door was open, then at the cap where it rested against the nearside wheel. He bent for it. He put it on his head and it fit pretty well. He took a look in the mirror fixed on the door.

Dressed in the cop's uniform, he left him in his shorts and socks. His own clothes he stuffed in a large paper sack he found in the back of the cruiser. Stowing that in the foot well on the passenger side, he climbed behind the wheel and sat for a moment with his head bowed and hands clasped in his lap.

Two

Perched on a rock, Quarrie had his shirt off and the heat of the sun on his back. Mud-colored waves danced where the breeze sculled the surface of the river; they held his attention for a moment before his gaze shifted to his son. Sitting cross-legged in the dirt James watched Pious where he too had his shirt off; six feet of middleweight muscle, he studied the water's edge.

Picking his way across the stones Quarrie came alongside and they both looked on as a trout jumped close to the bank.

'Pious,' Quarrie said, 'we got us a ranch-sized fish fry to take care of and hand fishing's illegal in Texas. You got any holes in mind this side of the river, we can't be grabbling in them.'

Pious indicated the northern shore. 'She's legal in Oklahoma, John Q, and yonder is Oklahoma. I got a place in mind a mile downstream where a train wrecked forty years back. More holes over there than you could shake a stick at, and flathead love that kind of thing.'

'Train wreck?' From where he was sitting James looked up.

'Yup.' Pious glanced over his shoulder. 'Bridge came down one night in a rainstorm and nobody knew it had happened till the train left the rails and wrecked.'

'Did anybody die?'

Pious squinted at Quarrie. 'Can't tell you that for sure on account of it was so long ago, but I don't see many getting out.'

Leaning to the side Quarrie spat. 'Hell of a place to fish for flathead, Pious. You're talking about a graveyard I guess.'

Pious pointed downriver towards the next bend. 'You want to fish this waterway with your conscience intact then the best place

4

is that wreck. You want to forget about being a Ranger for a few hours that's fine with me, because there's plenty sweet spots right here where we're at.'

Together the three of them hiked the clay-colored river that marked the border between Texas and Oklahoma, though where one state ended and the other began was still something of a moot point. Some said the border was the middle of the river itself and others the southern shore. Until a definitive statement was made by someone, Quarrie figured on halfway across.

Memorial Day, he and Pious had been talking about Korea while James asked lots of questions and he hadn't done that before. It occurred to Quarrie that for the first time maybe, he really understood.

'Pious,' the boy said, 'how come you know about this place?'

Pious looked down where James walked between him and his father. 'Fact is I found her when I first got out of Leavenworth. You were still a baby back then, only just gotten back from where you lived up in Idaho with your dad. Me, I learned how to grabble catfish when I was a kid growing up in Georgia. Fresh out of prison like that, I figured a hand-caught fish ought to taste pretty sweet, and this old boy in the cell house told me about that wreck.'

Brows knit, James looked up. 'And Leavenworth was where you were after my daddy wrote the president, right?'

'Federal penitentiary, yes it was.' Pious laid a hand on his shoulder. 'Army gave me the death sentence for disobeying an order over in Korea. I guess we done told you that. Well, your daddy was laid up in the hospital and had some time on his hands. He took to writing and after he was done the president changed that sentence to life with hard labor, and I could've been there yet.' He glanced briefly at Quarrie then. 'But nobody figured on a bunch of attorneys from back east taking my side, and they found out the government never did declare war in Korea. We told you this story, right?'

5

'Yes, you did,' James said. 'But I don't mind hearing it again. It meant it was peacetime, didn't it, on account of the president not saying how we was at war?'

'Yup, technically that's what it meant. It also meant that all they could throw my way was five years for telling an officer how I wasn't about take a bunch of soldiers I'd just gotten safe back to their certain deaths.'

'On account of all the Chinese gunfire going on?'

'Yes, James: on account of that.'

'But they sent you to prison anyway?'

'Yes, I'm afraid they did. It didn't matter that we'd been under the kind of fire where you got no choice but to fall back. Fact of the matter is I'm a black man, and back then there were plenty in the army didn't think a black man had the stomach for a fight. The captain was dead and so was the LT. It was up to me to make the decision and I brought the men off the hill. CO didn't want to hear about it, said to me how I was a coward and that I had to take those men right back.' Gesturing, he made a face. 'I told him I wasn't going to do that and if he wanted to take that hill he better pick up a gun hisself.'

They walked to where the river curved and Quarrie considered the trees crowding the Oklahoma shore. On this side the woodland was not so dense, scrubland climbing where bunch grass grew and rattlesnakes made their nests. On the other side the foliage was much thicker, with branches overhanging the water and strings of roots cutting through the mud.

The Red River: threading through the canyons that split Texas and Oklahoma, it carried mile after mile of shallow bends before forming another short border with Arkansas. As they rounded that last elbow they could see the first of the railroad cars jutting from the water, like some kind of warning perhaps. Rusting hunks of metal that seemed as old as the river itself, and Quarrie wondered if the forty years Pious had been talking about wasn't considerably more. Spilling from the Oklahoma side he could make out remnants of wall panels, bits and pieces of roof, the partial turn of a wheel, and all of it the same ochre color as the water.

Harsh-looking shanks reached up from beneath the surface, girders lying exposed where the cars had been reinforced and all that was left was the steel. It was all that remained of the train: half a dozen cars in bits that lay scattered across the banks and buckled into cottonwood trees. There was nothing left of the bridge.

Beyond the banks more bits and pieces of wreckage hugged the waterline and there was no way of telling how much metal was actually hidden underneath.

'Son,' Quarrie said to James, 'now that we're here, I ain't so sure this is the place for you to learn where to be a catfish grabbler. All that wreckage and everything. You see what we got going on?'

The boy looked up at him with a pained expression on his face.

'You know what?' Pious too was considering the maze of sharpened steel. 'Your daddy's got a point. It's been a while since I fished down this way and I guess I forgot just how much of a wreck there actually was. Going to be some real sharp edges down there and I didn't allow for you getting cut.'

'I tell you what,' Quarrie laid a hand on his son's shoulder, 'me and Pious will check her out and if it's safe then you can swim on over, but not until I tell you, OK? Meantime, I want you to set here on the bank and if you spot any snakes in the water you go ahead and holler right away.'

James did not say anything. Working the muddy bank with his toes he kept his gaze downcast as his father passed a palm over his hair.

Wearing just their jeans, he and Pious waded into the cool of the water.

'Man, that is sweet against the skin,' Pious murmured. 'Memorial Day, John Q, and it feels like she's July.'

Together they made their way to the middle of the river. 'OK, bud,' Quarrie said, 'we're on the Oklahoma side now so we're legal, but she's narly as hell underfoot.'

'Yes, she is.' Alongside him Pious was chest-deep and moving very slowly, drops of river water clinging to his close-cut hair. 'You-all follow my lead, OK? See if I can't remember where the worst hazards are at and where the best holes used to be.'

Tucking in behind him Quarrie came to the first hunk of wrecked railroad car and felt sheared metal brushing against his leg. He cursed softly as Pious eased around the side of another wasted panel where a massive water spider was keeping watch.

'Best have one eye out for snakes,' Quarrie said. 'I figure we got copperhead and cottonmouth both.'

'Yeah we do, and sure as hell we don't want to get snake-bit, not all the way out here.'

They were right in amongst the wreckage now, with bits of old railroad car on all sides, a maze of metal both above the water and below.

'Pious,' Quarrie said, wading up to his chin, 'there better be some decent-sized flathead back here because this is worse than any string of trotlines, I swear.'

'Quit bleating, will you? I know what-all I'm doing.' From where he was picking his way through the wreckage Pious looked back. 'I'll let you know when we find what we're looking for. Just keep following my lead.'

'So how big are these flatheads anyway?' Quarrie asked.

'You think I'd bring you-all in here if they were tiddlers? Biggest I caught was fifty-nine pounds seven ounces and that's a lot of fish right there.'

They were close to the bank now, in among trees where the roots had broken through, and Quarrie was feeling his way with his toes. As he moved to his left he felt the opening of a large hole and stood there easing his foot across the muddy entrance pretty gingerly, for fear of cutting a toe on some piece of sharpened steel. He was searching for any kind of vibration in the riverbed, the thump of a flathead's tail.

'Pious,' he said. 'Think I might have something here. A hole any-ways. You want to see if you can't find where she comes out?'

Pious swam alongside him; closer still to the bank, he was in among the overhanging branches where they clustered around smaller fragments of wrecked train. It took him a few moments, then he located the other end of the hole, and he was up to his chin where the current was pressing him back.

'John Q,' he said, 'I reckon this right here where I'm at is actually the entrance. You got the back end I think, any movement at all down there?'

'Nope. If he's in there he knows not to thump his tail. You want me to go down and take a look?'

'No sir, this here's my party. You-all stay where you are.'

They were ten feet apart, the hole the catfish had taken for its den feeding the length of the bank.

'Take care now,' Quarrie said. 'Lots of roots to tangle you up in, and a whole bunch of metal to boot.'

'I know it, so don't be making it a long count before you figure I might need some help, OK?'

'Long count?' Quarrie said.

'Grabbling term we got back in Georgia. You got a long and a short depending on what-all you got going on. With me the long is one hundred and fifteen seconds because that's how far I can hold a breath. Short is about forty-five, and in water like this, if I ain't up by then I ain't coming up, so best you come on down.' Pious made a duck dive and disappeared.

Down in the depths he was feeling his way with outstretched fingers before he came to the lip of the hole. Mud rising in swirls from the riverbed, it silted up the water and he was barely able to separate the tangled mass of roots from shards of rusting steel. Easing his way a little further he had his hands where his feet had been and was working the lip of the hole. Making a fist he reached inside but no catfish latched on, and he peered through the murk to see if there was anything there. He could find no trace of whiskers waving in the water, but there was something moving, he just could not make out what it was. A patch of yellowed white; inching a little closer, it bobbed right in front of his face.

Quarrie counted forty-two seconds and was about to make the dive when the water boiled and his friend came up thrashing and gasping for air. There was no sign of any fish and Pious had a haunted look in his eyes. He took a moment to catch his breath; chest-deep in the water still, he was panting hard. He did not say anything. He just looked at Quarrie and Quarrie looked back at him.

'What's up, bud? Swallow a little river water there then, did you?'

'Yeah, I did. And we got us a graveyard for sure.'

Quarrie dived, feeling his way as Pious had done moments before. He came to the edge of the den and stared through the gloom with his heart lifting against his chest. White and bulbous, a human skull; empty eye sockets, they stared at him like a sentinel guarding the hole.

It was all he could do not to swallow water, and he could see it was not just the skull, but some partial vertebrae as well. A little of the neck was still attached and what looked like part of the clavicle. A child: from the size of the skull and that collarbone he figured it had been a child that drowned here and they'd not been much older than James.

For a macabre few moments he just trod water, then reached out to gather up the bones before he remembered his son was waiting on the southern bank. Leaving the bones where they were, he surfaced and looked at Pious in exactly the same way that Pious had looked at him.

'You see it?' Pious said.

'I saw it. And whoever it is, they've been there since the train wrecked, I guess. I'll call it in when we get home.' He nodded to where James was skimming stones from the other shore. 'In the meantime I don't want him knowing about it. I'll tell him when I'm ready, OK?'

'Whatever you say, John Q. But the fish and all – we got people relying on us to bring a flathead home.'

'I know it. But we're done here, bud. We'll go fish the Texas shore.'

Three

Dawn, and he drove the Winfield City cruiser towards the state line. So far nobody had looked his way and that included a sheriff's deputy who passed on the highway and barely lifted a hand. Up ahead he saw a sign that read *Henry's Diner* and he eased his foot off the gas.

Pulling into the parking lot he stopped outside an old slat-board shack that was built on shallow stilts. Climbing out of the car he stretched his shoulders, then shifted the weight of the Colt where it hung on his hip. He cast an eye over the three other vehicles parked up: an old Ford pickup, a Lincoln and a Buick sedan. Adjusting his cap he crossed the dusty parking lot, climbed the steps and went in.

Sitting on a swivel stool at the counter he drank coffee and forked scrambled eggs into his mouth, considering the half-dozen or so customers at the tables and the short-order cook working the hatch. The waitress was efficient, moving up and down the counter with the coffee pot; no sooner was he sipping and setting down than she was right there topping him up.

Quietly he cased his fellow diners: two good old boys in coveralls, a middle-aged couple, and a guy of about thirty wearing a shirt and tie who was well into a plate of ham and eggs. He had a Coke going alongside his coffee cup and when he was finished eating he reached for a pack of Lucky Strikes.

From his stool he watched as the man palmed a few bills onto the table then slid from the booth. Through the window he saw him button his jacket as he trotted across the parking lot. Taking a couple of dollars from the money clip he had stolen from the cop on the station platform, he laid them down on the counter and watched as the Buick pulled away.

He followed that car up the highway, passing a sign that indicated there was a swimming hole called Henry's Bathtub a mile further on. The driver of the Buick could not have been watching his mirrors because he was fairly ticking along. Flicking on the roof light, he checked the dashboard for a siren switch.

Within minutes he was tailgating the Buick, then backing off as the driver pulled into a turnout fifty yards from the dirt road that led to the swimming hole. Easing the prowl car in behind, he turned off the engine but remained in the seat. He was wearing the police officer's gunbelt and next to him a pump-action shotgun stood upright in its stirrup. As he climbed from the car he could see the man in the Buick with his eyes riveted on the rear-view mirror.

The driver's window was rolled down and the guy had both hands hooked around the steering wheel. His gaze was nervous, darting, sweat across his brow as if he were high on dope.

'Officer, is everything all right?'

'Guess you weren't concentrating on your speed.'

Tongue shifting the length of his lips the man's gaze locked onto the shotgun. 'Was I going too fast? I'm sorry. I guess I was listening to the radio and just got carried away.'

Moving back from the car door he shifted the shotgun to his other shoulder. 'Would you mind stepping out of the car? I need you to sit in the back of my cruiser while I run a check on your license and registration.'

Still the man sat where he was with his fingers encircling the wheel. 'Registration, right. The car isn't mine. It belongs to the company I work for.'

Stepping back from the door he indicated for the driver to get out. 'That's all right. If you'd just take a seat in my car for a moment I'm sure everything is going to check out fine.'

The man did as he was asked, walking ahead of him to the

13

cruiser and waiting while he opened the rear door. Seated in the back with the door closed he was a prisoner, locked in and going nowhere. Stepping over to the Buick again he took the keys from the ignition and slipped them into his pocket.

Back in the cruiser he fired up the engine and watched the color slide from the young man's face. Beyond the metal grille he was sitting on his hands saying nothing, though he swallowed hard when they pulled out onto the highway and drove fifty yards to the sign for Henry's Bathtub.

They drove the dirt road for a hundred yards before it climbed a short rise then dipped into a gully, where a natural swimming hole filled the stubby valley beyond. He let the cruiser roll all the way to the bank and then he put on the parking brake. Reaching for the shotgun he swivelled in the seat. 'Sir,' he said, 'I'm going to have to ask you to get out of the car.'

'Why? What's this about?' the man stammered. 'What're we doing back here? I don't understand. I mean if it's a ticket you're writing what're we doing back here?'

'Sir, if you'd just get out of the car.'

He stood with the shotgun resting on his hip once more and asked the man to take his jacket off and toss it on the back seat. First, though, he had him take out his wallet, check book and driver's license. Walking around to the back of the cruiser he unlocked the trunk.

'Yeah,' he said, peering inside. 'I figure there's enough room.'

'Enough room for what?' Trembling, the young man stared.

'Me and the boys back at the station house, we had a bet to see if you could get someone in the trunk along with all the gear.' He indicated the traffic cones. 'You see, with only the back seat there on a busy night it's a case of holding a suspect where you can. Oblige me, sir, please, would you?'

Still the man stared. 'Are you kidding? You want me to get in the trunk?'

'You're about average size: what do you weigh, one sixty; one sixty-five?' He racked a cartridge into the chamber and pointed the shotgun at the man's stomach. 'Go on now, do as I say.'

The man was shaking badly but he did as he was told, climbing over the fender and crouching down in the cruiser's trunk.

'Curl up on your side.'

'What?'

'Like a baby now. Curl up on your side.'

The man lay down and looked up.

'That's good,' he said, nodding. 'That's real neighborly.' Closing the trunk he walked around to the passenger door and fetched his own clothes from the paper sack.

He could hear the man hammering on the trunk lid as he changed out of the uniform and slipped on his T-shirt and jeans. He tugged on the sleeveless Levi jacket then pocketed the man's wallet and check book. The driver's license said his name was Kelly, and the Buick was owned by a company called Mission Farm Supplies. There was thirty-six dollars in cash in the wallet and half a dozen checks in the book.

He kept the pistol but not the holster, which he left with the uniform on the passenger seat. Taking the shotgun and extra shells he reached across the column and slipped the cruiser into neutral. Releasing the parking brake he stepped back and watched as it began to roll.

Four

When Quarrie went to sleep that night all he could see were those stone-washed, sightless eyes. When he woke at dawn he could see them again, and again as he drank his coffee outside.

Tossing away the dregs of his cup, he found James at the kitchen table in his pajamas, shaking grape-nut cereal from the box. Quarrie fetched a quart bottle of milk from the refrigerator and ruffled a hand through the boy's hair.

The phone rang on the wall and he picked up.

'Van Hanigan here, John Q.'

'Captain. What's up?'

'Got a job for you over in Marion County.'

'Marion County? Are you kidding me? That's clear across the state.'

'I know it. But somebody put a call in to Austin and that call made it to me. City of Winfield, they got a cop been beat half to death, and the fact is we got nobody over there right now on account of all the protests going on. Headquarters told me they had to send everybody we got down to Houston because of those college kids kicking off. The draft and all – nobody wants to fight for their country anymore. Anyway, whatever. The perp used the cop's own billy on him and stole both his uniform and his car. It's a fact he's quit the county most probably and could be in Louisiana by now.'

Quarrie wore a pair of flesh-hugging Levi jeans and his tan-colored boots with no pattern tooled on either on the leg or toe. All his life he'd favored plain boots, and if he couldn't have bought them off the shelf like that he would have paid for them to be hand-made. His hat hung on the back of the kitchen door along with his gunbelt and pistols. A pair of three-fifty-seven Ruger Blackhawks in silver with polished wooden grips. He slid each one from its holster and took a moment to check the loading gates.

'James,' he said to his son. 'Bud, I'm sorry but that was the captain on the phone. I've got to go east for a while.'

The boy spoke through a mouthful of cereal. 'When will you be back?'

'Don't know right off. It won't be tonight though. Tomorrow maybe, or the day after that.'

Head down, James nodded. 'That's OK, Dad. I got school.'

'Yes, you do. Eunice will drive you down to the bus stop and Nolo or one of the other hands will be there when you get back.'

Barefoot and still in his pajamas, James followed him outside. Quarrie had an overnight bag in his hand and his guns strapped on his hips. His son opened the driver's door on the Riviera and flipped the seat forward, and Quarrie stowed his bag in the back. Knocking the sun visor down, James reached for his father's sunglasses. Neck craned a little, he studied the photograph of the mother he had never known where it was pouched where the glasses had been. Blonde hair and blue eyes, she was smiling from where she sat the rail of a fence.

'That was taken in Idaho, wasn't it,' the boy said. 'That picture of Mom.'

Quarrie polished the Ray-Bans on his tie. 'Yes, it was.'

'I know I never knew her but I think about her every day.'

'That's good, son. She'd like for you to do that,' his father said. 'It doesn't matter that you didn't know her. It doesn't change the fact you're her son. You're a lot like her, kiddo. Same kind of instinct, especially when it comes to horses. She'd be proud of you, I know.'

Eyes a little misty, the boy stepped back a couple of paces as Quarrie slipped into the driver's seat.

'Dad,' he said, 'we haven't been up to the house in a while. When school's out this summer can we go up there d'you think?'

'Sure we can. I already got her planned.' With a smile, Quarrie nodded towards the kitchen door. 'Now go on and get ready. Don't want you being late on my account and Miss Munro bawling the two of us out.' Closing the driver's door he rolled down the window. 'And stay in class, you hear? No more lying in the dirt watching ants trail dirt when you're supposed to be studying math.'

With that he twisted the key and the Wildcat 425 Pious had sweetened thundered into life. For a moment he sat there watching as James climbed the step and went in through the screen door. Shaking a Camel from his pack Quarrie tapped the inscribed end against the base of his thumb then looked once more at the picture of his wife before folding the visor back. Nursing the motor a little he clicked a gear and backed the car around, then drove the dirt road three miles out to the blacktop.

Picking up some coffee from Cabells, he headed east on 82 with the light flashing under the clamshell grille. It was long drive and he wasn't quite sure how it was that he could be the only Ranger available, but it was a fact there were only sixty-six covering the entire state. With all the anti-war protests going on, for a while they'd been stretched pretty thin.

He was into Fannin County beyond Sherman and heading for Paris, Texas, when a call came in.

'Dispatch calling any sheriff's unit on Route 82.'

Quarrie listened to see who would pick up.

'Dispatch calling any sheriff's deputy. Do you copy? Come back.'

Still there was no answer.

'We got an incident at a house south of Monkstown,' the dispatcher went on. 'Possible B&E. Does anybody copy? Come back.'

The location she'd named was up in the Caddo Grassland about ten miles north of where Quarrie was driving now. Turning the volume a little higher on the radio he waited for a deputy to pick up.

'Does anybody copy?' he heard the dispatcher say. 'Highway 82: is anyone out there at all?'

With a shake of his head Quarrie unhooked the transmitter from its housing. 'Dispatch, this is Ranger Unit Zero-Six.'

'Ranger?' the dispatcher said. 'I'm looking for a sheriff's deputy. How come you're the only one picking up?'

'I don't know. But I'm south of Monkstown right now so you better tell me what you got.'

'Look, this is a county deal. I don't want to hang it on you guys – not with what-all you got to deal with. Fact is I took a call from a gardener and it might be nothing at all.'

'Could be nothing, but then again it might not. I'm here now so you might as well go ahead.'

'Well sir, this gardener said his name was Gonzalez and he's working a house up there by the lake. Said how he showed up to cut the grass as he usually does only he found the door wide open and no sign of the owner, and nobody answered when he called. It doesn't sound like a hell of a lot, but it's remote over there, and with the door open the old man didn't like what he could smell.'

'What he could smell? You mean from inside the house?'

'That's right. Told me he could smell something and it didn't smell good.'

'Did he take a look?'

'Not that he said. Just told me how the vehicles are in the garage and the owner would never go out and leave a door open like that. There's a phone in the garage apparently and he used that to make the call.'

'OK, copy that. I'm only a few miles south right now. Go ahead and tell me where it's at.'

The dispatcher told him the house was on its own at the end of a dirt road not far from the lake. Clipping the handset back on the hook, Quarrie flipped the switch for the siren and stamped his foot down hard on the gas.

Heading due north he located the road where the clouds hung bruise-like across the sky. Flatland up here, it was salt brush and wheat grass and it shimmered like the sea until the road was swallowed by the stands of trees. Hot and sticky, the drought had broken finally, and the weather report said there was a storm coming. Judging by the weight of those clouds it was going to hit pretty soon.

He drove deep into the trees before finally coming on a mailbox fixed by the side of the road. The name *Bowen* printed on it, he turned into the gravelled drive. There he spotted the gardener, an old Tejano leaning against the door of a bull-nosed Chevy with his equipment loaded on the bed. Quarrie peered beyond him to the house. Built in yellow brick, it was single-story with a pitched roof as well as a separate garage made from the same colored bricks. The garage doors were open and inside two vehicles were parked side-by-side. Pulling up next to the gardener's truck, Quarrie reached for his hat.

'Howdy,' he said as he got out. 'You the feller called the sheriff just now?'

The old man nodded.

'My name's Quarrie. Texas Ranger. What's going on?'

Gonzalez seemed to inspect him for a moment before he nodded towards the house.

'The kitchen door is open.'

'Yeah, that's what they said.'

'It never happens.' Gonzalez wagged his head. 'Mr Bowen, he don't ever leave a door open. I been working here three years and he don't go anyplace unless he locks up.'

Quarrie nodded to the car and pickup parked in the garage. 'You sure he ain't about here somewheres? Vehicles in the garage like that, he could be up at the lake.'

'No.' Again Gonzalez shook his head. 'He's not here. I know he's not here. Nobody answers when I call, and the door is open, and then there is the smell.' He wrinkled his nose as if to emphasize the point. 'I know Señor Bowen. He would not go out and leave a door open. That's not the way he is.'

Quarrie started towards the house. 'All right,' he said. 'I'm going to take a look. Stay where you're at and don't come in the house lessen I call.'

Crossing the driveway he climbed the short flight of steps to the paved patio and went around the side of the building. The fly screen was sprung to but beyond it the kitchen door stood open. On first inspection it did not look as if it had been forced but, using just his index finger, Quarrie hooked the screen back to get a better view. The lock was intact: no wood splintered or paint stripped. He could see the kitchen was set with a stone-tiled floor and worktops made from granite. No marks on the floor that he could pick out, he was struck by the scent of burnt coffee and wondered if that was what the Tejano had smelled.

'Mr Bowen,' he called. 'Are you here, sir? Is anybody home?'

There was no answer. All he could hear was the hum from the Frigidaire. Casting another glance, he took in an antique range-style stove in enamel that ran on propane gas. A single cup and its saucer were upturned on the draining board with a dishcloth folded neatly beside.

The kitchen opened onto a living room and he could feel a moist kind of warmth rising now. Inside he saw the glimmer of a flame from a river-rock fireplace where fake logs burned beyond the chain-link guard.

'Mr Bowen?' he called again. 'Sir, my name is Quarrie and I'm a Texas Ranger. Are you OK?'

Nobody answered and he took a look around the room. A leather couch cut in the style of a Chesterfield, two matching armchairs and coffee table in between. Back of that was a circular card table with a green felt top. A bar area was built to the side with a couple of stools and a cooler fixed to the wall. A twenty-six inch Admiral color TV occupied one corner with a remote control box placed on top.

Pictures hung on the walls, western scenes painted by Russell, or somebody trying to emulate him perhaps. On the mantelpiece above the fire was a single eight-by-ten-inch photograph of a man and a woman with a couple of dark-haired boys.

Another scent struck him, a sickly sweet kind of odor that was a little weighty, Quarrie knew that smell and it wasn't coffee burned in the pot. Without touching he photo he studied it for a couple of moments then he turned once more. The far wall was entirely made of glass, a set of sliding patio doors. They overlooked a barbecue area furnished by cane-style armchairs that were actually made from steel. They were gathered around a glass-topped table, and a brick-built barbecue was set into the wall.

To the left of the fireplace an archway opened onto a spacious hallway that had various oak doors leading off it and all of them were closed. At the far end a casement window offered the same view as from the living room and, though it brought in some natural light, the hall felt gloomy still. Falling away beneath the window a set of stairs led down to the basement and the smell was much stronger now.

Unfastening the hammer clip on his right-hand holster, Quarrie started along the hallway towards the head of the stairs. He opened the first oak door and found another, smaller living room, set with a couch and TV, though this one was black and white. Two more doors opened onto two more single bedrooms that were both bare and functional: there was nothing homely here. It was regimented, and a little like his cottage back at the Feeley ranch, he could sense no woman's touch. The last door opened onto the master bedroom with a queen size bed where the sheets were tucked in and the pillow slips newly pressed.

At the head of the stairs the smell was even worse. A chill seemed to gather from below. Palm on the butt of his pistol, Quarrie started down.

'Mr Bowen?' he called. 'Are you there, sir? My name's Quarrie. I'm a Texas Ranger.'

Nobody answered. He was at the foot of the stairs in a narrow corridor that peeled fifteen feet to a single door. That door was closed and Quarrie remained where he was long enough to pick up any sound. He could hear nothing though, and doubted he would, so he started for the door. Pausing outside the smell was thicker still.

Easing the door open he took in oak boards on the floor and oak panels on the nearest wall. It was replete with bookshelves and books, and where there were no books there were a few photographs scattered here and there. Beyond the shelves a glass-fronted gun cabinet was built as part of the wood. Stepping inside Quarrie saw a desk in shadow in the corner that had been hidden as he opened the door. A man was sitting at the desk. Hunched a little to one side, his head was angled; both hands thrown out before him, one of them fisted and the other one holding a gun.

Five

He did not move. He did not speak. The rank odor lifted directly from where he sat. Moving closer Quarrie could see how his eyes had sunk in their sockets, his stare as sightless as the skull they had found in the river. He looked about fifty; hair clipped so close it appeared to graze his scalp. Jaw slack, a trail of dried blood had leaked from his temple where the hole was small and round. The automatic cupped in his palm looked like a twenty-two and with no exit wound visible, the slug had to be lodged in his brain. Looking closer still, Quarrie could see purple colored marks like bruises on the skin just above his collarbone.

Apart from the dead man there was nothing wrong with the room, no sign of a fight or struggle or anybody else having been there. Nothing looked out of place. Quarrie could see no obvious marks on the floorboards. A blotter was placed centrally on the desk with a gold pen set just ahead of it. A wire file holder perched to the right of the dead man's hand, an empty in-tray of sorts.

Studying the bullet hole more closely, he could see where pinpricks of black powder scattered the skin. The dead man's gaze was fixed; he seemed to peer almost, as if he could not quite get a handle on something in the corner of the room.

The sound of footsteps in the passage broke the silence, heavy and weighted; a shadow filled the doorway. As Quarrie turned he had a pistol drawn.

'Jesus, whoa! Hold up there – I'm a cop.' A sheriff's deputy not wearing his hat. He stood with his eyes wide and palms outstretched.

Shaking his head, Quarrie let the hammer down. 'Don't be doing

24

that,' he said as he holstered the pistol. 'Creeping up on a feller, it's not a very smart thing to do.'

'I'm sorry,' the young man said. 'I should've hollered from up-stairs. My name's Collins, Fannin County sheriff's department.' He stared at Quarrie's gun. 'You know what, I never even saw that piece till it was pointed at me. Have you always been that fast?' He was young and skinny, and when he stepped into the light he looked pretty raw. Spotting the dead man in the chair he lifted a hand to his mouth as if he was going to throw up.

'Jesus H,' he uttered. 'Thought I could smell something. How long's he been like that?'

'I figure maybe two or three days.'

'All that time with the fire going up there in the living room. No wonder this place stinks.' The deputy crossed the room now hold-ing the cuff of his shirt to his nose. At the desk he bent with his free hand pressed to his thigh.

'Shot hisself. Never could figure why anybody would want to do that. You come across many suicides before?'

Quarrie did not answer. He moved from the desk to the shelves where he considered the photographs more carefully and could see they were all of the dead man in uniform and clearly taken some years ago.

He studied the gun case, which housed an assortment of rifles as well as handguns and a razor sharp-looking bayonet. They were se-cured on hooks and one of those hooks was empty. Stepping to the side Quarrie ran his eye down the crack between the edge of the cabinet and the door and saw that though it was closed, the door wasn't locked.

'You figure that?' From behind him the deputy was still talking. 'How anybody would want to take a gun to their head? Hell of a thing. Got to be a reason I suppose.'

'You'd think so,' Quarrie said. 'Sickness, loneliness maybe, all kinds of stuff a man might be going through that he ain't going to talk about to anybody else about.' He looked back at the desk. 'That's how it is sometimes, only this guy didn't kill himself.'

'Do what now?' the deputy said.

'Someone was here and they put that bullet in him,' Quarrie stated. 'Afterwards they fixed the piece in his hand and I imagine they wiped their prints. From what I can see, they sat him a little more upright in that chair.' He pointed. 'That's post-mortem lividity you can see there at the base of his neck.'

Back at the desk the deputy stared.

'Those purple marks,' Quarrie said. 'What looks like bruising, that's where blood settled after he was dead.' He glanced towards the basement stairs. 'It doesn't look like they disturbed a whole lot, but there was someone here all right, and when they left the kitchen door wasn't closed. This ain't a suicide. It's is a homicide, so be careful where you put your hands.'

The deputy had an uncertain expression on his face. 'Sergeant,' he said, 'I ain't about to argue with you, you being a Ranger and all. But are you sure? It looks for all the world like he took that piece to himself.'

'Course it does.' Quarrie crossed to the desk where he dropped to his haunches. 'That's how it's meant to look but that's not how it was. Come over here and I'll show you.'

Pacing around the desk the deputy crouched down next to him.

'Hand me your flashlight,' Quarrie said.

The deputy unhooked it from his belt.

'All right then.' Quarrie shone the beam across the dead man's skin. 'Take a look at that bullet wound right there and you'll see how the skin is lifted but only a fraction. You can see the pinpricks of powder where it burned.'

'Got it,' the deputy said.

'That ain't a contact wound,' Quarrie told him. 'That's a shot been fired from a couple of inches away at least. Deputy, when somebody takes a gun to their head they press the barrel right up to the skin. They do it because they're scared they'll miss and wind up still alive but with half a face. Happens every time and you get a star shaped wound on account of it with four or five points and each of the points is flared. When you look real close you see that the skin is pressed inwards ever so slightly, as if somebody kneaded it a little with their fingers.'

Rising to his full height he passed the flashlight back to the deputy. 'It's caused by gases from the cartridge spreading between the bone and subcutaneous tissue. What the coroner would call an overpressure.' Taking off his hat he worked a hand through his hair. 'You got yourself a homicide all right, so best you secure this room.'

Six

Leaving him to call it in, Quarrie returned to his car and drove back to the highway once more. He kept his foot down hard, travelling east towards Paris before heading through Mount Pleasant, making for Winfield in Marion County.

It was not a place he had been to before and the rain arrived long before he pulled up where the railroad crossed at the bottom of Main Street. It was dark now, and after all day in the car he was stiff in the back as he waited for the freight train to pass.

A sheet of lying water on the street, it flared indigo under the lamps. All the stores were closed and few vehicles filled the spots between the twin rows of parking meters. Unsure where the police department was, he pulled up outside the pool room and asked a young man for directions. The man sent him another couple of blocks, then he made a right and a left before coming up on a station house that looked underfunded and rundown. A squat, flat-roofed building cast in old brick, it was hunched between two much smarter offices and that only added to the air of decay.

Parking the Riviera, Quarrie tickled the throttle one last time and the V8 shuddered into silence. He sat there yawning, then reached for his pack of Camels on the dashboard and stuffed it in his breast pocket. On the sidewalk he shook out a leg where cramping had set in and worked at the toe of his boot. The sign above the station house door was painted rather than electronic, and even the paint seemed a little weary. The rain still fell and with his hat at an angle he pushed open the door.

He was greeted by a fan trying to cut through the dampened heat where it perched atop a tired-looking file cabinet. A high desk out front with an overweight man in uniform squatting behind it, a low gate in the fenced-off section where two more cops in light blue shirts and black pants,lounged at a couple of desks. The type-writers looked pre-war, as did the stack of arrest report dockets. A door to his left read *Chief*, and Quarrie assumed the cells lay beyond the far door where a glass panel offered the glimpse of a corridor. The three cops cast their collective gaze from his pistols to where his tie was fastened with a longhorn pin.

'Evening boys,' Quarrie said. 'Sorry it took so long to get here but I had to make a stop on the way.'

The chief's door swung open and another man came out wear-ing the same black trousers and tired-looking shirt. His name tag said he was Billings, and he beckoned Quarrie inside.

An air-conditioning unit was flattened into the glass of the grimy window, and apart from that there was an ancient wooden desk with a swivel seat as well as an armchair that was moth-eaten and ugly. Behind the desk a rack of rifles was fixed to the wall. Another fan sat on another file cabinet but that looked as though it was broken. The chief indicated the armchair but Quarrie shook his head.

'No, thanks,' he said. 'I'm just about seized up right now on ac-count of being set on my butt all the way from Wichita Falls.'

Approaching fifty, the chief looked like he was carrying a few pounds he didn't need; his hair greased high on his forehead with a single lock that wanted to droop between his eyes. He looked more than put-upon, as if the mayor had been giving him a real bad time, and seeing as how they had lost a cruiser and had a cop in the hos-pital, it was a fact he probably had.

'That's not all we got going on,' he admitted when Quarrie probed. 'This used to be a sleepy little spot on the map but I guess it's not anymore.'

He nodded to the twin-rig gunbelt Quarrie was wearing. 'You always port a pair like that? I've seen pictures of Rangers from the thirties and forties wearing a two-piece but you rarely get to see it anymore.'

'Well,' Quarrie said, 'this is how it was with my godfather, Chief, and this is how it is with me.'

'Your godfather a Ranger too then was he? Would I know him at all?'

'Frank Hamer,' Quarrie said. 'He's dead now but at one time there wasn't a soul in Texas hadn't heard of him.'

'That's a fact. Man who divided opinion for sure.' Arms across his chest the chief looked a little speculative. 'So Frank Hamer was your godfather, uh? Him that shot Clyde Barrow and settled the town of Navasota back when there was a shooting on the street every day. That place hasn't been the same since he left and he left a long time ago.'

'Yes, he did.'

'He wore a twin rig too then? I didn't know.'

'He did back then, Chief. And I ain't the only one still packing a pair. There ain't that many of us and we work alone most always, and a set of twelve at the ready gives a man a little more confidence than six.' Quarrie sat down in the chair now and the cushion sagged under his weight.

'So anyway,' the chief said. 'We called you up on account of we had an officer down and now that officer is dead.' His expression had grayed a little further. 'His name was Michaels and he died at two o'clock this afternoon over in the hospital at Queensboro.' Reaching to his top drawer he took out a bottle of cheap Bourbon. 'I guess the least we could do is drink to him. You ready for one now that it's dark out?'

Taking his cigarettes from his pocket Quarrie shucked one out and offered the crumpled pack. Shaking his head the chief found two dusty-looking glasses, poured the whiskey and passed a glass across.

'The fallen,' he said.

Quarrie drank and placed the empty glass on the arm of the chair. 'So, what else you got going on, Chief? You said your guy wasn't the whole story.'

'No, he's not. Just this afternoon we find ourselves with another dead body.' The chief poured himself a second shot. 'Woman name of Mary-Beth Gavin who'd only been here six weeks. Neighbor found her around the same time Michaels died down there in the hospital. Middle-aged and living on her own, beaten up bad she was. On that, sir, you can quote me.'

Quarrie sat forward. 'Same perp you're thinking then, are you?'

'Could be. I don't want to pre-empt anything you might come up with.'

'But you think so?'

The chief gestured. 'I'm not a detective, Sergeant, but the way Michael's had his skull fractured and how she's all busted up around the face.'

'Where do you have her body?'

'Right now they got her laid out at the funeral parlor over on 4th Street.' Finishing his drink the chief got to his feet. 'Nearest morgue is Queensboro, thirty miles south, and I didn't want to bring her down there till you had a chance to take a look.'

They drove across town in his Plymouth, Quarrie peering through the windshield as they came to 4th Street, where lights still burned in the single-story building that housed the funeral parlor.

'Nobody saw anything?' he said.

The chief shook his head. 'No sir, not at the Gavin house nor down at the railroad depot either.'

They got out of the car with the rain falling harder and Quarrie asked him what time Michaels had been found.

'Not till the four-oh-five rolled in for Houston, though nobody was boarding the train. Engineer saw something lying on the ground at the far end of the platform and when he went to take a look he found the poor bastard stripped to his shorts.'

They walked up the steps to a wooden door with a glass panel in the center.

'So,' Quarrie said, 'right now we got us a cop killer driving a Winfield City cruiser. Somebody must've spotted it, right?'

'We've only had one call.' The chief pushed open the door and they went into a small wood-panelled hallway. 'Early this morning that rig was seen down the road at Henry's Diner. One of ours was in there for breakfast apparently, only our patrol ends with the city and we got nobody living out that way.'

The dead woman was laid out on the embalming table. As far as Quarrie could tell she was in her early fifties, fully dressed she was covered with a white cotton sheet. Red hair, freckles scattered across her forehead, though her face was pulp. One cheekbone had been crushed completely, her nose little more than a flattened swelling, her eyes were purple around the lids. The already pale skin of her shoulders was paler still now that the life had left her.

'Doctor's been and gone,' the chief told him. 'Had him come out to the house as soon as the call came in.'

Quarrie was still considering the body.

'Took her brain temperature and figured she'd been dead at least twelve hours.'

Stepping closer to the table Quarrie studied the bruise marks in blue and mauve that gathered at the base of the woman's throat. 'What time did you say this was reported?'

'Around two thirty this afternoon.'

'And your Officer Michaels, they found him at four this morning?'

The chief nodded. 'You're thinking he swung by the depot following his usual route and found himself with her killer?'

'Could be.' Quarrie still studied the dead woman's neck. 'Fingers,' he said inspecting the bruising. 'Crushed her windpipe with his fingers and that takes a lot of doing.' He drew breath audibly through his nose. 'I've seen a few strangled with cord or a

32

length of chain, but not many killed with fingers.' Eyebrow cocked he indicated the lower body.

The chief shook his head. 'No sign of anything going on down thataway, or at least that's what the doctor said. Guess it'll be confirmed by the autopsy.'

Quarrie looked more closely at the dead woman's mangled features. 'Chief,' he said, 'I might be wrong but this kind of beating – looks to me like the perp was pretty pissed off. You see what I'm saying? A whomping like this, and to a woman – it smacks of anger. Is that how it looks to you?'

Glancing at the woman's face the chief pursed his lips. 'Sergeant,' he said, 'we haven't had a murder in this town since God was in britches, so if that's how it looks to you then that's how it looks to me.'

With a smile Quarrie nodded. 'What about her family? Have you been able to talk to anybody?'

'Not so far. It's like I said back at the station house: she showed up in town maybe six weeks back and rented a house over on Osprey. Kept herself to herself and from what the neighbor said it doesn't sound like she had many visitors. No sign of any previous address in the house so we haven't been able to trace a next of kin.'

Quarrie worked fingers across her jaw and remaining cheekbone where rigor mortis had thickened the skin. Moving around to the side of the table he considered her hands and specifically the fingernails. Trimmed short, they were not bitten but shaped with a pair of nail scissors and he could see where they had been filed with an emery board. There was no trace of nail polish and no hint of anything obvious hooked underneath.

'Where did she work at?' he said.

'According to the neighbor she was a secretary for old man McIntyre. Got him a shop down on Orchard and Main. Maintains farm machinery and folk come from miles around on account of there ain't anything his boys can't fix.' The chief let go a sigh. 'I haven't told him she's dead yet. Gutted he'll be; hates any kind of disturbance and this used to be—'

'A sleepy little spot. You said.'

Outside Quarrie stood on the porch staring into bands of falling rain. All was quiet; nobody on the street, and when they drove back across town there was no one on Main Street either.

'Always this way is she?' he asked. 'After dark I mean, or is it on account of the rain?'

Billings worked his shoulders. 'Rain doesn't make any difference. Apart from a few kids kicking off like they are right now, we're not so busy come sundown.'

Osprey was a quiet residential street scattered with small one- and two-bedroom homes built in weathered clapboard that were either open onto the sidewalk or set behind fences of chain link. The Gavin house was even more dilapidated than the police department and whoever the landlord was he was clearly not big on mainten-ance. No fence, the yard overgrown with yellow grass where a single willow tree hunched like a porcupine with its bristles up.

Quarrie stood for a moment looking up and down the street. Silent apart from the rain, there was not so much as a cicada singing as the chief grabbed a cape from the trunk. He offered it to Quarrie but he didn't mind the rain, and there was never enough of it up in the panhandle. It ran off his hat and splashed onto the already soaking sidewalk while he took a minute to consider the dead woman's home.

'Nobody heard anything?' he said. 'Last night when this was go-ing down, nobody heard her scream?'

'Not that anybody said.' The chief stepped onto the sidewalk. 'We started door to door this afternoon but we haven't spoken to everybody.'

Quarrie approached the house along the overgrown footpath with a flashlight the chief had retrieved from the trunk. The stoop was cut from rough-looking wood and two of the steps were rotten, the edges turned to mush. He picked up a scraping of mud that seemed to have been deposited at an odd angle. Coasting the beam from the flashlight across the grass he saw where it was flattened in places and that was not due to the rain. Moving away from the stoop he looked more closely and picked out where the grass was splayed more deeply and shone the torch on the turned earth under the window.

'Got you something there, do you?' The chief spoke from where he was sheltering on the inadequate porch.

Close to the wall Quarrie made out a full-sized footprint that was partially hidden by weeds. Next to it was another print where a step had been taken, and that was almost as flat as the first one. It shouldn't be. He knew tracks, had studied them for as long as he studied anything, and he could tell when a man was running or walking, when he was agitated and when he was calm. He knew when he was making a turn, or pausing to think about making one maybe. There was something about that print that seemed a little odd and it took a moment before he knew what it was. The first one made sense being as flat as it was, but with the second the angle was wrong. That kind of movement ought to leave a mark where only the ball of the foot flexed, but that's not how it was. There was more of the print showing than there should be.

'What is it?' the chief said. 'What you got there?'

'Boot print,' Quarrie told him. 'US Army issue: I can tell that from the pattern on the sole because that ain't changed since World War II and I wore a pair myself.'

'You fight then, did you?'

'Korea.' Quarrie looked up at him. 'Chief, I think your perp was standing right here checking out Ms Gavin through the window. He's wearing a military boot and the left one's got a nick in the heel. I can't say about the right, but the way it's flexed I'd say those boots have a steel shank running the length of the sole.' Thumbing back his hat he dropped to his haunches. 'That means the boots are second-phase. The eyelets are distinctive in that they're screened to keep out water, and I can tell you that the cuff is made from nylon. In my day it was canvas but they changed it when they put the shank in.'

'What's the shank for?'

'Punji stake mantraps.' Quarrie rose to his full height. 'Stops a grunt getting impaled if he steps on one. The sole is pretty rigid though, and on account of that it makes them much less flexible to walk in.'

Scratching his head the chief took his flashlight back and shone it on the ground himself.

'You know all that from a couple of footprints?'

'Sure.' Quarrie was smiling. 'Even ants leave tracks in their wake, Chief. I thought everybody knew that.'

The chief had the house keys. Opening the door he reached inside for the light switch. A Chinese-style paper shade clung around the inadequate bulb casting macabre looking shadows on the walls. No door to the living room, just a squared-off archway, Quarrie stood with his hands in his jacket pockets.

The living room looked like a bomb site, furniture thrown over, the table smashed; the cushions had been pulled from the couch. Every drawer in the cheap bureau had been tossed and the contents tipped on the floor.

'Somebody looking real hard for something,' Quarrie said. 'What's missing? What did he take?'

The chief pursed his lips. 'I don't know. There's no cash lying around, so if she had any he took that, but there's jewellery still in the bedroom.'

Quarrie considered the body-shaped outline chalked on the wooden floor. He could see blood drying on a rug, blood on the walls, and more scattered in strings across the front of the bureau. A purse lay among the ruins of the broken table. Inside he found the victim's driver's license as well as a check book with a balance of eighty-seven dollars listed on the accounting slip.

He could tell by the amount of white powder still lying that the lab team had been through here already, but as he moved about the room he was careful just the same.

'Chief, how many sets of prints did your boys raise?'

'Seven,' the chief said. 'She lived on her own I guess, but this place is a rental.'

'Seven?' Quarrie said. 'That's a lot of fingerprints, even for rental. How many were fresh, were the lab boys able to tell?'

'They weren't absolutely certain, but they reckoned on probably two.'

Quarrie moved from the living room to the hall and bedroom. Again it was turned upside down, the mattress half on the bed and half on the floor, the drawers from the nightstand thrown over. The dressing table was trashed, all the drawers on the floor and their contents scattered. The jewellery box was open and had been rifled but there were some nice pieces lying there so robbery hadn't been the motive.

'Are you talking to the NCIC?' he spoke to the chief where he hovered in the doorway.

'Up there in Virginia, sure. Teletype of the prints already been wired.'

Quarrie nodded. 'Do me a favor and ask them to have a copy sent to the Department of Safety in Amarillo.'

Outside again they stood on the porch where Quarrie lighted a cigarette and stared into the rain. He had looked through the rest of the house but found nothing that told him anything other than that whoever killed Mary-Beth Gavin had done it in a violent rage. She ought to have been screaming and somebody should have heard that. If this was Dallas or Houston he might accept the fact that it could have been ignored, but not in a town this small.

Back in the car he asked the chief to drive him over to the railroad depot and they parked close to where the fallen deputy's body had been found. Any blood lying had long since been washed away by the rain and there were no traces of footprints or tire marks.

'Part of his route,' the chief explained. 'Michaels patrolled this area every night and he always made a sweep of the depot.'

'What about trains?' Quarrie asked him.

The chief shrugged. 'Nothing till the four-oh-five. Like I told you, it was the engineer that found him.'

Quarrie took a room in a family-run motel a block east of Main Street. There was a phone by the bed and he called Amarillo, leaving a message for Van Hanigan about the incoming teletype. Then he telephoned the ranch.

'How you doing, kiddo?' he said when his son came on the line.

'I'm fine, Dad. When you coming home?'

'Don't know yet. Fact is it took me all day on the road and I only just got here. You can blame those students you see on the TV. On account of them I'm the only Ranger available to get over this way and that's a pretty poor state of affairs.'

'Yes, it is,' James said.

'So how was school today? Did you learn anything?'

'Sure. Miss Munro told us we have to come up with a project on some kind of history.'

'Did she now? So what're you thinking of doing?'

'Well sir, I talked to Pious and he said he's going to help me.'

Sitting up straighter Quarrie reached for his cigarettes. 'You-all going to write something about what happened to him? What went on in Korea?'

'No, sir. I thought about that. I thought about how he saved your life that time too, the story you told Nolo and the others at the fish fry. Pious told me he don't want that dragged up again, not even for a school project.'

'So what're you thinking?'

'We talked about it and he figured I ought to do something on that train wreck up on the Red?'

'Did he tell you what it was we found there?'

'No, sir. What was it?'

Quarrie did not answer. Shaking a cigarette from the pack he rolled the wheel on his Zippo. 'I tell you what,' he said. 'You go ahead and see what you come up with. When you got something I'll tell you what we found up there and we'll see if we can't fit all the pieces together.'

'OK, Dad,' the boy said. 'By the way, I asked Miss Munro about looking stuff up in the newspaper and she said they kept the records on some kind of fish.'

'Fiche,' Quarrie corrected with a smile. 'F-I-C-H-E. It's a piece of plastic, son. They shrink all the text and pictures down and transfer them onto the plastic. They call it a microfiche, James. What's the name of the newspaper?'

'Don't know yet. I guess I'll have to ask Pious.'

When he put the phone down Quarrie lay back with his boots crossed at the ankle. Thinking about what James had said he stared at the wall and all he could see was that skull where it hung in the river.

Seven

He woke to threads of sunlight creeping around shabby drapes: a grubby motel in Fairview; one street with a supper club, mercantile and bank. Working the heel of his hand into his eyes he climbed out of bed, crossed to the window and eased aside the drape. A handful of vehicles had been parked in the lot last night but only the Buick he had stolen was left.

In the bathroom he splashed cold water over his face. There was a coffee pot and some packages of coffee on the side and he added water from the faucet. While the coffee perked he got dressed. The shotgun was resting against the wall where he had left it and the Model 10 Colt he had taken from the deputy's holster lay on the nightstand by the bed.

Driving down the street to the mercantile, he went inside and hunted among the shelves till he found a two-foot hacksaw and roll of duct tape.

'Don't be cutting yourself now,' the girl at the counter warned him. 'That there tape won't work on a missing finger.'

Back in the motel room he moved the folding luggage rack into the middle of the floor and placed the twelve-gauge shotgun lengthwise across canvas bands. Keeping it steady with his left foot he sawed the barrel off half an inch in front of the magazine. He had no file to square the cut with so he took a wet towel to the burr instead.

Taking up the saw a second time he sectioned the stock so it left only a pistol grip and he bound that carefully with tape. Then he folded the rack once more and set it against the wall by the closet. Sliding the six bullets from the chamber of the Model 10 he cleaned that with the towel then reloaded and stuffed the pistol in his waistband. He had a few dollars left from the money he had taken from the dead salesman's wallet but he still had the check book as well.

The bank was not busy, only one customer ahead of him as he waited in line. Filling out a check for a hundred dollars, he passed it across and the teller told him she would have to call the bank in Little Rock to check the account. He waited while she crossed to the manager's office.

When the teller came back she told him there was actually only sixty-one dollars in the account right now, so he wrote another check for sixty. The woman cashed that and he pocketed the money then walked back out to the car.

Behind the wheel once more he drove out of town, keeping to the speed limit, and headed for the freeway. Driving south he pulled off at the exit for Marshall and stopped at a diner across the road from the library and Army/Navy.

*

Out front of the station house in Winfield, Quarrie took a good look at the tire tread on one of the department's cruisers while the driver looked on with a puzzled expression on his face.

'What you doing there, Sergeant?' he said.

Quarrie considered the tire: a Goodrich Radial, he memorized the pattern of the tread.

'Tell me something,' he said. 'Do all your vehicles carry this make and model of rubber?'

'I don't know. I guess so. I really couldn't say.'

Quarrie squinted at him. 'Go inside and ask someone for me, would you? It's important.'

The rain had stopped; the skies much clearer this morning and the sun beat down on the sidewalk. Sweat was beginning to mark

41

Quarrie's shirt at the armpits, and already he had his top button undone and his tie stowed in his overnight bag. Leaning against the door of his Riviera he polished the toe of one boot against the back of his leg. A moment later the young officer came out and told him that as far as anybody knew, all their patrol cars had the same tires.

'Thanks,' Quarrie said. 'I got another question for you. Where can I find Henry's Diner?'

He drove south-east on Route 49 heading for the Louisiana state line and thinking about the four-oh-five to Houston and what Mary-Beth Gavin's killer had been doing on the depot platform. They had no idea whether he was local or from out of town, but given he had stolen the cruiser Quarrie thought it more likely to be the latter. This morning the chief had called to tell him the victim's body had been shipped down to Queensboro right after they saw it. Since then the coroner had been on the phone to inform him the head trauma had occurred post-mortem. That only added fuel to Quarrie's theory that the perp had been looking for something. It seemed clear that he did not find it, and whatever it was it was either still in that house or had never been there at all. Frustration, that's what the head trauma indicated, and especially now they knew it had happened after the victim was already dead. So who was this guy and what had he wanted from Mary-Beth Gavin?

These were questions had no answers to right now, and his thoughts shifted as the sign came up for Henry's Diner. He had not had any breakfast, his stomach was rumbling and he turned into the parking lot. Taking off his hat he took a seat at the counter where the waitress poured out a cup of coffee. She looked like she was in her twenties, wearing a white housecoat with the name *Nicole* printed on a plastic tag.

Quarrie ordered some bacon and fried eggs. Adding cream and sugar to his coffee he took a long swallow.

Nicole served another customer and then she returned with the steaming coffee pot.

'Nicole,' he said, 'my name's Quarrie. I'm a Texas Ranger.'

'The cruiser,' she said. 'You want to know about the Winfield city police car?'

Returning her smile, he nodded. 'Yes mam, as a matter of fact I do. Was it you that called it in?'

'Yes it was; yesterday morning, early. There was a Winfield city cop came in and I thought it odd because this is a long way out for those guys.' Setting the pot back on the warmer she rested her elbows on the counter. 'It's not often we see cops from Winfield in here and I didn't recognize this guy.'

'Did you talk to him at all?'

Nicole shook her head. 'No sir, I didn't. I mean other than to say good morning and ask him what he wanted.'

'Do you remember what that was?'

'What he ordered? I don't know; I'd have to think about it. Maybe some scrambled eggs.'

He smiled again. He nodded. 'You got a good memory. Tell me, do you recall what he looked like?'

Pursing her lips she looked a little speculative. 'He wasn't a real cop, was he?'

'No, he wasn't. Do you remember him at all, Nicole?'

She took a moment to think about that. 'I don't know, a little maybe, I guess. He was about thirty I'd say. No, actually, I think he was younger. It's hard to tell when a man's in uniform. He was younger than you though, if that's any help.'

'I'm thirty-six years old,' Quarrie told her. 'How much younger than me do you think he was?'

'Mid-twenties then maybe. He was clean-shaven and I think he had blue eyes. Yeah, blue eyes. They were about the same color as yours.'

'OK, Nicole, thank you. That's helpful. Was there anything else you noticed? How did he act? Was there anything that stuck out at all? Anything that caught your attention?'

Nicole shook her head. 'No sir, nothing odd. He was just like any other customer. He ordered and ate. Then he left.'

'Were you busy around then? I guess if it was breakfast time you probably were?'

'Actually,' she said, 'right around the time he was in we were a little slow.'

'The other customers, do you remember any of them?'

'Sure, I notice most of our customers. I like people – in this job you have to. There was an older couple I'd never seen before. Then there was Willy and Ellis from the breakers' yard and a handful of regulars I guess. One guy on his own who comes in from time to time: he's not from around here. I think he's some kind of salesman.'

Taking another sip of coffee Quarrie set the cup down. 'OK,' he said. 'Thank you, Nicole, that's useful. The cop though, when he left out: could you tell which way he was headed?'

'No sir, I didn't see. But I remember he left right after that salesman.'

Quarrie ate his breakfast and when he went back outside he considered the floor of the parking lot. The ground hard-baked and covered in dust, it was littered with an assortment of different tire tracks. The rain hadn't made it this far yet and the coating of dust lay like powder. Leaving his car for a moment, he walked to where the parking lot met the highway and studied the marks at the lip of the asphalt. It took a while to pick it out but finally he spotted a partial tread that had been crossed over by a number of others.

Climbing behind the wheel once more, he reached for his sunglasses and Mary-Clare smiled at him where she sat on the fence at the cabin he still owned in the shadow of the Grand Tetons. Set at the end of a narrow dugway, they'd found it purely by chance when they moved north not long after they were first married.

He let the engine idle for a second or so before selecting a gear and cutting out onto the highway. He drove at a steady forty-five;

one hand on the wheel, he was taking in every ranch and airline road, every single sign that was posted. Spotting one for Henry's Bathtub his eyes narrowed a fraction. A swimming hole about a mile down the highway, that young cop had mentioned it when he told Quarrie how to get to the diner. He said the bathtub had been named after the old guy who first opened the place, how he always had so much grease on him from flipping hamburgers the only time he ever got really clean was when he went for a dip. Somebody named the swimming hole after him and eventually the county put a sign up.

There was a gravel turnout about fifty yards ahead of the sign for the turn-off to Henry's Bathtub. Instinctively Quarrie brought the Riviera to a stop and got out. This was just a hunch but that waitress had said the bogus cop had left the diner straight after a guy she thought might be a travelling salesman. Right now Quarrie was wondering just how far the perp thought he'd be able to get driving a Winfield City prowl car. Standing on the edge of the highway he hunted down a cigarette and smoke drifted as he studied the surface of the turnout. No scenic overlook, nowhere for a picnic, this was the kind of spot where people would stop only if they had to adjust something on their vehicle. It was where a trooper might pull someone over.

Stepping closer to where the asphalt gave out he considered the packed gravel, the layer of dust and mess of tire tracks that fouled it. There were quite a few tracks here as there had been at the diner, and it took him a moment to locate it. But there it was: the same tread he had seen at the diner.

Back in the car he rolled down to the turning and eased up just ahead of the cattle guard. From where he sat he could see the same tire tracks marking the dirt beyond the metal grille. He still wore his pistols on his hips and, instinctively, he worked the hammer clips loose. Then he put the Riviera back in gear and rolled across the guard, following the trail for a hundred yards as it snaked towards a shallow rise. At the top of the rise he halted. Nothing but the flat, gray waters of the swimming hole, fifty yards down the slope to a stubby little bank of mud and rocks where the water was lapping gently. A little breeze in the air, as he got out of the car he could feel it cool on his face where it coasted off the water.

He followed the tire tracks all the way down the hill to the bank where they disappeared. He stood there with his hat in his hand, scrutinizing every inch of dirt where the tires dug deeper with the weight of the car and that told him it had been stationary. He could see the wall of the track where a little dirt had lifted then collapsed again and that indicated the car had moved some after it came to a halt. No reversing marks though: the trail ended there at the water.

As well as the tire tracks he located two sets of footprints, flat-soled shoes on them both, that had to be the perp wearing Officer Michaels' uniform and whoever it was he had with him. Moving a few paces into the brush, he picked up another set of prints that led back up the trail to the rise. No flat sole now, he recognized not only the pattern of the jungle boot, but also the nick in the heel.

For a moment he stared at the water then went back to his car. Unhooking the radio handset he rested an elbow on the roof.

'Zero Six calling Marion County sheriff.'

It took a moment before a disembodied voice crackled back. 'Copy that, Zero Six.'

'I'm at Henry's Bathtub, the old swimming hole on Route 49. Need you to put a call in to the police department in Winfield. Tell Chief Billings I think I might've found his cruiser.'

Eight

From his third-floor office Dr Beale could see the checkered barrier at the main gates where a young man in military uniform climbed into the back of the hospital Jeep. Below the window some of the male patients not confined to their cells were tending the lawns and flower beds under the watchful eye of an orderly.

From where he stood Beale was party to both sides of the ten-foot wall that separated the men from the women and he cast his eye across the grounds then looked back at the Jeep once more. At his desk he picked up a fountain pen and scribbled a couple of notes on a fold-over yellow pad, then screwed the top back on the pen and considered the telephone as if he was waiting for it to ring. After a moment he got to his feet and went back to the window. This time he concentrated on the far side of the wall where some of the female patients were gathered.

On his desk the phone rang and for a moment Beale seemed to study the little red light where it flashed at the base.

'Yes, Alice?' he said as he picked up. 'What is it?'

'Dr Beale, there's a man downstairs to see you. He's says his name is Isaac Bowen.'

The doctor seemed to hesitate. 'All right,' he said carefully. 'Have one of the orderlies bring him up.'

He waited now, standing behind the desk with a little perspiration marking his brow and his eyes wrinkled at the corners. A few minutes later there was a knock on the door and orderly Briers came in wearing a short, white housecoat and green T-shirt: a big man, he was balding and heavyset with tufts of gray hair lifting from the neck of his T-shirt.

'Doctor,' he said. 'Isaac Bowen is here to see you.' He stepped to one side and the young man in uniform came in. Still the orderly hovered, but Beale was intent on his visitor. Blue-gray eyes, his hair slicked back from his forehead, the dress uniform he was wearing looked a little care worn but it was neatly pressed and there was shine to the toes of his shoes. For a moment Beale studied him and the young man looked back with neither of them saying anything, then Beale indicated for Briers to close the door.

When he was gone the young man approached the desk. 'Thank you for seeing me, sir,' he said. 'My name is Isaac Bowen and I'm looking for my brother. I think he might be a patient here.'

Beale indicated an empty chair across the desk. 'Take a seat, Mr Bowen. You look as if you've come a long way.'

'I have, sir. From Vietnam.' Wearily Isaac sat down. 'My final tour. That's three now and I guess they figure I'm done.' Spreading a palm he gestured. 'Did Ishmael tell you about me? My brother, sir, Ishmael Bowen. He doesn't know I'm back yet. I wanted to surprise him before I go home to my dad.'

'I see,' Beale said.

'Dad doesn't know how I'm done over there yet. I was going to surprise him but only after I visited with Ish. The fact is our ship docked in San Francisco and the army flew me to Houston. I spoke to my dad on the phone he told me Ish had been moved to a place called Trinity. I never got to see him the last time – he was still in the hospital in Houston – and I didn't know about this other one, not till I spoke to Dad.' His eyes were pinched, a puzzled expression on his face. 'I had no idea there'd been a fire. I went down there and found the hospital in the woods like Dad said, but it was deserted, all burned up. I spoke to the caretaker, an old Mexican guy who told me the whole place went up and everyone had to be evacuated.'

'Yes, I'm afraid that's pretty much how it was.' Beale looked a little tentative. 'It was six weeks ago now. The fire took hold very quickly though nobody seems to know what set it off.'

'What happened to the patients?' Isaac asked. 'The caretaker said they were moved to other hospitals. He told me some of them came here and I ought to talk to you. He said that if Ish wasn't here you'd be able to tell me where they sent him.' He looked up, a hopeful expression on his face. 'Is he here, sir? I'd really like to see him.'

Beale seemed to think about that. Picking up his pen he made another note then replaced the pen on the desk. 'Your last tour, you say? You're home for good now then, are you?'

Isaac nodded. 'Yes, sir. Home for good, though if truth be told I wasn't sure I was going to make it.' He let a little air escape his cheeks. 'I guess it's always like that for someone who knows they're going home. They tell you ahead of time and it's all you can think about and yet you're still out on patrol.' Hunching a little forward in the seat he gestured. 'Everybody tells it the same. As the time gets close you just get more and more nervous. It's on your mind, how if you step in the wrong place or duck the wrong way . . .' He broke off for a second then he said, 'That last fire-fight . . . Just after they said I was coming home we were on the march – six hundred of us on the road about sixty miles north of Saigon. I kept telling myself it would be all right, how my number wasn't up and I was going to stay lucky. But then we came to this clearing and there they were there, waiting where we couldn't see them. Hidden in the sawgrass, they let go with everything they had, and all I could think about was avoiding bullets, leave alone firing back.'

'Sawgrass?' the doctor said.

Isaac nodded. 'Thick as a wheat field, reaches right to your waist.' Again he looked at the floor. 'I was walking the point, the tree line just ahead, and we could see nothing for all that grass. I guess they let go with heavy machine guns, ripped into us like you wouldn't believe. Thirty-one dead and a hundred and twenty-three wounded. We killed a hundred and seventy Vietcong, dug in real deep and waiting for back-up, and finally they sent in air support. Anyway,' he said, looking up, 'that's all done with now, thank God. Ishmael, sir, my brother: I really need to see him.'

Beale's expression was fixed. 'I'm afraid you can't. He's not here. The fact is not all the patients at Trinity were accounted for, and I'm sorry, but one of those was Ishmael.' He watched as Isaac's features stiffened. 'We're missing seven patients in all right now and until we have the final report we won't know how many bodies were actually recovered. It's not an easy identification process because with the way that fire took hold, the intensity of the heat, there wasn't much left.' He was staring intently across the desk. 'I'm sorry, but your father will know more. I imagine the investigators have been touch.'

He watched from the window as the Jeep took Isaac back to the gates. Brow a little sweaty, he plucked a key from the top drawer of his desk. On the far wall a picture of Sigmund Freud dominated the office. Taking it down Beale revealed an inset safe. Two shelves holding various reels of tape in cardboard boxes, they were labelled carefully and on top of them was an address book.

Back at his desk Beale flattened a page with the heel of his hand then picked up the phone. He hesitated a moment before dialling. Sitting back in the chair he waited for the phone to be answered. It rang and rang but nobody picked up and no answer machine cut in. Beale hung up, sought another page in the address book and dialled another number.

Once more he waited; three rings, four, five. Then the call was answered and he hunched a little closer to his desk.

'Hello,' he said. 'This is Dr Beale. I'm sorry to call you again so soon and I know you asked me not to. I thought you should know that he just showed up here at the hospital.' Listening for a moment he nodded. 'Bellevue in Shreveport, yes. He told me he'd been to Trinity and he's on his way to his father's house. Look, there's no need to worry. I'm going to go up there myself.' Again he listened and again he nodded. 'Yes, she is. One of the ones we brought here. Look, I know I said I wouldn't call, but I figured you ought to be aware. It will be fine though, there's nothing to worry about. I'm telling you just in case.'

For a while after he'd put the phone down he sat with his hand on the receiver where it rested back in the cradle. He looked long and hard at the notes he had made, then collected the pad of paper and his pen and placed them in his briefcase. Replacing the address book back in the safe he locked it and re-hung the photo.

From the bottom drawer of a file cabinet he retrieved a twin-reel tape recorder together with a hand-held microphone. Locating another set of keys, he left the office and locked the door. He told his secretary that something had come up and he would be away for a few days and she should cancel his appointments. Then he rode the elevator down to the ground floor.

In the lobby he left the tape recorder behind the desk, then used his keys to open the first of the adjoining doors. Cast from metal, the window was laced with wire mesh. Closing that door he locked it again, then walked the short corridor to another door with a similar pane of reinforced glass.

Now he was in the women's wing and he passed beyond a set of double doors into a common room where some of the patients played checkers while others stared at the TV. Women of all ages: pale in the face, lank-haired; wearing robes and baggy pajamas. Beale made his way through the common room and unlocked the far door. Opening and closing two more locked doors, he was in a corridor with linoleum on the floor and heavy oak doors with unbreakable panels were staggered on either side. He walked almost as far as the nurse's desk at the end before he paused outside a door on the right.

He could see the patient through the glass. Around fifty, she was bone-thin and bug-eyed, her hair weak and sparse with her waxen-colored scalp visible in places. A single bed, the walls covered in pencilled drawings of stick children. The woman was sitting on the bed cradling a baby in her arms, only the baby was a porcelain doll, and its hair was as thin as hers. On the other side of the room a narrow bureau was laid with a vinyl changing mat, next to it a Moses basket supported by wooden legs. Rocking back and forth, the woman suckled the doll at her breast.

Turning from the door Beale called to the nurse who was seated behind the desk at the end of the corridor.

'Nancy,' he said, 'can you let me into Miss Annie's room?'

A grim expression twisting her lips, the nurse got up from the desk and walked the corridor carrying a set of keys. Selecting one, she fit it in the lock but before she opened the door she paused.

'Dr Beale,' she said, 'don't you think I should fetch an orderly?'

He shook his head. 'No, that's all right. I'm not going to be very long.'

'Even so. She's not been herself just lately.'

He gave a hollow laugh. 'Nancy, when has Miss Annie ever been herself?'

'You know what I mean.' The nurse was peering through the panel to where the wizened-looking woman stared back. 'Are you sure you want to go in there? You know how she's been. Look at her. Look at her eyes; she's got that look in her eyes, and if you're going in there she really ought to be strapped.'

Beale too now looked through the window. 'In a jacket you mean? I don't think so. She trusts me, Nancy. She won't try anything. She never does.'

'She used to trust you,' the nurse said. 'She doesn't trust you anymore. She doesn't trust any of us anymore, and she remembers, Doctor. There's nothing Miss Annie forgets.'

Finally she unlocked the door and Beale went in. Nancy closed the door behind him but she did not lock it and she did not move away. The doctor leaned with his back to the panel of glass while Miss Annie remained where she was. She held the baby doll in her arms, its chill features pressed to a tired nipple where it poked through her pajama top.

'I'm feeding,' she said. 'You shouldn't be in here, not when I'm feeding my baby.'

'I know that and I'm sorry. How is he, Miss Annie?' Beale asked. 'How's your baby?'

She did not reply. She just looked at him. 'If you touch him, if you try and take him away from me, I'll kill you.'

Nine

Quarrie was still at Henry's Bathtub. Prising another cigarette from his pack he felt in a pocket for his lighter. The wrecker down by the water's edge was in position with the winch hooked up to the chassis of the submerged cruiser. The driver flipped the switch and the winch started rolling and a couple of minutes later the vehicle surfaced. The same steely blue as the car he had inspected back in town, it was dripping water and weed and hissed like some ancient leviathan. The driver's door was not locked and the keys were still in the ignition. Grabbing them, Quarrie opened the trunk.

The dead man's face was the color of a gutted fish, his clothes fastened to his skin. He looked flattened, as if the weight of the water had squashed him, where he lay curled in the foetal position between the traffic cones and wheel-jack. The Marion County sheriff stood with his arms folded and alongside him Chief Billings.

'Don't look like he took a bullet,' the chief said. 'Jesus Christ, do you think this sumbitch had him climb in?'

Briefly Quarrie glanced at him. 'Like you say, Chief: it don't look like he's holed any.'

He went through the dead man's sodden pockets. No driver's license or wallet, nothing that could identify him. Nostrils flared, he wiped his hands on his jeans.

'That gal you talked to from the diner,' the sheriff said. 'Did she have any idea what it was he might've been driving?'

Quarrie shook his head. He looked beyond the two men back towards the highway. 'Whatever it is, he's but a few hours ahead of us. We've traced him this far so I'm going to follow my gut and see if I can't get any closer.' He glanced at the sheriff again. 'Nicole,' he said, 'the waitress. Have somebody walk her through a detailed statement and call me if she comes up with anything.'

A few hours later he was south of Marshall, Texas, heading for the freeway and listening to the regular radio where the newscaster was relating a casualty report.

'Thirty-one Americans and one hundred and seventy-six of the enemy were killed in a three-hour battle in a jungle clearing sixty miles north of Saigon. Of the six hundred Americans involved, one hundred and twenty-three were wounded. There was no estimate for wounded among the Vietcong.' The man's voice was crisp and clear, staccato, like the firefight he was describing. *'The Vietcong struck first with heavy machine guns from the brush and tree line shortly after the American battalion hiked into the knee-high sawgrass. US soldiers returned fire and within fifteen minutes artillery began to pound the enemy positions...'*

The shortwave crackled where it was housed under the dash and Quarrie turned the regular radio off.

A woman's voice lifted through the speaker. 'Harrison County dispatch calling Ranger Unit Zero Six?'

Reaching for the handset Quarrie picked up. 'Copy that, Harrison County. What's up?'

'The sheriff up in Marion told us you might be in our neck of the woods and that you'd want the heads up on anything we got.'

'Yes, mam, go ahead.'

'The Sheers Motel in Fairview, one of the cleaning staff found the partial barrel of what she thinks is a shotgun dumped by the side of the road.'

Twenty minutes later he was driving Main Street, Fairview, passing the bank and mercantile. A little further he came to the Sheers Motel. A flat-roofed concrete block housing two dozen rooms together with a tiny reception area like a kiosk out front. The manager was sitting behind a tall counter reading a copy of

Sports Illustrated and the sawn-off barrel of a shotgun was lying on a sheet of brown paper. Bald-headed, when he got to his feet the man stood around five and a half feet with suspenders keeping up his pants.

'You the Ranger?' he said, glancing at Quarrie's guns.

Quarrie nodded.

Stepping back from the counter the manager wedged a fist against his hip and jutted his chin at the truncated barrel. 'Grace found it walking into town this morning.'

'Grace is the cleaner?' Quarrie was inspecting the roughly sawn barrel carefully.

'Colored woman, yeah. She's gone for the day right now; got kids at home to take care of.' The manager gestured vaguely in the direction Quarrie had just come from. 'I had her run to the store real quick to pick up some stuff we needed, and she came across this here piece of metal. Said it was back from the road aways but the sun caught on it and she went to see what-all it was. Just lying in the brush, she said, like somebody tossed it out of a car window.' Taking a hunk of chewing tobacco from his pocket, he peeled a sliver off with an overlong thumbnail that looked to have been cultivated for just that purpose. 'She brought it back here to me because she figured I'd know what to do.'

Again Quarrie considered the barrel. 'How far down the road did she find it? How far away from the motel?'

'I can't tell you exactly. About a hundred yards I reckon.'

'If I asked her could she show me the spot?'

'I don't know. She's pretty sharp. Yeah, I imagine she probably could.'

Quarrie cast another short glance his way. 'You busy right now? Got many people staying?'

'I guess there's one or two.'

'What about last night?'

'Five, I think there was.' Spinning the register around where it was laid on the counter, the manager took a look. 'Yeah, we had five people staying last night.'

Quarrie turned the book so it faced him again. 'What about vehicles? There're no license numbers written down here.'

The manager shook his head. 'This is a small place and people pay up front and usually it's with cash. I don't bother with license plates or stuff like that; it ain't as if we ever need to trace anybody.'

Looking through the window Quarrie studied the concrete block of rooms. 'Was one of your guests a young guy with dark hair?'

'Maybe. We had one young guy, I think. Can't tell you what-all color his hair was. I don't notice stuff like that.'

Quarrie squinted at him once more. 'You want to show me his room?'

Grabbing a key from the metal locker behind the desk, the manager led the way across the parking lot. He unlocked the door to room 13 and was about to go inside when Quarrie checked him with a hand on his shoulder. 'Grace cleaned this room already, is that what you said?'

The manager nodded. 'Last one before she went home.'

'OK, thanks. I can take it from here.'

The room was not very big and it was basic, a nightstand beside a narrow-looking double bed, a black-and-white TV and a tiny bathroom at the back. The bed was freshly made and the drapes at the window tied back. Yellow flowers had been painted directly onto plain blocks of blue cinder that made up the walls. The carpet was threadbare and patchy and in places he could see a hint of concrete showing through.

It looked as though everything had been vacuumed thoroughly and he imagined if Grace was sharp enough to spot the barrel of a shotgun by the side of the road then she would be more than fastidious in her work. Standing in the doorway still, he cast an eye across the nightstand, the bedclothes and the little table where the

TV was set. Nothing jumped out at him initially; he could see no marks on the table or nightstand to indicate where someone might have taken a saw to a shotgun. But then his gaze fastened on the luggage rack.

Moving into the room now he shut the door and considered the carpet again. It was clear Grace had worked it hard, but he kept to the edge of the room as he sought the luggage rack. Folding metal legs with canvas bands running in between, taking care to open it up he inspected those bands and could see nothing at first, but then he picked up the tiniest slivers of what looked like shavings of steel. In the bathroom he tore a piece of toilet paper off the roll and gently smoothed the shavings onto it. Folding the paper over, he took a pen and marked it with the room number and name of the motel.

Back in the parking lot he opened the trunk of his car where his 7mm hunting rifle was clipped to the underside of the lid. Lying on top of a folded sheet of tarpaulin was a briefcase and inside that a stack of evidence envelopes. Carefully he slipped the fold of toilet paper into one of those then sealed it and scribbled a note on the front. Grabbing a roll of police tape from his tool box he sealed the door to the motel room, then went back to reception for the barrel of the gun.

Back in the little kiosk he called the sheriff's office and requested that a lab team be sent down to dust the room. He told them he wanted a teletype of any fingerprints they recovered forwarded both to the National Crime Information Center and his captain's office in Amarillo. Then he went back to his car and drove the short distance into town.

The mercantile was on the right-hand side and he pulled into the parking lot and went in. A young woman was sitting on a stool at the checkout chewing gum, and he asked her if she remembered anyone coming in to purchase a hacksaw.

'Yes, sir,' she said. 'Young guy about my age came in here first thing.'

'What was it he bought exactly?'

'A hacksaw like you said. That and a roll of duct tape.'

Thanking her, Quarrie went back to the parking lot and was about to get in his car when he noticed the facade of the local bank. He stood there for a second or so chewing his lip and thinking how there'd been no wallet on the dead man in the trunk of the cruiser.

Inside the bank, he talked to the cashier and she showed him the check she had cashed for sixty dollars. A little red-faced, she admitted she had not asked the young man for any identification.

Using the manager's phone Quarrie spoke to Ranger Headquarters in Austin and then he went back to the mercantile to get a cup of coffee while he waited for somebody to call him back. He was sitting in his car outside the bank with his hat over his eyes when the manager came out and Quarrie followed him.

A dispatcher was on the phone and he took it at the manager's desk. 'John Q,' the woman said, 'we got the information you wanted. The body you found in the trunk was a salesman called Kelly, working for a farm supplies company out of Little Rock, and it's the company that owns the vehicle. 1966 Buick sedan, it's black and the license plate is five, double-three, double-one.'

'All right,' Quarrie told her. 'I want an APB out on that car and someone from Arkansas needs to call on Kelly's next of kin.'

Ten

Isaac Bowen spent the night in Shreveport, Louisiana, and in the morning he took a train to Texarkana and a bus from there to Paris. Late afternoon, he walked five miles west on the county road until he came to the junction where it forked with Route 38. Perched on the top rail of a fence he looked up at the sky where rain was threatening to fall. A few minutes later he heard the sound of an engine in the distance and saw the speck of gray as a vehicle approached. Straightening his tie he fixed the collar on his tunic, picked up his duffel and stuck out his thumb.

A pickup truck, it rumbled towards him but did not slow and Isaac lifted his hand. An older guy at the wheel, he was wearing bibbed denim overalls and a battered-looking hat. Spotting Isaac finally, he came to a halt ten yards further on.

'Where you headed, son?' Leaning across the seat he opened the door.

'Up towards Monkstown; house not far from the lake.'

The old guy indicated through the windshield. 'I'm driving 38 so I can only take you as far as the T.'

'Thank you, sir: the T junction will be just fine.' Throwing his duffel over his shoulder Isaac got in.

They drove west across flatland, the old man working the wheel while Isaac sat upright at the other end of the bench.

'Got us a little rain blowing in,' the old man said. 'Ain't been so bad over this way but out west they ain't seen a drop since fall.' He nodded to Isaac's uniform. 'I guess you wouldn't know too much about that, though, huh? I guess you been overseas. Good to see a man in uniform, son, especially right now what with all them kids waving placards and shouting the odds. Don't know what the world's coming to.'

'Was always going to happen,' Isaac told him. 'The service I mean. When I was growing up a soldier is all I was ever going to be. My dad was in the army and his dad before him, his granddaddy before that.'

'Is that a fact?' the old man said. 'Just get back from over there then, did you?'

Isaac nodded.

'So where is it you live?'

'Right now I'll be staying with my dad.' He pointed. 'Our place is way up there in the woods.'

The old man looked the width of the cab. 'Me, I farm a few acres a little ways south. Don't know many people up thataway anymore, though if I was a sight more neighborly I would. Wife died a few years back and I kind of got took up with being by myself.'

Isaac looked ahead. 'Well, sir, maybe you can come visit. I only just got back and I aim to surprise my dad.'

The old man said nothing further. He concentrated on the road ahead until they came to the T junction and he dropped Isaac before turning south.

Isaac walked in the opposite direction, making his way deep into the woods with the wind getting up and the first traces of lightning scattering the landscape ahead. Dry still here, he stepped up his pace and came to the mailbox at the bottom of the drive. He paused now, squinting at a car parked a little deeper into the woods. A Ford Fairlane, two-door with Louisiana license plates, he walked over to take a closer look. There was nobody around, but he could see a briefcase on the back seat and a weighty-looking tape machine with a reel of tape loaded and a microphone clipped to the side.

When he got to the house the front door was locked so he rang the bell but nobody came. He rang it again and still nobody came so he walked the length of the patio to the kitchen door only to find that was locked as well. With a shrug of his shoulders he crossed to the garage and found the door closed but not locked. Inside, his father's Pontiac sedan was parked next to the old pickup truck, the keys to which were hanging on a hook. Fetching those, Isaac climbed behind the wheel and backed the truck out then switched off the engine and left the truck on the drive. Inside the garage again he paused to consider the metal trapdoor in the floor that was visible now the truck was gone.

A storm shelter. He lifted the trap and climbed down the ladder into the darkened passage below. He stood there listening for a moment then he sought the light switch on the wall. The passage led to a large, square room made of concrete where his father kept sleeping bags and camp beds as well as water coolers, a propane stove and lots of canned food. From there another passage carried under the drive to another door with no lock, only a handle. Opening that, Isaac was faced by a panel made up of oak boards running lengthwise bottom to top. Working his fingers-down the right-hand side he found the spot and the panel swung in.

His father's study. He stood there catching the stale scent in the air and sniffed like a dog. The door to the basement corridor was open and as he moved around the desk he caught his foot against the leg. On one knee now, he retied a loose shoelace and noticed some tiny stains on the floor. He stared at them then flicked on the lamp but that did not give off enough light so he crossed to the wall and the switch for the overhead spots. Again he paused; the passage that led to the foot of the stairs was dark and chill, no sound of a TV or radio playing and no light shining from above.

'Dad?' he called. 'Are you home? It's Isaac, back from Vietnam.'

There was no reply. With light flooding the study now he went back to the desk and considered those stains again. A little air escaped his lips. A few blackened-looking dots, scraping at one with his fingernail he tasted it and his expression was grim. His attention was taken by the weapons cabinet fixed on the wall where one of the hooks was missing its gun. He looked at the floor once more and then back to that empty hook, then he heard the doorbell sound from above. Closing the wooden panel he cast another short glance at the gun cabinet then made his way along the basement passage and climbed the steps to the hall.

Through the window he could see a Fannin County prowl car parked in the drive outside. A skinny-looking deputy in his twenties was at the door in his light brown uniform with his hat in his hands, hair cut close and his cheeks carrying old acne scars.

'Mr Bowen?' he said, looking closely at Isaac's uniform. 'Sir, are you Isaac Bowen?'

Isaac nodded.

'We've been trying to find you, sir, through the Army. Is it all right if I come in?'

Isaac ushered him into the kitchen and the deputy stood there shifting his weight.

'Last couple of days,' he said, 'we were making a whole bunch of calls to see if we could track you down.'

'Why?' Isaac said. 'What's up?'

The deputy worked a palm around the brim of his hat. 'Well, sir,' he began, 'the fact is I have some bad news. Mr Palmer from the farm down the road there, he called the department just now and told us he'd given you a ride. He figured who you were but he didn't let on, on account of how he didn't think it was down to him to be the one to tell you. That had to be one of us.'

Isaac's gaze was taut. 'One of you – tell me what?'

The deputy looked him in the eye. 'Mr Bowen; there's no easy way to say this. I'm afraid your father is dead. I'm real sorry, sir; but it seems he took a gun to his head.'

Isaac stumbled backwards into the living room as if he'd been hit. One hand to the mantelpiece he leaned his weight before bending double as if he was about to throw up.

'Are you kidding me? My father – dead?'

The deputy avoided his eye.

'A gun to his head? But why? Why would he do that? Why would he shoot himself?'

The deputy lifted his shoulders. 'I'm not qualified to say, I'm afraid. I don't know is the fact of it. I said as much to the Ranger.'

'Ranger? What Ranger?' Isaac stared at him now.

'Well sir, it was a Texas Ranger that found his body and I have to say his first reaction was that your dad had been murdered, but the county doesn't see it like that. I'm real sorry, but he took his own life.' A little helplessly he gestured. 'This house is pretty isolated and it seems he was very much on his own. We've asked around but there wasn't anybody that knew him real well and none of them had ever met you.'

'I haven't been here,' Isaac said. 'I've done three tours, been fighting in Vietnam.'

'Yes sir, I can see that, and I'm sorry you had to come home to this.'

Isaac stared hard at the floor. He was biting down on his lip. 'I don't understand,' he said. 'A Ranger said someone killed him and you're telling me he killed himself?'

'That's what he told me,' the deputy confirmed. 'The Ranger I mean. But it was a first reaction and he wasn't here very long, and it's a county matter anyhow. Detective Crowley was here much longer than he was and he sees it as suicide. There was no sign of anybody else ever being here and no indication of a struggle. And your dad – well, I'm sorry, but he had a gun in his hand when I saw him and that gun was registered here at the house.'

Isaac had tears in his eyes, they were weighted and shining. He was shaking as he stood there looking from the deputy to the photograph and back.

'Is there anything I can do for you, sir?' the deputy asked. 'Anyone you want me to call? What about your mother?' He regarded the photo himself. 'Where's she at, sir? Would you like for us to try and get a-hold of her?'

'I don't know where she is,' Isaac said. 'She left when my brother and me were kids.'

'Oh, I'm sorry about that. I guess it's best if we leave it to you. I can see how this is a terrible shock.' The deputy shook his head. 'I never had to tell nobody nothing like this before and I'm sick to my stomach, I swear.'

Isaac did not seem to hear him. He was staring into space.

The deputy flapped his hat. 'Anyway,' he said, 'your daddy's body is in the mortuary over in Bonham. If you want to see him you'll need to call the coroner but I'm sure it would be OK. There'll be an autopsy of course, but I figure you'll want to make the funeral arrangements and there's a parlor on Chestnut and 5th.' Turning to go he glanced again at the photo. 'I guess that's you and your brother there, am I right?'

Isaac nodded.

'You look alike. Not identical, but about the same age.'

'We're twins,' Isaac told him. 'He was born fifteen minutes ahead.'

'Listen, sir, why I'm asking – we tried to get hold of him as well. Your brother. When we couldn't trace you we tried to find him, but there's no address for him anywhere about. We got his name from letters you wrote your dad, which are back in his desk, by the way. We couldn't find an address for him though. I guess he's over there in Vietnam too?'

Isaac shook his head. 'No. Ishmael isn't in the service.'

'Oh, OK. It doesn't matter. I guess you know where he's at and you-all can get in touch. It'd be better him finding out about this from family rather than us.' Again he flapped his hat. 'You have our condolences, sir. Everybody at the department, we're all real sorry for your loss.'

When he was gone Isaac went back to the living room as the clouds let go and rain started to rattle the windows. For a long time he stared at the photo on the mantelpiece and then he got to his feet. He was about to go back down to the study when he heard another car in the drive. The Fairlane he had seen parked on the dirt road, he watched as it pulled up and Dr Beale from the hospital climbed out.

Brows deeply furrowed, Isaac had the front door open before Beale could ring the bell. 'Doctor,' he said. 'I didn't know that was your car out there. What're you doing all the way out here?'

Beale stared past him into the hall. 'I came to see your father,' he said. 'I meant to offer you a ride yesterday and I don't know why I didn't. Your dad's been calling the hospital to see if we'd heard anything from the fire marshal. When you showed up, I guess it prompted me to drive on out.'

Slowly, Isaac nodded. He was gazing beyond Beale to the garage where the trapdoor was lying flat.

'Is he in?' Beale said. 'Your father, I'd like to talk to him. Is he here?'

Pacing around him Isaac strode across the drive to the garage and stared at the hole in the floor. For a moment Beale hesitated on the step. Then, with a short glance inside the house, he followed Isaac across the drive.

'What's down there?' he said, indicating the trapdoor.

'A storm shelter my dad put in.' Eyes glassy, Isaac's voice was distant. 'He was clever like that, learned how to do stuff, what with all those years in the army. There's a room down there with cans of food and that, first aid and water. Dad, he ... Dad ...' He was sweating suddenly, lines of perspiration running from his hair all the way to his jaw.

'Are you all right?' Beale asked. 'Where is Ike? I need to talk to him. Is he here?'

'No.' Isaac's voice cracked as he spoke. 'He's not here. He won't be here. He's dead, Doctor. A sheriff's deputy told me he killed himself.'

For a moment Beale just stared. Mouth open he lifted a hand as if to gesture then he let it fall.

Isaac was trembling, he was shaking his head. 'He came by just now – you must've passed his vehicle. He told me my dad shot himself.' He had tears in his eyes. 'I don't believe it. He wouldn't do that, not my dad. He was a soldier. All his life in the army and what reason could he have?' The pitch of his voice was rising and Beale took a short pace back. 'That deputy told me a Texas Ranger found his body and he said somebody shot him, only the detectives from the sheriff's department think he killed himself.' Again he shook his head. 'My dad would never do that. He's no coward. He's the toughest man I ever knew.' Spreading his fingers he gestured. 'Suicide, Doctor. No Bowen would do it. We're soldiers. We trace a line all the way back to when we carried colors in the war for the South.'

Beale looked down at the open trapdoor. 'But if that's what the sheriff's department said?'

'It doesn't matter,' Isaac stated. 'They don't know my dad and I don't care what they think, he would never take his own life. My mother left years ago and he survived that. He brought me and Ish up on his own and he's dealt with Ish being in and out of the hospital. There's no way he'd abandon us. It doesn't matter that we're grown. If he was shot in the head then somebody shot him. He would not shoot himself.'

He paused for a moment then he murmured, 'They must have been watching the house.' He glanced towards the tree line then stabbed a finger at the hole in the floor. 'They must've found out about the passage. They must've seen Dad down here when the trapdoor was up and this is how they snuck in.' He was nodding to himself. 'There's a passage down there that leads all the way to a wood panel that opens into Dad's study. He put it in as an escape route so we wouldn't have to cross the yard if a tornado hit. That's where they found him, sitting at his desk in his study.' Again he paused and then again he gestured. 'There's a switch down there in the passage and you have to know where it's at, but I reckon if somebody was down there long enough they'd be able figure it out.

There's a door that opens onto this wall of wood and that'd tell you there's got to be something behind it. Come on, Dr Beale. I'll show you.'

Sliding down the ladder he dropped to the floor then beckoned the doctor to follow. For a moment Beale seemed to hesitate, then he too climbed down to the passage.

Underground, he followed Isaac through the storm shelter to the second passage. He followed him to where the door was closed and Isaac indicated the wooden panel.

'See what I mean?' he said. 'That's the back side of the oak Dad used to line his study.' Placing his palm on the wall he worked his fingers down the right-hand side and stopped when he found the switch.

'Isaac,' Beale said as the panel clicked open, 'that's really intricate. I don't think anyone who didn't know how to do that would be able to open it, really – do you?' Through the half-dark he offered a smile. 'Look, I know it's tough and you don't want to believe it but perhaps the sheriff is right.'

Eleven

When he left the bank in Fairview Quarrie drove back to the station house in Winfield, where he found the chief in his office wading through a pile of papers with the air conditioner barely working and perspiration lacing his brow.

'You're back then,' Billings said.

Quarrie perched on the arm of the ratty chair. 'I got as far as Fairview and that shotgun barrel before the trail ran cold. It's almost certain our boy crossed the state line so we ought to get onto the Feds.'

'Already taken care of.'

Sitting back in the chair Billings laid down his pen. 'You know, since you found that cruiser so quick I've been asking a couple of questions about you.' He indicated Quarrie's holstered guns. 'From what I hear you're pretty special with that pair of irons. More than special: they say there ain't a cop in Texas can beat you when it comes to combat examination. They told me how you can draw and kill a man before he can pull the trigger even if he's holding?'

Quarrie nodded. 'I can do that.'

The chief arched both eyebrows. 'Throwback to the old days, huh? Old-school Ranger like your Uncle Frank.'

'They say prevention's better than cure, Chief – ask any hospital Doc.'

With a smile then Billings gestured. 'So, if I had a piece pointed at you right now – my old Model 10, say – all cocked and ready to go, you could draw and fire, kill me before I had time to get a round off?'

Evenly Quarrie looked back. 'Chief, I could put a pair in you and holster again before you could get the message from your brain to

69

your trigger finger.' His eyes were a little dull. 'Frank Hamer took a bullet seventeen times and on four occasions he was left for dead. It was him taught me to take care of myself, and if you've been checking you'll know I got a son to bring up on my own. Right before she died, I promised his momma I'd take care of him so making sure nothing happens to me is something I study on.'

Billings puffed the air from his cheeks. 'Seventeen times, eh? Is that a fact?'

'And four times left for dead.'

'You know, I think I read somewhere how old Hamer wrote the king of England during the war, something about a bodyguard of retired Rangers going over there in case the Germans made it as far as London.'

Quarrie nodded. 'Yes sir, that's what he did.'

'Big letter writers then, your family.' Billings seemed to be musing now. 'I hear how your best friend is a black guy and you wrote President Truman about him. Something about a court-martial in Korea?'

Quarrie held his eye. 'His name is Pious Noon, Chief. They said he was a coward, but he risked his life to drag me off a hill after I was gut shot and bleeding out.'

Eyes bright Billings nodded. 'That's what I heard. It's what you told the president in the letter they published in the *New York Times*. From what I read, on account of it that boy's sentence was commuted to life in prison but he ended up with just five in the federal pen.'

'What's your point, Chief?' Quarrie said.

Adjusting his jacket, the chief got to his feet. 'I don't have a point. Just like to know who it is I'm working with whenever I'm partnering up.'

They drove back to Mary-Beth Gavin's place only this time in Quarrie's car. Parking outside the darkened windows of the run-down house, he looked up and down the street.

'Must've been a hell of a racket going on in there and nobody heard a thing?'

The chief shook his head.

'That's the neighborhood for you I guess.'

Getting out of the car they walked the path to where Billings unlocked the front door.

Inside the house everything was just as it had been before. Nothing had been touched only Mary-Beth's outline was fading a little where it had been chalked on the floor. Quarrie stood in the hallway with his thumbs hooked in his belt. Head to one side he considered that mark and the way the furniture had been knocked about. He was talking as if to himself. 'He comes here because he knows who she is and she has something he wants.'

'Quarrie, that's your supposition, not mine.'

Quarrie looked sideways at him. 'You got another idea?'

Billings shrugged. 'B&E gone wrong; intended rape victim – maybe he couldn't get a hard on.' He threw out a hand. 'I don't know, Sergeant. I'm just playing devil's advocate here like one of us is supposed to.'

With a smile Quarrie stepped into the room. He stared at the floor, the rug and walls where the spots of spattered blood had dried. Picking his way between the drawers, the broken mirror and smashed leaves of the table, he paused where the room opened into the kitchen.

'Probably you're right,' Billings said from behind him. 'He wanted something from her. We just have to figure out what it was.'

Quarrie took a few moments to look over the kitchen. Compared to the rest of the house it seemed relatively untouched. Opening the refrigerator he found milk and butter, a package of bacon wrapped in waxed paper as well as an unopened bottle of wine.

The cupboards yielded nothing but crockery and some cookware; a few cans of food and a sack of ground coffee. Mary-Beth had kept a little cork noticeboard pinned to the wall, though nothing was pinned to it and it hung askew. Nothing stood out. Nothing spoke to him and he eased his hat a little higher on his brow.

'Chief,' he said, 'did you come across an address book or anything like that? Something with phone numbers in it?'

'No sir, we did not.'

Quarrie looked back at him. 'Doesn't that strike you as odd?'

'Not really. Not everybody keeps an address book. She was new to town and according to the neighbor that found her, nobody ever seemed to come visit.'

The neighbor's name was Jane Perkins and she actually lived three blocks down the street, and wasn't a neighbor so much as a woman who also worked for MacIntyre's Farm Machinery. Opening the door when they knocked, she showed them into an identical one-bedroomed house, only it was neat and clean. About Mary-Beth's age, she told Quarrie that her husband had died of cancer and she'd been on her own the last five years.

'I been working for Mr McIntyre almost ten,' she added. 'He owns these houses and I don't know if you knew that, Mr Billings?' She glanced at the chief. 'They come as part of the job and that's why Mary-Beth was so keen to get it. It's why she worked that first week without any pay and I had her staying here with me because she didn't have money for a motel.'

Quarrie squinted at her. 'She roomed here?'

'Yes, she did, but only for a week.'

'Where did she come from?'

'I don't know, sir. She never told me.'

Quarrie raised an eyebrow. 'A couple of girls rooming together and the two of you didn't talk?'

'Oh, we talked plenty, but Mary-Beth never really said where she was from or what she'd been doing before. I asked all right, but when she didn't tell me right off I didn't figure it polite to be asking again.'

'Did anybody ever visit with her?'

'Not that I know of,' Mrs Perkins said. 'At least nobody she ever talked about anyway. I don't recall seeing any cars parked at her place, other than hers I mean. But then she was only here six weeks. She was nice enough, I guess. But she was quiet. She kept herself to herself.'

Sitting back in the chair, Quarrie crossed his ankle on his knee. 'While she was staying here did she call anybody on the phone?'

'I don't think so.' Mrs Perkins twisted her lips. 'She certainly didn't when I was home and she never asked to use the phone. But then I wasn't home all the time. Sometimes she was here on her own.'

'Do you still have the bill from back then? When she was staying with you, I mean.'

'From the phone company? It might be around somewhere but I don't hang on to them as a rule.'

'But you read them though, right? The numbers I mean, check for any mistakes?'

Mrs Perkins made a face. 'I don't know as I do so much actually. Not especially now you mention it, no.'

'But you have long-distance?'

'Yes sir, but only if I call the operator.'

Quarrie looked closely at her then. 'Mrs Perkins,' he said, 'if it's all right with you I'm going to need to sequester your records from the phone company.'

Billings looked sideways at him.

'What do you need those for?' Mrs Perkins seemed a little puzzled.

Quarrie indicated the window. 'You found Mary-Beth's body. You saw how badly she'd been beaten up?'

With a shiver Mrs Perkins nodded.

'Me and the chief here,' Quarrie glanced at Billings, 'we believe that whoever did that to her wanted something. We don't think they got it and that's why they beat her up. We think that was done out of frustration, and if she had something they wanted then it's possible she knew them from somewhere. It's possible they might've spoken to her on the phone.' He looked at the chief once more where he was sitting across the room. 'The police department's already asked for Ms Gavin's records, isn't that right, Chief?'

Billings colored a little before he nodded.

Where she sat on the couch Mrs Perkins tucked her legs underneath her and looked from one of them to the other.

'Right now we know nothing about her.' Quarrie's tone was gentle but firm. 'We have no idea who she was or if she had any family or where she lived before. You say she didn't really talk?'

Mrs Perkins shook her head. 'Like I said just now, she kept pretty much to herself. I asked of course, made conversation, but she wasn't one for giving much away. She wasn't married – I know that much – because she was on her own of course, and she had no ring on her finger. Whether she'd ever been married I can't say. She only stayed with me that one week and it wasn't even a full week now I come to think on it. It was only four days before Mr MacIntyre told her she had the job permanent. After that she moved into the house down on the corner and I only ever saw her at work.'

Twelve

Dr Beale spent the night in a motel in Bonham a few miles west of the Bowen house. Fetching some food from the local diner he ate in his room and when he'd finished he got up and went to the window. Easing the drape aside he gazed across the darkened parking lot. Nothing moved; nobody out there. Even so, he checked the dead bolt to make sure the door was secure just the same. The tape recorder was on the bed and he unhooked the microphone.

'May thirty-first, 1967. Dr Mason Beale in a motel room in Bonham – that's Fannin County, Texas.' He paused for a moment looking down where the spool still turned. Clearing his throat he sat straighter. 'Icarus Bowen is dead. According to the sheriff's department he shot himself, but his son is at the house right now and he believes it was murder.'

*

Isaac woke in his father's house. He lay in bed gazing at the white-painted ceiling then got up and took a shower. Combing his hair back from his forehead, he dressed in his uniform and went to the garage where the keys were still in the pickup. Climbing behind the wheel he drove the short distance to the town of Bonham.

The sheriff's department was a modern, flat-roofed building built across the street from the courthouse. A couple of cruisers in the parking lot, Isaac went in through the glass-panelled doors and found a young woman seated in front of a telephone switchboard.

'My name is Isaac Bowen,' he told her.

'Yes, sir.' She offered a shallow smile. 'I thought it might be, on account of your uniform. We're all so sorry for your loss.'

'Thank you, mam. That's kind of you.' Isaac rested a palm on the counter. 'I want to talk to the deputy who came by my house yesterday.'

'All right, sir. I'll see if he's around.' Plugging a lead into the switchboard the woman asked if Collins was back there and then she looked up at Isaac. 'He'll be right out,' she said and indicated a pair of plastic chairs set next to a fake orange tree. 'Why don't you take a seat?'

Isaac did that. Tunic buttoned, he straightened the flaps and sat with his head bowed and hands clasped together. A couple of minutes later the deputy with the pock-marked face appeared from behind the counter.

'Mr Bowen,' he said. 'You asked to see me, sir. What can do for you?'

Isaac was on his feet. 'The detective you told me about – the one who said my dad shot himself. I don't think that's what happened and I'd like to talk to him if that's OK?'

The deputy looked at him with his brows knit. Briefly he glanced over his shoulder at the switchboard girl and then he looked back.

'Lieutenant Crowley you're talking about. He ain't here right now, I'm afraid. They got him giving evidence in a trial down in Houston.'

Pushing open the glass doors he led Isaac outside. The sun climbing a cobalt sky, the heat shifted tar macadam into mush so it stuck to the soles of their shoes.

'Look,' Collins said, 'I know how this is for you. I lost my own father when I was fourteen and I understand, I promise you.'

Isaac stared at him. 'Did somebody shoot him?' he asked.

'No, sir.'

'Did anybody tell you that he killed himself?'

'No, he died of liver cancer.'

'Then I'm sorry, but you don't know how it is. I want to see him. My dad – where is he?'

The deputy drove him across town to the hospital off Rayburn Drive. Parking the cruiser he led the way through a side door where a coroner's ambulance was parked. They went down a flight of steps into a short corridor where a set of fire doors faced them. Collins opened those and beyond them they found a clerk in a white coat sitting at a metal desk. A white-tiled anteroom, he listened to the request the deputy made, took a swig from the coffee cup perched at his elbow, then led them into a smaller room at the back where a rack of metal drawers were fixed in vertical rows. Studying the names on the drawers he pulled out a gurney from the row at the bottom.

Isaac stared at his father's face. Colorless and empty, a tick started up at the corner of his mouth; he ground his jaws so the teeth scraped across one another audibly. At his sides his hands had knotted into fists. His father's eyes were closed; the skin on the right eye purple and puffy. Pacing around the gurney Isaac bent to study the hole at his temple where a hint of soot lay scattered in all but invisible pinpricks.

With a sigh the deputy folded his arms. 'The Ranger told me how that wasn't a contact wound, but the lieutenant said it didn't matter. Your dad had a lot of guns, Mr Bowen; he knew how to use them and it didn't matter that the barrel wasn't pressed right up to the skin.'

Isaac was still inspecting the wound. 'My dad was 82nd Airborne. He fought in Africa and took a bayonet in the stomach.' He was shaking his head, looking from the deputy to the clerk and back again to his father's body. 'There's no way he would've shot himself. I don't care what your lieutenant said.'

They drove back to the sheriff's department and Isaac sat with the window rolled down and his tie loose at the collar. He had his top button undone and sweat scrolled from his temple.

'Deputy Collins,' he said. 'I can't talk to your lieutenant right now because he's not here.' He looked sideways at him. 'That Texas Ranger you told me about – how do I get a-hold of him?'

*

When Beale drove back to the Bowen house he found the pickup gone and there was no answer when he rang the bell. He rang a second time but still nobody came to the door so he walked round to the back of the house and peered through the kitchen window. No sign of anybody inside. Walking back to his car, he seemed to ponder before he got in.

Back in Shreveport a few hours later he showed his pass to the guard at the hospital gates. Collecting the tape recorder and his briefcase from the trunk of the car, he walked the length of the road to the main entrance, glancing at the patients who were stable enough to work in the garden.

Inside the building it was cool as he crossed the polished parquet floor to the elevator where an orderly ensured no patient made it up to the suite of offices. He nodded to the doctor and Beale nodded back, and when he got to the third floor he spoke to his secretary.

'How are things, Alice? Has anyone been in touch?'

A middle-aged woman wearing pearl-white cat-eye spectacles, she looked up from behind the weight of her typewriter. 'Nothing that was urgent, Doctor: everything here is fine. There's nothing to report, though don't forget the meeting with the trustees later.' She paused briefly before she added. 'Unless you want me to cancel that, of course: I did tell them you'd gone away and that you might not be back.'

Beale had his office door open. 'Do that, Alice, would you? Tell them I am back, but I'm busy as hell right now so if it could be re-scheduled I'd appreciate it.'

Inside his office he closed the door then placed the tape recorder on the coffee table and unhooked the reel of tape. Sliding that into a cardboard case he marked the label then locked it in the safe with the others. Behind him the phone buzzed on his desk.

'Yes, Alice?' he said as he pressed the speaker.

'Orderly Briers is asking to see you.'

Beale seemed to think about that. 'Is he out there now?'

'No sir, he just called from downstairs. Said he saw your car in the parking lot and that he needs to have a quick word.'

Beale made a face. 'All right,' he said. 'Have him come up.'

A few minutes later the orderly was standing before Beale's desk and seemed to regard the doctor a little cautiously.

'Dr Beale,' he said, 'Alice told me you were away for a day or two but she didn't say where you'd gone.'

Beale looked up. 'That's because I didn't tell her.'

Briers colored slightly, hovering on the balls of his feet. 'I spoke to Nancy. We talked, the two of us. What's happening, Doc? What's going on?'

Beale looked at him for a moment longer then his expression softened. Allowing a little trapped air to escape his lips he sat back in the chair and gazed beyond Briers to the photo of Freud.

'I went to Texas,' he said. 'I went to see Ike Bowen.'

'Did you?' Briers's brow was furrowed. 'And what did he have to say?'

'Nothing,' Beale shifted his attention back to the orderly. 'He's dead, Charlie. He blew his brains out.'

Thirteen

When he left Mrs Perkins house Quarrie told Billings he would be back when the phone records came in and then he made the long drive home.

It took him a little over five hours and he found James watching TV in the cottage with Eunice keeping an eye on him. The house was one of three Pick Feeley had built in whitewashed adobe, set alongside the bunkhouse on a piece of flat land a little way below the remodelled ranch house. Quarrie slipped Eunice an extra ten dollars and asked if her brother was about. Eunice told him that he'd been in Houston with Mrs Feeley but the airplane was back in its hangar and he was probably over at the bunkhouse now.

When his son was tucked up in bed, Quarrie crossed the yard to the low-lying building where he found Pious playing cards with the Uruguayan foreman. At twenty-three years old Nolo Suarez was the single most accomplished horseman Quarrie had ever seen. His father had been a gaucho all his life, working a spread south of Montevideo, and his mother was part Comanche and part Tejano. The bearer of an American passport, Nolo had come north when he hit eighteen and ended up in the panhandle. Pick Feeley was still alive back then and he gave the kid a job. Now Pick was gone Mrs Feeley couldn't do without Nolo, not unless she decided to turn all the land she owned over to oil and get rid of the stock completely.

Mama Sox had a half dozen bottles of Falstaff sweating in the fridge. Pious's mother, she ran the bunkhouse along with Eunice, and Quarrie had known them since he was a fourteen-year-old kid. When Pious was locked up in Leavenworth, Quarrie found his mother and sister work at the ranch and they had been there ever since. Grabbing a long neck he snapped off the top and sat down at the table.

'You look beat, John Q,' Nolo said.

'Do I? Fact is I been on the road so long I could sleep on a chicken's lip.'

Nolo laughed. He indicated the cards. 'You want to play? We could deal you in?'

'No, sir.' Quarrie shook his head. 'I'm a worse poker player than Pious even and that's saying something.' With a grin he glanced at his old friend. 'James told me he talked to you about that train wreck up on the Red.'

'Yes, he did.' Pious was concentrating on his hand.

'You never said to him what we found there?'

Pious shook his head. 'Nope. You told me how you'd tell him when you were ready and I figured you meant what you said. Did you talk to the sheriff yet?'

In his mind's eye Quarrie could see those bones in the river again. 'Not so far,' he said. I was going to but then this business kicked off in Marion County. James told me he's going to write something up for school though, and I figured I wouldn't tell him about the skull until I saw what it was he had. Meantime I'll get a-hold of Sam Dayton and have one of his boys come up here so you can show them where we were fishing at.'

'You know what?' Pious said. 'We could bring those bones up and give them a proper burial, but the way I see it they're pretty much buried as it is. I guess I told you that wreck happened forty years ago but I was wrong about that. On the way down to Houston Mrs Feeley said to me how that bridge actually came down in nineteen hundred and three. That's sixty-four years, John Q, and those bones been there ever since. If this was up to me I'd leave them where they're at rather than go disturbing them over again.'

'I'd kindly like to oblige you, Pious, but the fact is I'm a cop.' Taking another swig of beer Quarrie got to his feet. 'I can't be leaving human bones lying around for someone else to come up on. You ain't the only catfish grabbler knows about that wreck. Sooner or later somebody else will make the same discovery we did. We need to gather those bones up and I should've done it right off. I'll get hold of the sheriff first thing in the morning. And you never know, if James does this project thing properly, maybe he'll come up with a name for the kid.' He took another pull at the bottle. 'He told me you said you might help show him how to look stuff up, and seeing as how I'm on the road right now, I'd be obliged if you did.'

After he dropped James off at the bus stop the following morning, Quarrie drove to Wichita Falls and Sheriff Dayton's office where he was able to commandeer a desk. He had the sawn-off section of twelve-gauge barrel as well as the slivers of metal he had recovered in two separate evidence envelopes and he sent them to the forensic lab in Austin. He was about to wire the newly formed National Crime Information Center to see if they had anything on the fingerprints, when a call came in.

'Dispatch here, John Q. We got someone on the line wants to talk to you.'

'Yeah?' he said. 'Who is it?'

'He says his name is Bowen and he's calling from Fannin County.'

Quarrie waited for the operator to put the call through with his knee resting against the lip of the desk.

'Sir, I'm sorry to bother you.' The voice sounded a little emotional. 'My name's Isaac Bowen. My dad was Icarus Bowen, though everybody called him Ike.' He broke off for a moment then he said. 'The deputy from Fannin County told me it was you that found his body.'

'That's right,' Quarrie said. 'I was passing when your father's gardener called the sheriff. It's their deal though; you need to be speaking to them.'

'Yes sir, I know that and I have done. The thing of it is Deputy

Collins said you told him my daddy was murdered but they think he killed himself.'

Back at the ranch Quarrie found Pious working on one of the trucks. 'Bud,' he said, 'does Mrs Feeley have any plans right now for the plane?'

Standing tall Pious wiped his hands on a rag and glanced from the barn to the hangar up on the plateau where the ranch house was built. 'Not that she told me.'

'I need for you to fly me to Fannin County. You figure you could do that? Department's paying for the gas.'

'Sure.' Pious jerked a thumb at the truck. 'I'd rather be flying that plane than working on this piece of shit. Just give me a minute to make the checks.'

Thirty minutes later they were in the cockpit of a '63 Piper Cherokee – a model that had been brought out to compete with the Cessna. A two hundred and thirty-five horsepower unit with a pair of tip tanks holding seventeen gallons a piece. Pious said they did that to enhance the load capacity, and along with the existing tanks that made a total of eighty-four gallons. Quarrie wasn't up on the pay load or any kind of avionics, but when they were kids Pious had been able to fix just about any ailment on any engine that was placed in front of him. A couple of years after he started working the ranch, Pick Feeley had been so impressed he paid for him to get his pilot's license.

Seated at the controls Pious glanced across the cockpit, a pair of mirror-lens Ray-Bans pressed high on the bridge of his nose.

'So,' he said, 'tell me if I got this right. The sheriff is saying suicide and you reckon homicide. Is that about how it is?'

Quarrie nodded.

'You sure he's wrong and you're right? I mean, I know how you like to think you ain't ever been wrong, but I've known you twenty-two years, John Q, and you been wrong a bunch.'

'Pious, do I tell you how to fix this plane?'

'Nope.'

'Do I tell you how to take off or land?'

'Wouldn't pay you any mind if you did.'

'So, I've seen enough gunshot wounds to know when it's a suicide and when it ain't, and people don't shoot themselves with a gun held two inches away from their head.'

Pious eased the sunglasses a little lower. 'And that's how it was with this guy?'

'That's how it was with this guy.' Quarrie stared through the spinning prop. 'Somebody took a twenty-two automatic from his gun cabinet and stood alongside him as he sat at his desk. After he was dead they sat him a little more upright and put the gun in his hand. I know that not just from the powder burns but the way blood settled after he was dead.'

Pious put the plane down a few miles south of the lake. On the phone Isaac had told Quarrie that a farmer named Palmer had an alfalfa field that had been sheared right back to the dirt. Quarrie knew Pious could land on that and he settled the Piper on its wheels before rolling to a stop just ahead of a ragged-looking barn where most of the paint was peeled off.

Quarrie got down and Pious got down and they could see Isaac Bowen in dress uniform leaning on the fence next to an old boy in a pair of denim overalls. Quarrie wore a Carhartt jacket with his twin-rig shoulder holsters underneath, but neither man was looking at him.

'Something, ain't it?' A little sadly Pious wagged his head. 'How a black man can be flying an airplane. Never would've guessed it, a damn-fool thing like that.'

The old man did not say anything, he just looked on with faint hint of color in his cheeks.

Quarrie was studying the man in uniform. 'You Bowen?' he said.

Isaac nodded. 'Yes sir, I am.' He indicated the older man. 'This is Mr Palmer.'

84

They walked across the dust-blown yard to an old Ford pickup, and by the time they got there Palmer was picking Pious's brains about the plane. Isaac got behind the wheel with Pious next to him and Quarrie on the far side. He drove them north to the woodland and the mailbox with the Bowen name.

Talkative to begin with, Isaac slipped into silence as they closed on the house. By the time they turned into the gravel driveway he was silent and the color had gone from his face.

'You-all just hit back in the world then, did you?' Pious asked him.

Pulling up out front of the open garage Isaac killed the engine. 'Yes, I did.' He looked sideways. 'You in the service, were you?'

'Triple volunteer like you.' Quarrie indicated the insignia on Isaac's sleeve. 'Old Pious might fly an airplane these days but there was a time we were jumping out.'

Standing on the gravel driveway he could feel the heat of the breeze coming up from the south. Above them no clouds billowed, there was only the sun; a yellowed ball, it seemed to echo the yellow brick of the house.

Isaac led the way into the kitchen where he had coffee going in a new pot. He poured three cups and passed them round. Pious wandered through to the living room where he noticed the green felt table. 'Texas Hold'em, or five-card stud?'

'Blackjack is what it was.' Isaac followed his gaze. 'My dad used to play blackjack when he was first married. I guess that table is just a reminder though, because I never once saw him deal a hand. There's an alcove underneath with chips and all, got a deck back there that's still wrapped up.' He looked at Quarrie. 'Somebody shot him, that's what you said?'

'That's what I figured when I saw him.'

'So why is it the sheriff's telling me he took the gun to himself?'

Quarrie thought about that. 'Beats me,' he said. Looking beyond Isaac he considered the family photograph. 'I found marks where blood settled in his neck. That indicates post-mortem movement and he couldn't do that by himself. Hasn't the coroner seen the body?'

'I don't know,' Isaac shrugged. 'Nobody said.'

'OK, I'll check that out when we're done.' Quarrie considered his uniform again. 'So how much time did you get in?'

'In Nam you mean? Three tours.'

'You weren't drafted then? You volunteered? Where was it you were fighting at?'

'No, I wasn't drafted,' Isaac told him. 'I was regular Army and it was the Fishhook I was based at. Fought in the Crow's Foot valley, places like that. Long-range recon – they liked to have me walk the point.' Loosely he gestured. 'Last detail ended up as a firefight sixty miles north of Saigon.'

Quarrie was still looking at the photograph.

'Ambush from the sawgrass, had us pinned down up there with thirty-one dead and a hundred and twenty-three wounded.'

'Your last detail huh?' Quarrie studied him again. 'After that you were on your way back?'

Wiping a line of perspiration from his brow, Isaac nodded. 'Last detail of my last tour. Took the boat home to surprise my dad only, it was me got the surprise of my life instead.'

Quarrie glanced briefly at Pious. Then he looked back to where Isaac was trembling ever so slightly. 'You OK there, Isaac?' he said.

'Yes, sir,'

'You staying here at the house?'

Isaac nodded.

'Kept it spotless, didn't he? Your dad, I mean: stickler for that kind of thing.'

With a half-smile, Isaac nodded. 'Yes, I suppose he was. Learned how to be like it in the army – his whole life the army; Africa then Korea, fighting in the jungles, he was always saying how easy it was for infection to set in. Kept everything clean on account of it, and

86

he was so obsessive I guess that was one of the reasons Mom left.'

Crossing to the fireplace Pious took a long look at the photograph. 'That your mother there?'

Isaac nodded.

'How long ago did she leave?'

'I guess not long after that picture was taken. Maybe a year or so – I can't recall exactly.'

'That your brother there with you?' Quarrie said. 'Where he's at?'

At that Isaac faltered. His lips seemed to form words but none came out, as if he was just about keeping his emotions in check.

'I don't know,' he said. 'That's something else I've got to deal with. I can't find him. I can't find Ish.' He pressed the air from his cheeks. 'He was at Trinity, the hospital. There was a fire and . . .' His voice seemed to break all over again. 'The whole place went up and they told me a few of the patients still aren't accounted for.'

Sinking into an armchair he looked helpless. 'That's why this whole thing is as bad as it is. I mean coming home from all that shit over there to find your family . . .' He lifted his palms once again. 'All anybody wants over there is family. But I come home to find I don't seem to have one, not anymore, not unless I can find Ish.' Tears built. He seemed to be fighting them where he sat. 'I get off the boat after six weeks at sea and fly to Houston to go to the hospital because it's a year since I saw Ish. I wanted to do that before I came here. I wanted to check on my brother. I wanted to see how he is. But when I get there, when I get to the hospital, I see the whole place is burned and I have to go up to a place called Bellevue. That's Shreveport, Louisiana; and when I get there they tell me that Ish is either dead or missing. I get home here and my dad . . . Him and me, Dad and me . . .' Eyes closed now he shook his head. 'Well, anyway, the fact is my dad is dead and they're telling me he killed himself.'

Blowing out his cheeks he gestured. 'I'm sorry, but there's no way

87

I believe that, despite the way he was.' He paused for a moment then he added, 'What I mean is – the thing with my dad, he was different after Mom left. I guess that was only natural. All my life he was a little distant, and maybe that's how he was around her. Maybe that's why she left. But after she did – after that it was just the three of us and he was even more distant then.'

'How do you mean?' Quarrie said.

'I don't know, I guess he never said a whole lot, and I wrote him all the time but he never once answered my letters.'

Pious was staring at him with his brows knit. 'You wrote your old man and he never wrote back?'

Isaac nodded.

'From Nam you talking about?'

Again Isaac nodded.

Quarrie shifted to the edge of his seat. 'But why?' he said. 'He used to be a soldier. He must've known what it's like to be in a combat zone and how important mail from home is.'

'You'd think so,' Isaac said. 'He was a soldier all his life. Got wounded a couple times. When he was in Africa he took a bayonet in the gut and it almost killed him. The fact is I wrote all the time – I'm talking three full tours and he never once wrote back.'

Fourteen

He showed them the entrance to the storm shelter, Quarrie standing in the garage with Pious at his shoulder while Isaac lifted the trapdoor.

'I think whoever it was shot him got in this way,' Isaac said. 'They must've been staking out the house from the woods.'

Quarrie looked doubtful, head to one side and his hands in his jacket pockets. 'Mind if we take a look?'

Isaac told them about the panel leading to his father's study and how to open it, then Quarrie and Pious climbed down. They walked the short passage to the storm shelter and took in the camp beds, sleeping bags, and the cans of food stacked on the shelves. From there they followed the second passage to the other door and the back side of the wood panelling. For a moment Quarrie considered it, then worked the tips of his fingers down the right-hand side as Isaac had suggested. Nothing happened. He sought another spot, pressed that and still nothing happened. Locating a third spot he tried again and still nothing happened. At the fourth attempt nothing happened but at the fifth they heard the faintest of clicks and finally the panel swung in. Quarrie cast a glance at Pious.

Inside the study they moved around the desk where Quarrie's eye was drawn to the tiny spots of dried blood that still marked the floor. He studied the chair where it was pushed under the desk and he looked at the blotter and pen set, the empty wire in-tray.

Pious was at the gun cabinet where one of the hooks remained empty. He raised an eyebrow at the bayonet. 'Do you figure that's the blade he was talking about?'

Quarrie shrugged. He was considering the photographs on the

shelf where Ike Bowen, a good-looking man in his younger days, gazed rather proudly back.

'Career soldier,' Quarrie stated. 'All his life in the service, must've been a shock to the system when they told him it was time to quit.'

'Yeah, I guess.' Pious moved alongside him and he too cast an eye across the photos. 'John Q,' he said, 'what kind of father is it that don't answer letters written him by his son?'

'I have no idea.'

'Don't make any sense.'

'No, it don't.'

'So what about the brother, the hospital he was talking about?'

'I don't know,' Quarrie said. 'When he's calmed down some I figure I'll ask him.'

Pious looked back at the open panel. 'Saw a few like him in Korea. Poor bastard, he's just about holding it together.'

Crossing to the other door he looked the length of the basement corridor. 'You got to feel for him, what with the sheriff's detective telling him his old man took a gun to his head and you telling him that ain't how it was.'

'His daddy was murdered, Pious,' Quarrie stated. 'He was setting that chair yonder with powder burns on his head.'

'So who'd want him dead, and how would they know about that passage?'

Quarrie shook his head. 'They didn't get in through the passage. When the gardener got here the kitchen door was open. I figure whoever it was they just showed up, knocked on the door and Ike Bowen answered. Could've been anybody – drifter, somebody watching the place as Isaac said – but whoever they were, Ike must've let them in.'

'So Isaac – what's his fixation with the passage?'

'It's like you said he's just about holding it together. His old man is dead and he has no idea what happened to his brother. He ain't thinking straight, Pious. In his condition I don't know many who would.'

'So what're you going to do?' Pious said. 'Swing by the sheriff's department and tell them how they got this wrong?'

'Not right away. Later maybe. Isaac said how the lieutenant is in Houston right now so I'll probably just wait on the coroner.'

With a nod Pious returned his attention to Ike Bowen's picture. 'So whoever it was knocked on the door they had to have had a weapon. Old soldier like that, he would've been suspicious of anybody just showing up, so they had to be already holding.'

'Yeah,' Quarrie said. 'What's your point?'

Pious gestured. 'Why bring the man down here? Why use his own piece and why make it look like he used it himself?'

'Simple.' Quarrie pointed to the chair. 'If this is suicide then nobody's looking for anybody else and the trail ends right where he was sat.'

Upstairs they found Isaac sitting out on the patio. Shaking a cigarette from his pack, Quarrie tapped it against the heel of his thumb then took a seat in a metal cane chair. He smiled encouragingly.

'You OK?' he said. 'I guess this whole deal has you pretty hopped up.'

'I'm OK,' Isaac told him.

'Listen,' Quarrie went on. 'That passageway, the storm shelter – there's no way that's how the intruder got in. It's too intricate, too complicated. Whoever it was killed your daddy, I figure they just had him come to the door when they knocked.'

Isaac looked from him to Pious and back.

'That's how it happened,' Quarrie assured him. 'The gardener found the kitchen door open and I figure they left the same way they got in.'

Pious sat down and Quarrie laid his unlit cigarette on the table. 'So anyway, I have to ask you some questions. Your father, did he have any enemies you can think of? Anybody he might've had a beef with?'

Isaac did not answer right away. Sitting with his hands in his lap he shifted his weight in the chair. 'I don't know, I guess it's hard to say with me being away all the time. You kind of lose touch with what's going on.' Again he glanced from Quarrie to Pious. 'I guess he might've had enemies. Plenty of people do and it's a fact he could be pretty ornery.'

'How long had he been up here?' Quarrie said. 'This house I mean, all on its own like this with no near neighbors. I guess that's how he liked it, but how long had he lived here?'

'Seven years almost. This was my base when I was in the army but I never really lived here myself.'

'What about your brother?'

'Ishmael?' Isaac worked his shoulders. 'He was here some of the time I guess, but then he was in and out of the hospital.'

Quarrie nodded. 'Yeah, you mentioned that. What was he doing in the hospital?'

Isaac tapped his temple. 'He had issues; it's a fact my brother's got problems.'

'What sort of problems?'

'Hard to say really. I guess when he was younger he used to talk to himself, hold conversations, you know, when nobody else was with him.'

Quarrie reached for his cigarette. 'Where'd you live at back then?'

'Oklahoma City.'

'And your mom was already gone?' Pious said.

Isaac nodded. 'Long gone. She took off when we were kids.'

'Why'd she do that, leave out on her family?'

Isaac sat forward. 'Beats me,' he said. 'Why does anybody leave anybody? Why do people get divorced? It's not like Dad had to give her anything. Money, I mean. I don't think she walked with a dime. You'd have to ask her why she took off. I'd kind of like to find out myself.'

'So do you have any idea where she is?'

Isaac shook his head. 'She was never in contact, not with me or my brother, and my dad . . .' He was struggling again. Shifting his gaze to the floor his voice seemed to fall away.

'These hospitals,' Quarrie said. 'Your brother, you told us his troubles started when he was younger. How was it that kicked off?'

Eyes glassy, Isaac peered across the driveway towards the woodland that broke up the flatlands ahead of the lake. 'I don't know,' he said. 'I guess it started around the time Mom left. I asked Dad what it was set Ishmael off and he said he'd tell me when I was older.' Lifting a hand he gestured. 'I'm older now and I still don't know so I guess he never did.'

Fifteen

Instead of going home, Quarrie had Pious fly him to a crop-dusting outfit just outside Winfield in Marion County. From the duster's office he called Chief Billings and asked him to send someone out to pick him up. When he got into town Billings was on the phone and he waved Quarrie to the broken-down armchair.

'That was the highway patrol,' he said when he finished his call. 'They just found that stolen Buick a block from a Baptist mission cottage in Marshall, Texas.'

Quarrie sat for a moment without saying anything. He peered across the desk. 'Why would he do that?' he asked finally. 'A town like Marshall. That ain't anywhere to be at.' He was quiet again, then he added, 'He had to believe we wouldn't know what he was driving, not with the way he drowned your cruiser. The fact we found it hasn't been broadcast – the radio I'm talking about – has it?'

Billings shook his head. 'No, it hasn't.'

'So why would he do that, Chief? Abandon the car he made such an effort getting hold of?'

The chief had no idea but he said he would find a vehicle for Quarrie to use then he opened a drawer and handed him two sets of phone records. One was for Mrs Perkins and the other Mary-Beth Gavin. Quarrie pored over them while Billings got back on the phone.

'There are no long-distance calls here,' Quarrie stated when the chief hung up. 'Not from Mary-Beth's phone anyway. In the six weeks she was here she didn't make a long-distance phone call.'

Billings seemed to ponder that for a moment. 'Six weeks isn't very long,' he said. 'And maybe there was nobody to call. Or if there was, maybe she called from work or a payphone.'

Quarrie turned his attention to the Perkins bill. There were numbers for Dallas and Houston, as well as Santa Fe, New Mexico. He found one call to an area code he did not recognize and it had been made around the time that Mary-Beth would have been staying. Perched on the edge of Billings's desk, he picked up the phone and dialled the number. He had to wait for the connection and it took a moment before he heard the dial tone.

Nobody answered and he was about to hang up and try again later when the line clicked and a woman's voice sounded. 'Hello?' she said. 'This is Carla.'

'Afternoon, mam,' Quarrie said, glancing at Billings where he walked around the desk and squatted on the arm of the chair. 'I didn't think anybody was picking up. I'm a police officer calling from Texas.'

'Police officer?' She sounded a little nervous.

'Yes, mam. My name's Quarrie. I'm a Texas Ranger.'

'What do you want with me?'

'Well, first off, if you don't mind, I'd like to know who it is I'm talking to. You said your name was Carla? What's your last name?'

She seemed to hesitate, the line went quiet and for a moment he thought the connection had been lost.

'Mam, are you there?'

'Yes, I'm here. It's Simpson. My last name is Simpson.'

'And where am I calling you exactly?'

'You don't know?'

'No, I don't. Like I say, I have the number not the address and I don't recognize the area code.'

'Tulsa, I'm in Tulsa, Oklahoma.'

'Tulsa, right,' Quarrie said. 'Look, I'm sorry to bother you like this, but I need to ask about a woman named Mary-Beth Gavin.'

Again she was silent, the line so still this time he was sure he had lost the connection.

'Mam, are you still there?'

'Yes, I'm here, but I was on my way out. I'm late right now. Can you call back another time?'

'Ms Simpson, I need to know about your relationship with Ms Gavin.'

'There is no relationship. I don't know her. I never heard the name.'

Quarrie was frowning. 'But she called you. Six weeks back, your number is right here on the phone bill from the house where she was living at in Marion County, Texas.'

'I don't know her,' the woman repeated. 'I've never been to Marion County. I'm sorry. This has to be a mistake because I don't know anyone called Mary-Beth . . . What did you say her last name was?'

'Gavin. Mary-Beth Gavin. Are you married, Ms Simpson?' Quarrie said. 'Maybe your husband—'

'No, I'm not married. Look, I'm sorry. This is all some mistake. It was probably a wrong number. Now,' she was sounding flustered, 'I really do have to go. I'm awfully late. I'm sorry I wasn't able to help you.'

She hung up and Quarrie looked round at Billings where he was still sitting on the arm of the chair.

'I guess you got most of that,' Quarrie said, glancing once more at the phone number. 'Told me how she doesn't know Mary-Beth, said she doesn't remember the call.' He stood up. 'She knows all right; the name at least – it was a bolt from the blue when I told her.' Dialling again he called Austin. 'This is Sergeant Quarrie,' he said when headquarters answered. 'Got a telephone number here for a Carla Simpson in Tulsa, Oklahoma, and I need for you to get me the address.'

The following morning Billings brought an unmarked Ford to his motel and gave him the keys.

'I spoke to old man McIntyre,' the chief said. 'Told him how you wanted to talk to him about Mary-Beth and you'll find him at the shop down there, a block off Orchard and Main.' He stuffed his hands in his trouser pockets. 'What about the Buick? You want to go take a look?'

Quarrie made a face. 'Not right now. In fact maybe you could do me a favor and have somebody load it onto a flatbed and ship it to Austin. We got pretty good forensics up there these days so maybe they can come up with something.'

Leaving the police department he drove through town, making the turn on Orchard and pulling up out front of McIntyre's Farm Machinery. A workshop with an entrance twenty feet wide, a concrete floor with workbenches carrying both sides and beyond it, a couple of glass-fronted wood-grain offices. Showing his star to the man outside, Quarrie made his way past a couple of mechanics and went up to one of the offices where a thin-faced man was on the telephone. Next to that was a smaller office with room for little more than the secretary's desk and a couple of metal file cabinets. A young woman with thick, dark hair and a lot of eye make-up was typing a letter as Quarrie went in.

'Ranger,' he told her. 'I'm here to see Mr McIntyre.'

The young woman poked her head next door then she ushered Quarrie through. McIntyre was seated behind his desk, still on the phone; he indicated a chair directly across.

A minute later he hung up, looking a little flustered. It was hot and airless. Sweat seemed to drag at his shirt and his neck was rouge where the tie looked too tight at the collar.

'Sorry about that,' he said. 'Rushed off our feet right now, and since Mary-Beth . . .' He broke off and glanced at the plywood door. 'She tries hard that one, but it's a fact she's not used to typing more than a letter. Mary-Beth, now she really was something. Normally have them work a week's trial, two weeks sometimes if I'm not sure, but she showed what she could do in about three days flat, and it was all I could do to move her into that house I own by the weekend.' Pressing the air from his cheeks he sat back. 'A feller trying to run a tight little ship like this needs back-up and she was back-up, I promise you.'

'She was more than just a secretary then?' Quarrie suggested.

'I'll say she was. Started out that way, but by the end of the second week she was just about running this place. I'm talking book-keeping and records, invoicing, chasing up money owed from people who don't want to pay. Then this creep comes along and ruins everything.' He looked keenly at Quarrie. 'You have any idea who it was done that to her? Strangled, the chief said, and in her own house – my house if anybody's asking.'

Quarrie looked him in the eye. 'Right now we don't have much to go on.'

Grimly McIntyre nodded. 'Billings said how it wasn't just her. The sonofabitch killed a police officer.'

'Yes, he did, as well as a salesman from Arkansas.'

The older man gawped now, he was shaking his head. Taking off his hat Quarrie rested it on his knee.

'Mr McIntyre,' he said, 'I'm pretty sure Mary-Beth knew her killer. I'm pretty sure she had something of his or something he wanted, and when she couldn't or wouldn't give it up he killed her in a fit of anger. He was so mad he took a length of two-by-four, or a fire poker maybe, and left her just about unrecognizable.'

McIntyre's features had lost all color.

'I need to know who she was,' Quarrie said. 'I need to know where she came from. I'm going to need her Social Security number and anything else you got that might help me.'

'I can give you her Social Security number.' McIntyre pressed a finger to the buzzer on his phone. 'That's about all I've got, though. She didn't tell us where she was from and if I asked where she worked before, which I might not have, I don't remember what it was she told me.' Quarrie looked at him a little sourly. 'I know, I know. Hardly any way to run a business, but she was so damn capable I didn't think it mattered.'

'What about people coming by the shop to visit her?' Quarrie asked. 'Or calling on the phone. Did she ever mention anybody? A Carla Simpson maybe?'

McIntyre shook his head. 'I don't get involved in my employees' personal lives, Sergeant, and she was only here six weeks. I've got enough trouble just trying to deal with the customers. So long as the folks work hard, are on time and don't steal from me, that's about as far as my interest stretches.'

'Do you mind if I talk to your people?' Quarrie asked him. 'See if there was anything anybody noticed?'

'Be my guest. Talk to who you want, anything I can do to help catch this sumbitch, you got it. I tell you what,' he added, looking beyond Quarrie now through the window. 'There is one thing you might want to check out. Yonder is the grocery store and there's a colored girl makes sandwiches over there with home-made chillies and pickles. One of my boys told me that come lunchtime Mary-Beth would sit out back with that colored girl. It's the kind of thing gets noticed in these parts, but it was nothing to do with me so I never said anything about it.' Sitting back he pursed his lips. 'Maybe I should have, but she kept herself to herself and if she wanted to make friends with a Negro, what was that to me?'

Nobody in the workshop had heard of Carla Simpson and the new girl in the office had never met Mary-Beth. Leaving his car where it was Quarrie crossed to the store where a young black woman had a queue of people waiting for sandwiches. Making his way to the front Quarrie showed her his badge. Another girl took over and Quarrie and the young woman went out back of the store where a tiny courtyard was set with a narrow bench. Taking a seat the woman looked at him with her eyes darting.

'It's all right,' he told her. 'You haven't done anything. I just want to talk to you about Ms Gavin.'

The woman said her name was Patty and when he spoke about the murder her eyes brimmed with tears. She fished in her apron pocket for a tissue and Quarrie waited while she blew her nose.

'Listen,' he said, 'I'm reaching out here, Patty; looking for any kind of detail that might help me find who killed her.'

Hands clasped tightly, Patty nodded.

'Mr McIntyre across the street there told me that she liked to eat lunch out here at the back of the store.'

'That's right, sir: sometimes she did.'

Quarrie smiled. 'Looks like you build a hell of a sandwich. Queuing out the door like that, I guess you got yourself quite the reputation.'

Patty returned his smile but it did not seem to hold much humor.

'Patty,' he said, 'I guess the two of you would've been out here together and I need to know what you talked about.'

Patty seemed to think about that. 'Well, I don't really know,' she said. 'It wasn't that we ate our lunch together so much as Ms Gavin liked to eat out here. She told me it was too far to go home and she didn't want to set at her desk. I was out here just getting a little air is all, and black folks don't say a whole lot to white folks – not in this part of the country.'

'No, I get that,' Quarrie said. 'But, right now the fact that she did talk to you is all I have. I can't seem to find another person in town Mary-Beth was friends with and by all accounts she was a nice lady. I know she was only here six weeks, but to not have any friends, no family visiting – it doesn't make a whole lot of sense.' He smiled now. 'I'm a police officer and I guess people like me we're kind of suspicious. When I see a situation like that, when somebody new comes to town and nobody knows anything about them, I wonder if they're not hiding or running away from something.' He looked squarely at her then. 'You saw her most every day: did she look to you like she was hiding?'

Patty shook her head. 'I can't say as I noticed anything like that, sir. She was nice to me is all and I never figured it any more than that.' She looked across the alley to the rear of the buildings opposite where a black man was folding sheets of cardboard into a dumpster. 'She talked to me like I was her equal and that ain't like anybody else; not with white folks anyhow.' She gestured to the door of the store. 'White folks they just want what they want and they tell you what it is and you go get it for them.'

'But Mary-Beth was different?' Quarrie said. 'So what did the two of you talk about?'

'Oh, not much. I guess she asked if I was going to get married, if I wanted to have any kids. She was an older lady and she talked to me kind of like my momma. She heard me humming one time and said I had a nice voice. She asked if I went to church, if I liked to sing in the choir. I told her I was Catholic so come Sundays I'd be at Holy Trinity and there wasn't any choir there.' Breaking off Patty narrowed her eyes. 'That's something, maybe. She told me she used to know a place called Trinity.'

'She did? A town was that? Did she say whether it was in Texas?'

'No sir, she never did.'

Back at the station house Quarrie called the ranch and asked Eunice to go and find Pious. A minute or so later the phone was picked up.

'John Q,' his friend said. 'I'm underneath that old wreck of a feed truck again and she's leaking oil all over.'

'Then I guess I better make it snappy. Isaac Bowen.'

'What about him?'

'He said how his brother was in a hospital, a sanatorium that burned, right? What did he say was the name of it?'

Sixteen

In the women's wing at Bellevue, Nancy watched Miss Annie through the glass panel in her door. She was sitting on the bed, cradling her baby to her breast whilst rocking back and forth making little crooning sounds that could just about be heard through the glass. She did not look up. Concentrating on what she was doing she lifted the doll to her shoulder and paced small circles between the bed and the changing mat. Patting the doll's back as if to wind it, she laid it down and set about loosening the tiny strip of cloth she had tied as a diaper.

From the corridor Nancy watched as she switched from clucking sounds that were gentle and soothing to a sort of quiet admonishing. Taking off the diaper she made as if to wash it, scrubbing with the heel of her hand, using an imaginary piece of soap and working it hard, then rinsing the cloth and wringing it out before she hung it over the end of her bed. It was only then that she seemed to be aware she was being watched and her eyes dulled briefly before she flung herself bodily against the panel of reinforced glass.

Nancy was so stunned she stepped back as if she had been struck. On the other side of the door Miss Annie was at the window, skeletal under her pajamas, the malice in her pale blue eyes accentuated by the veined and waxen scalp that was visible through her hair.

Back at her desk Nancy smoothed lightly perspiring palms down the front of her uniform. Next to the desk on a small table she had a plastic pitcher of ice water that she kept topped up for the patients. Pouring a glass now, her hand shook a little as she drank it down.

A few minutes later the door at the end of the corridor opened and she looked up to see Briers making his way towards her. He paused when he got to Miss Annie's room and pressed his face right up to the glass.

'Don't,' Nancy said. 'For pity's sake, don't do that. I don't want her any more worked up than she already is.'

Briers puffed the air from his cheeks. 'Like that's even possible. Since the good doctor's little scheme went sour she's been worse than she ever was.' With another glance through the panel he came down to the workstation where he rested his weight on his fists.

Sitting back in her chair Nancy worked a hand over the pin where it fixed her hair.

'Everything he told us,' Briers went on, 'all that stuff about how it was going to come good and his theory would be proven finally.'

'I know, I know. You don't have to remind me. So what're you doing here anyway? You know you're not supposed to be in this wing unless it's to take Miss Annie outside and she's staying right where she is.'

'Yeah, I know that, but you're going to want to hear this. You know about Ike Bowen shooting himself?'

Nancy nodded. 'Yes, you told me.'

'And how Isaac showed up the other day?'

Again she nodded.

'Well, last night I talked to a buddy of mine back in Texas and he told me what he read in the newspaper.' The orderly looked warily at her. 'You haven't heard anything about that, have you?'

'No, I haven't. What're you talking about? What newspaper?'

'Town called Winfield in Marion County: Mary-Beth Gavin, that's where she ended up after leaving us all when she did.'

'After the fire you mean, when she took off? What was she doing in the newspaper?'

'She's dead, Nancy. Mary-Beth was murdered.'

When he went back for the car it was gone. He had left it parked behind the Baptist mission cottage but it was not there now. He stood in the street, jeans hanging a little low at the waist, he wore the sleeveless Levi over his T-shirt and the laces on his boots were undone.

Two blocks from the cottage he spotted a diner set back from the road. Taking a seat in a window booth he gazed at the spot where the car had been as if he expected it to suddenly reappear. A waitress came over and he ordered a hamburger and ate it slowly. No French fries; chewing every mouthful of bread and meat and sipping from a glass of water. When he was finished he remained at the table until the waitress cleared his plate away.

He could see the thicket of bushes about ten yards further on from where he had left the automobile. A quiet road, that cottage was the only house among a block of business premises. Leaving a dollar on the table he went back now, passing the bushes where he could see the sawn-off twelve-gauge and the pistol still lying where he had hidden them before. Grabbing the Model 10 Colt he stuffed it into the back of his jeans but left the shotgun where it was. Taking a moment he looked at the sky then scanned the assortment of buildings. His gaze shifted to the mission cottage where a sign highlighted the fact that orphaned children were saved from a life of crime by the work of the church. No cars parked; no vehicles in the yard, a garage set on its own with two wooden doors pulled all the way across.

With a glance back the way he had come, he walked right around the house and up to that garage. Through the gap in the aging doors he could see an old Chevrolet with a bed sheet partially covering the bodywork. He looked over to the house where a path led to a front door set back on a stoop with a glass panel covered by a purple drape.

When he rang the bell the door was opened by a black maid in her teens wearing a blue dress with a crisp, white apron tied at her waist. Wiping her hands on the apron she looked up at him and was about to smile when she saw the Model 10.

Seventeen

According to the Panola County welfare officer what was left of the old Trinity Hospital lay at the end of a dirt road deep in the Piney Woods. When Quarrie spoke to her on the telephone, the lady told him it had been a private residence for eighty-odd years before it was converted to accommodate the patients. Some super-rich industrialist from back east had built himself a whole complex of buildings so he could entertain his friends and keep a boat on the lake. When he died he left the complex in trust, and a few years later a ten-foot wall was built and it opened as an asylum for the criminally insane.

The welfare officer could tell him nothing about the fire except that it had happened six weeks previously and that the patients had been shipped to various other secure establishments throughout the country. She told him that if he wanted to know any more he would have to talk to the fire department's investigators. Their initial reports indicated kerosene, but given the hospital kept a massive store of the fuel, they could not say whether it had been used to start the fire deliberately or not.

It was something at least, and when he hung up the phone Quarrie was considering the fact that Mary-Beth Gavin had mentioned a place called Trinity to the girl at the grocery store. It might be nothing, but then it might have been something she let slip to someone she thought would not be talking to anybody else.

Picking up the phone again he called McIntyre's shop and asked to speak to Jane Perkins.

'Mrs Perkins,' he said when she came on the line, 'did Mary-Beth ever talk to you about a hospital called Trinity?'

She seemed to think about that. 'No,' she said. 'The only Trinity I know is the Catholic church on Merrill Drive – and a hospital, you say? I guess I'd remember that.'

'What about Carla Simpson. Does that name mean anything to you?'

'No sir, it doesn't.'

'So you didn't call her in Tulsa, Oklahoma?'

'No, I didn't.'

She transferred him to the office and he asked McIntyre about Trinity but he'd never heard of the hospital either.

Hanging up once more, Quarrie sat back in the chief's chair as the door opened and Billings came in. 'Quarrie,' he said, 'I hoped I'd find you here. What're you doing right now?'

Quarrie caught the weight in his expression. 'I'm planning on a road trip. Why?'

'Marshall, Texas,' the chief said. 'I think our boy came back for the car.'

The door to the Baptist mission cottage was standing open and two city cops occupied the path between it and the gate. The area was not taped off yet and the children were home from school. Five of them divided between the back seats of two Marshall City prowl cars. Two more cruisers blocked the road and Quarrie followed Billings as he pulled over just ahead of where an ambulance was parked. Quarrie was driving the Ford the county had loaned him. Fitted with a shortwave radio, but unmarked, he looked through the windshield where the two paramedics were waiting with a gurney.

Together he and the chief passed between the cars that were stopping traffic and Quarrie glanced at the pale-looking faces of the children. 'Who found her?' he asked. 'Who was it called this in?'

A grim expression on his face, the chief nodded towards the children.

Inside the house all was silent. Quarrie made his way along the hall to the kitchen where he could see blood spattered in the open doorway. He could smell it, the metallic tincture where it caught in his throat.

The maid was sitting with her back to the sink and her head flopped so her chin seemed to balance on one shoulder. Her mouth was open, blood smeared across her lips and one of her front teeth was broken. Blood and tissue, brain matter coated the units and the base of the sink where the back of her skull had shattered. For a long time Quarrie studied her, then he turned to the window and garage across the yard where two beaten-looking doors hung open. Again he looked at the maid sitting there with her hands upturned at her sides and her legs thrown out where her heels had scuffed up the floor. He could see a puddle on the linoleum where her bladder had emptied. Her eyes were glazed, vacant pools fixed on a patch where wallpaper was peeling.

Outside, he worked a cigarette from his pack and hunted for his lighter. The chief followed him across to the garage where Quarrie paused with the unlit Camel in his mouth and his hands in his pockets, looking at a patch of oil on the concrete floor.

'Do we know what was in here?' he said.

The chief moved alongside. 'We're waiting on the pastor to tell us.'

Taking his Zippo Quarrie put the flame to his cigarette. 'I'm headed south right now, Chief. Panola County. As soon as you get a handle on what this sumbitch is driving, I'd be obliged if you give me the heads up.'

He drove the blacktop with an image of the dead girl in his head, thinking about how Isaac had told him he had a brother with issues that were serious enough to put him in a sanatorium, but had said nothing about an asylum for the criminally insane.

Crossing the freeway he drove Route 59 through the wetlands with Martin Lake to the west and passed beyond the city of Carthage. He had been there once before, though that was a few years ago, when they had been investigating vote rigging during the county elections.

South of town he drove beyond the dirt road that led to Murvaul Lake and took the east fork towards the hamlets of Paxton and Joaquin. At Joaquin he was on dirt himself heading deep into the woodland and with the way the trees pressed the lake, he was reminded of the Bowen property.

A dozen miles further the road forked and he made a right turn, passing through stand after stand of mast-straight hardwood where a breath of wind toyed with the upper branches. Nothing on the road out here and the thought of an asylum so deep in the woods made the hairs stand up on the back of his neck. Finally he came to an opening in the trees where the road was pot-holed and weeds were beginning to overtake the gravel. Hunting trails led off both left and right and he picked out an old deer blind built for bowmen.

Spotting a sign up ahead, he slowed the car and considered where the dirt road threaded into a narrow causeway.

Trinity: he could make out the printed letters, a little worn and weathered, on a piece of painted plywood. Turning onto the causeway, he rumbled deeper into the woods. Half a mile farther and a red-brick wall overgrown with lichen and moss formed a barrier among the trees. Twin gates in heavy scrolled iron hung between a pair of brick pillars with the causeway winding between. Quarrie nosed the Ford through those gates and fifty yards deeper the trees gave out and he was in a meadow where the grass was knee-high, and he was reminded of what Isaac had said about his last firefight.

A little lopsided to look at, the building appeared to stagger, almost as if it wavered on loose foundations. Only half of it still intact, the panels that remained were scorched the color of charcoal. Southern clapboard, it still bore the Gothic imaginings of its architect. Built over three floors, or at least it had been, the top floor was all but gone and what remained of the squared facade seemed to hang like some kind of suggestion.

Stopping the car, Quarrie let the engine idle for a second before he shut it off. He remained where he was seated behind the wheel peering up at the ironwork balconies. Beyond them windows that were glassless and empty were marked with more iron, only these were vertical bars. The second floor was supported by a pillared veranda that seemed to work its way around the entire building. Clearly there had been a number of smaller buildings but all that was left were the stone foundations.

Climbing from the car he put on his hat and stood with his hands in the pockets of his jacket, gazing across the tumbledown grounds to the darkened remains that seemed so stark against the trees. Movement behind him, a sound from the gates, instinctively his hand snaked inside his jacket. As he turned he saw an old Mexican pushing a bicycle. He wore a beaten-looking hat and a Mackinaw and he stopped when he spotted Quarrie.

For a moment they just looked at each other, then the Mexican came on, wheeling that bicycle along the overgrown road with a squeak sounding every time the wheels made a revolution. A bushy, gray beard seemed to shuck from under the stampede string of that hat, the old man with a kind of nonchalance about him as he stopped next to the car and rested the bicycle. From somewhere in the pocket of his Mackinaw he produced the stub of a cigar and, palming his Zippo, Quarrie tossed it.

'*Gracias,*' the man said.

'*De nada.*'

'*¿Habla español?*'

With a nod Quarrie continued. '*¿Quien es usted?*'

'*Un viejo, joven; un hombre viejo.*'

'I ain't that young, and you ain't that old come to think on it.' Still speaking Spanish Quarrie caught the light in the old man's eye as he considered the pair of Blackhawks pouched under his jacket.

'Texas Ranger,' he said. 'I'm here on account the fire.'

'Ah.' The Mexican nodded now, his gaze shifting from the guns to the burned-out building. Working the cigar stub between his teeth he rolled it from one side of his mouth to the other. 'A terrible blaze, and if there had been any kind of wind that night the smoke jumpers would still be back here.' Wheeling the bicycle closer he peered inquiringly into Quarrie's face. 'You must have come a long way, señor. I left a pot of coffee on the stove when I went out and there should still be some if it's not already burnt to the bottom.'

With the old man pushing his bicycle Quarrie fell in beside him and together they made their way along the pathway that veered to the left of the building where various other paths bisected the over-grown grounds. It was only then Quarrie noticed the saddlebags the man had fixed over the back wheel and how they were bulging with groceries.

'What's your name?' Quarrie asked him.

'Pablo. My name is Pablo Mendez.'

'I'm John Q,' Quarrie told him.

Pausing for a moment the old man wiped the palm of his hand over the skirt of his jacket, and when they shook Quarrie noticed that his little finger was missing at the first knuckle.

'What brings a Ranger all the way out here when there's nothing to see but a burned-down building?'

Quarrie hunched his shoulders. 'I don't really know, to be honest. Guess I was hoping to find out a little about what happened.'

They crossed the grounds to the wall where it was split by a heavy gate. The old man led the way through and they were in the trees briefly, before the path spilled into a clearing. Quarrie picked out a low-lying shack on the far side that was so well camouflaged it was all but swallowed by the forest.

'*Mi casa*,' the old man stated with a certain solemnity. 'I used to pay rent but I don't pay anymore. They charged me rent when the hospital was here, but then they paid for my power as it came off their generator. Now there is no power so I don't pay rent anymore. I just mind the place as I did before, only there is less to mind of course.' Leaning the bicycle against the wall he pushed open the door.

A single room dimly lit by a fading sunlight that was just about breaking through the unwashed windows. A stone fireplace at one end, the old man had firewood stacked and an assortment of wax candles covered almost the entire expanse of the mantel. Two seamy-looking armchairs were set before it, and against the other wall was an old-world wood-fired stove where a coffee pot was warming.

'They're still paying me,' the Mexican stated. 'The trustees, they pay me to watch that old ruin in the hope that one day someone will drive up here and see its potential. Meantime, the insurance company is taking care of the trust so I imagine I'll be here for a while yet.'

Taking off his coat he hung it on an iron peg behind the door and offered Quarrie a chair.

Sitting down, Quarrie crossed his ankle over his knee. 'Pablo,' he said. 'The fire, do you know what caused it?'

The Mexican made a face. 'I'm afraid I cannot tell you. I've had fire marshals here and the investigators, asking all kinds of questions. There was talk of the power shorting; some kind of outage that set sparks flying.' His eyes had darkened quietly. 'There was also talk of kerosene. This is an old place and not all of it was given over to electric. I mean, some of the outbuildings had no power and that's what the stocks of fuel were for.' Vaguely he indicated beyond the copse to the gate. 'None of those buildings are there anymore. Every one of them was razed, and with the way that blaze caught hold it's a wonder there is anything left.'

He took a cloth to the handle on the coffee pot and poured two tin mugs, dark and sugarless; he passed one over and Quarrie thanked him.

'Tell me about the hospital,' he said. 'I talked to a lady from Panola County Welfare and she referred to this place as an asylum for the criminally insane.'

'That's what it was.' Pablo settled in the other armchair. 'A place where dangerous people with mental illnesses were kept well away from normal people they might otherwise wish to harm. That's why they have the wall. It was never here back when this was a private house: the wall was built to keep the patients in, and this location was chosen specifically because it was so remote. If anyone escaped there would be plenty of time for the dogs to find them before they could get anywhere they might hurt somebody. Half a dozen Walker hounds the trustees paid for and a man called Briers took care of. Somebody told me they use Walker hounds to tree cougars, but they're just as good at hunting people.'

Taking a sip from his mug he nursed it between both palms. 'As far as I know nobody ever escaped from Trinity, at least not before the fire. The hospital was patrolled by armed guards just like a regular prison. The patients were allowed to exercise of course, and the regime encouraged hard work. I had a detail helping me with my chores, fixing doors, painting, clearing leaves in the fall.' He looked almost wistful then at the memory. 'But there were orderlies everywhere and, as I say, guards who were always armed.'

Setting his cup down on the hearth, Quarrie hunched to the edge of his chair. 'What happened to the patients that survived the fire? The welfare officer said that most were accounted for but not all.'

Pablo lifted his palms. 'That's right,' he stated. 'People are missing and only two bodies were found – at least two sets of badly charred bones. There were no other bodies recognizable but that does not mean they didn't succumb, and I imagine they did. Kerosene you see, with that fuelling the flames the heat would've been incredible and even bones would be incinerated. Nobody can say how many died. I was told that as of now there are seven people still unaccounted for and all of them patients. They might have got away of course, but it's much more likely they burned.'

Through the low window Quarrie could see the woodland outside and beyond the wall the sagging shoulder of the building. 'Pablo,' he said, 'how long have you been here?'

'Working as the caretaker? About twelve years.'

'I guess with what you did and all, you must have been around the patients?'

With a nod Pablo peered beyond him. 'Yes, I was. And they were all right, most of them. One of the things that changed after Dr Beale arrived was how the patients were treated and how members of staff were encouraged to interact with them.'

'Dr Beale?' Quarrie said.

'That's right; he was the chief psychiatrist here, though he also looked after another sanatorium in Louisiana. Shreveport, I think it is. He arrived about four years ago and just a few months after Dr Sievers resigned.' The old man's gaze soured a little. 'Nobody liked Sievers; not many of the staff and certainly not the patients. There was a cruel streak in that man and he treated the patients merely as prisoners, which of course they were. But he made no effort to deal with the afflictions that had brought them here in the first place.' Flaring his nostrils a little he sighed. 'He left after the orderly was stabbed.'

Quarrie shifted his weight where he sat. 'An orderly was stabbed? What happened?'

'One of the patients put a knitting needle through his eye, a woman considered to be one of the most dangerous.' A shudder seemed to cut between the old man's shoulders. 'A stick of a thing she was, I used to see her in the grounds sometimes, and yet she was strong enough to do that to a fully grown man.' He crossed himself. 'She was a special case, a patient who had been here since long before I arrived, and she wasn't allowed outside with the other women. She could only go out when they were inside on account of how she was so violent, and it was all to do with her baby. Leastways, that's what Ms Gavin said.'

Aware of a little tension in his shoulders Quarrie looked up. 'Mary-Beth Gavin you mean?'

Pablo nodded. 'A nice lady, she ran the office, records; kept all the paperwork, you know: details of the patients, staff, all the archives. None of it survived the fire. That patient though,' he said. 'The woman I told you about, her baby wasn't a real baby; it was a porcelain doll she pretended was real and she was never without it, not for a moment in all the years she was here. Somehow she got into the women's common room one day when she should never have been there. The nurse was new – the turnover of staff was always very high and that nurse hadn't read her notes properly.

'Anyway, this patient ended up not only in the common room, but sitting with some of the older women who had access to knitting needles.' His eyes were somber now. 'An orderly came in and he knew she shouldn't be mixing with the other patients so he tried to get her up from the chair, but he made the mistake of grabbing her doll with one hand while he reached for her with the other.' His voice puttered into stillness and he crossed himself a second time. 'That tiny woman, she got hold of a knitting needle from one of the other patients and jammed it through the orderly's eye.'

Quarrie wrinkled his brow.

'He survived,' Pablo told him. 'But of course he lost the eye.'

'And the patient? What happened to her?'

Pablo shrugged. 'Nothing. She was here for life already and it was a mistake by the staff. They just took her back to her cell, but Dr Sievers retired soon after.'

'And Mary-Beth Gavin: what do you know about her?'

'Not much,' the old man told him. 'She left right after the fire. Funny that, she was the kind of person any establishment would jump at recruiting and I'd have thought Dr Beale would've wanted to take her.'

'But he didn't?'

'No. She took off right after the fire. And I mean as soon as it was clear all the records had been destroyed. She just left and nobody seemed to know where she'd gone, and nobody seemed to know why she had gone so suddenly either.' He looked askance at Quarrie. 'Nobody ever said anything. But I'm not a fool: something had scared her badly.'

Quarrie was quiet for a moment as he considered whether to tell the old man about Mary-Beth's murder. 'The patients,' he said. 'You told me some of them were on work detail. Were there any in particular you remember?'

Pablo took a few moments to think about that. 'One or two I suppose.'

'What about Ishmael Bowen?'

Pablo looked at him again. 'I never spoke to him,' he said. 'But I knew about him. A young man, he arrived three months before the fire, and from what Mary-Beth told me, he was the only patient in the whole hospital who had no criminal record.'

'No criminal record? So what was he doing here?'

'That's a good question,' Pablo said. 'That's what his brother wanted to know when he showed up a few days ago. A soldier just back from Vietnam, he had no idea there had been a fire and I don't think he knew this had been a secure establishment either.'

Holding his eye, Quarrie nodded. 'So what happened to Ishmael?'

Pablo gestured. 'According to Dr Beale he was one of the patients they couldn't account for so I imagine he burned in the fire. I didn't tell his brother that though. I just suggested he talk to Dr Beale.'

Quarrie went back to his car. Pablo walked with him, one eye on the sky where a rash of plum-colored storm clouds were pushing up from the south.

'So much rain,' he muttered. 'Always so much rain blowing in from the Gulf, and after all these years I still can't get used to it. I'm from Sonora, desert country, and it never really rains down there.'

'How long've you been in Texas?' Quarrie asked as he opened the car door.

'I've been here as long as I've been living in the United States. Before that I used to drive a truck carrying fluorspar from the mines in Coahuila to Oklahoma City.' Lifting his hand he considered where his finger was missing. 'That's how I lost this, changing a wheel on that goddamn truck. Anyway, I got bored with going back and forth all the time – the only company I ever had were hitch-hikers and most of those were wetbacks.' Finally I sold my rig and that's when I came up here.'

'And you never learned English at all?'

At that the old man smiled. 'Of course I did,' he replied in perfect English. 'It's just that I don't see many people and the ones I do see speak English, and sometimes I like to hear my own language spoken to me.' He shook Quarrie's hand. 'Apart from the way you look perhaps, you could almost pass for Mexican.'

Eighteen

Quarrie was halfway along the county road when the storm hit. As if from nowhere the wind came howling through the trees bringing a swathe of brittle rain that seemed to shatter across the vehicle. Unfamiliar with the dashboard, he had to fumble for the wipers and a car passed coming the other way. It was the first he had come across and, checking his mirrors, he recognized the tail lights of an old Chevrolet.

*

Coming from the north he barely glanced at the Ford as he passed with rain tumbling in broken lines and the wipers switching back and forth. He drove with his eyes a little glazed and a fixed expression on his face. He drove deep into the forest, following the road to the gap in the trees and the causeway that led to the wall.

Spatters of blood still mottled the front of his sleeveless jacket. The laces on his boots were loose; he had the pistol on the seat between his legs and the shotgun in the foot well on the passenger side. No radio playing, no sound but the engine and that was labored. He slowed as he left the dirt road.

He did not drive through the gates. Instead he pulled up just ahead of them and sat with the engine idling. Sweat built on his palms and he worked them together before he headed up the drive. Making his way around back of the hospital he stopped the car and switched off the engine. Reaching for the shotgun he got out and walked back again with clouds unleashing their torrents. He walked with the gun gripped by the breech, keeping the tip of the barrel toward the ground so it would not take in water.

Standing out front he stared at the old mansion where it seemed to cower almost under the sky, weakened pillars and broken windows with bars running top to bottom. Climbing the short flight of burned-out steps he went in through the gap where the doors used to be and considered the darkened foyer.

Rain ran on the walls, it was breaking through the gaps in the ceiling. Transferring the shotgun from one hand to the other he shifted the pistol where it was chafing his hip then crossed to the flight of rotten stairs. Keeping close to the wall where the footing was surest, he made his way to the second floor. There he paused with twin sets of fire doors separating the landing from the corridors on either side.

Taking the doors on the right no rain dripped on him anymore. He could hear the sound of it above his head but the ceiling remained secure. A series of doors, or what was left of them, carried the length of the corridor. He counted: aloud he was counting and he came to the fifth door, only there was no door, just an aperture and the confines of the cell beyond. No glass in the window only vertical bars. Outside lightning toppled in ragged lines and he picked out walls covered in scribblings of stick children with large faces and over-large eyes. Stepping inside that tiny room he stood surrounded by those etchings in the middle of the floor. Trembling, he took in the walls, the floor and the cast-iron framework that was all that was left of the bed.

Darkness complete, he was at the gate in the wall, conscious of how the trees gave way to a clearing and a hint of light on the other side. Faint and flickering, a few dancing threads that were offset by the weight and shadows of the trees. Moving away from the wall he walked the path in his jungle boots where the laces seemed to drag once more. He made his way beyond the last of the trees and he was in the clearing and could see the shape of the cabin where the lights were fluid against the window.

Crossing to the weathered, wooden wall he stepped up to the first window where he made out a candle clustered with hanging wax; a single flame, it guttered and faded, glowed again then seemed to skitter as if it would die. Beyond the glass he could see where wood was crackling in the hearth, two chairs facing it and one of them was occupied.

For a minute maybe he watched the old man sitting with his back to him. Then he moved from the window to the door. Fingers encasing the aged handle, the door stuck as he pushed and he had to shunt it with his shoulder to get it open. As he did so the old man swung round.

For a silent moment they stared at each other. The old man parted his lips but did not speak. Eyes tight against the sagging skin of his face, he made no move to get up. He stared at the shotgun and finally cleared his throat.

'What do you want?' he said. 'I'm a poor man. There's nothing to steal.'

Door closed to the rain, he crossed the room and stood before the fire with the gun at his side, staring at the crusted wood, the light of leaping flames. He did not say anything. He was no longer considering Pablo. It was as if the old man wasn't there.

'Warm yourself.' Pablo was speaking slowly. 'It's a hell of a storm tonight, but we get them like that out here.' He made as if to get up from the chair, but his visitor looked round and he settled again. 'Who are you?' he said. 'I have nothing in the house – no money, I mean. No valuables. But I do have a little food. Are you hungry? Is that why you're here?'

For a few moments his stare remained fixed on the old man and then his gaze returned to the flames. He sat down. Wearily almost he slumped in the second chair.

'Do I know you?' Pablo asked quietly. 'I'm old. I've been around a long time so no matter what you might think, you cannot frighten me. I'm from Sonora, the desert. When I was fourteen I rode with Pancho Villa. I've seen a lot since then and there's nothing I'm scared of, not anymore.'

Silence, it filled the room as something physical and for the briefest of moments his eyelids fluttered where he slumped in the chair. Still he held the shotgun, both hands on the barrel where his knuckles were pale as bone.

'Were you a patient?' Pablo suggested. 'Were you a patient here before the fire?'

He seemed to focus and stared into the flames once more.

'Your face is familiar. I should remember you, but then I wasn't a doctor, or an orderly even. I was only the caretaker and I didn't know many of the patients by name.'

He looked round and his gaze shifted from the old man's face to his right hand where it gripped the arm of the chair. The little finger missing at the first knuckle, for a long time he seemed to stare.

'Do I know you?' Pablo followed his gaze. 'Have I seen you somewhere before?'

He was silent. His gaze shifted to the old man's face once more.

'My name is Pablo,' the old man told him. 'If you were a patient then you'll know I was the caretaker. I still am the caretaker actually, although there isn't much to take care of anymore.'

Blinking slowly he looked down where his boots dripped water on the floor. Pablo was still watching him, a hint of spittle sticking to his lower lip.

'What brought you here? You're sitting by my fire with a gun in your hand so I imagine you mean me harm.'

'Mean you harm?' He seemed to think about that. 'Why would I mean you harm?'

Pablo worked his shoulders. He gestured. He folded his hands in his lap. 'I don't know. But you're in my house with a gun and . . .' He tried to smile, ironically almost he laughed, but his tone was one of unease. 'So I have to ask if you mean me harm, or did you just want to get out of the rain?'

He sat back. Working the heel of a hand across his face he pushed at locks of soaking hair. 'I don't know,' he said. 'I don't know if I mean you harm or not. I guess that all depends.' He looked askance at him then. 'You're the caretaker. You cleared the yard of leaves.'

'That's right.'

'Why're you still here?'

Pablo offered half a smile. 'I ask myself that question all the time. I don't know,' he said. 'I never left when everyone else did. This cabin wasn't touched by the fire.'

'The wall.'

'What?'

'The wall, it's too high; the fire couldn't get past it. The wall acted as a fire break.'

'Yes, I suppose it did.'

'Kerosene,' he went on more softly. 'They kept barrels of kerosene in the store.' The light in his eyes seemed to die. 'The room, that room on the second floor . . .'

'What room?' Pablo said. 'Whose room? Are you looking for someone? If you tell me, perhaps I can help.'

'Help?' He stared at the old man again. 'Why would you want to help? Mr Briers,' he added, 'the orderly with those hound dogs they used to keep in the kennels by the wall. He was there that night, so was Nurse Nancy.' He nodded then, as if to affirm it to himself. 'They were both there and I figure one of them can tell me.'

'Tell you what?' Pablo asked him. 'What is it you want to know?'

Shifting round in the chair he stared. 'You were the caretaker. You must've seen them. What happened to them after the fire?'

*

Quarrie was almost back to the highway when the radio crackled with static. It had been doing that ever since he left Pablo and it was clear somebody was trying to get hold of him, but every time he picked up there was nothing but interference. The density of the trees began to lessen though, finally; and with the cloud cover not so complete he tried to get through.

'Ranger Sergeant Quarrie calling Panola County dispatch. Do you copy?'

A fresh belt of rain littered the windshield and yet more static issued from the speaker.

'This is Ranger Sergeant Quarrie. I got a lot of interference going on here. Anybody out there? Come back.'

'Chevy...' He heard the word then more static before the voice sounded briefly again. ''56 Chevy...said...you...'

For a few seconds Quarrie gripped the handset staring at the windshield where the wipers were flicking back and forth. He could feel how his mouth was dry and his heart a little high in his chest. For a split second he was back in the trees when the storm first hit and that car went rattling by.

Quickly now he swung the Ford around and headed back the way he had come. Driving as fast as he dared with falling water threatening to wash out the road he returned to the woods and the wind was buffeting the car. He passed no other vehicle and he came to the sign for Trinity and fishtailed along the causeway before bursting through the iron gates.

The grounds were just as he had left them, only they were rain-soaked and empty; darkness coating the landscape, there was no sign of any car. He did not stop. He carried half the length of the drive then swung across the grass only coming to a halt at the gate in the wall. Car door open, he had his hat pressed down to his eyes as he cut through the clearing in the cover of the trees.

Pablo's cabin, he could see a hint of light, the flickering of candles; tiny points that just about pierced the gloom. The door was wide open and it should not be like that, not with all this rain. A fire burning in the hearth, from the open door he saw Pablo with his back to him sitting in his chair.

'Pablo, it's Quarrie,' he called. 'What're you doing with the door wide open? Is everything OK?'

The old man did not stir.

He called again only in Spanish this time. '*¿Estas bien, Pablo? ¿Estas bien?*'

The old man did not move and he did not raise his head. Moving inside the cabin, Quarrie had a pistol drawn. Swinging left and right, he aimed at each corner of the room. Nobody there, but something on the floor caught his eye and he was aware of the way blood seemed to drag in his veins.

A boot print just a couple of yards from the door, he had seen that pattern before. A nick in the heel, he had seen it in the turned earth under Mary-Beth Gavin's window. He had seen it on the trail leading up from Henry's Bathtub, and it was there on the caretaker's floor.

Nineteen

The old man's eyes were open and almost absently he seemed to stare. A single hole in the middle of his forehead, the skin puffed up and a line of blood running down the side of his nose. His hands were in his lap as if he had been resigned to whatever was to befall.

Holstering his gun, Quarrie went back to the door and studied that print once more: the same boot, US Army-issue with a steel shank in the sole, and yet he hadn't passed the car. There had been no sign of it out front of the hospital building and he had not seen it anywhere on the road. There were plenty of other dirt tracks back this way though, and it could be just about anywhere by now.

Walking back to his car he lifted the radio transmitter from the dashboard and tried to call. He got no response however, the interference was too severe. Slipping behind the wheel he was about to close the door when lightning ignited the sky. Looking up, he saw a figure at a window on the second floor.

He cut for the main entrance at a run. With every step he was waiting for a shot to ring out but it did not come. Another bolt of lightning and he looked again but the window was bare. For a second or so he hovered on the steps then moved inside the ruin where shadows rippled with running water and the staircase climbed one wall.

He could feel adrenalin pumping as he made his way up the stairs. At the top he paused. Fire doors left and right, it was very dark up there and he could just about pick them out. Overhead thunder rolled and another streak of lightning hit. Pushing open the doors on his right he could see the length of the corridor. Slowly he paced, the sound of rain from above and the wind threatening to tear down what was left of the walls. He could feel the way his flesh had started to creep as if his skin had a life of its own. He came to the first room and it was empty. The next two were also empty. The fourth was empty, and when he got to the fifth he paused.

He stood there, gun in hand, as another sheet of lightning washed across the building and his gaze fastened on the walls. Children, images of stick children, hundreds of them scribbled from ceiling to floor. There was nobody there. Nobody at the window and he wondered if he had not been mistaken and it was only the drawings he saw. But then he heard the sound of an engine and he was at the bars of the broken window as a set of headlights sliced through the darkness below.

He took the stairs three at a time. Spilling out of the empty doors he ran back to the gate in the wall. At his car he was behind the wheel, fumbling for the keys in his jacket pocket; he had them in the ignition and the engine roared into life. Foot flat on the accelerator he spun the car around in an arc with standing water lifting in a curtained plume.

Moments later he was through the gates and giving chase. Back along the causeway to where it came to the wider road, the wind howling, wipers clicking back and forth, he was on that patch of dirt with the trees crowding him and the car skewing so badly he almost left the road. Spinning the wheel under his palm, he righted the car then fed power to the motor once more.

He drove as fast as he could without running off the road but could pick up no hint of a car. The road was a switchback that carried the trees and there was no sign of any tail lights, not so much as a reddened glow.

When finally he got to the asphalt he stopped. The nose of the Ford poking onto the highway, he looked both ways but there was no sign of any vehicle. He sat there trying to work out which way the Chevy might've gone. Making a right he drove half a mile to where lights flickered from an Esso station, gas at twenty-three cents a gallon with a cup of coffee to go.

The middle-aged man at the cash desk told him the phone was out because of the storm and Quarrie went back to his car. He drove as far as Joaquin where the supper club was open and their phone was working OK. He called Austin and asked them to beef up the 'all points' they already had out on the car. He asked them to contact the Louisiana State Police because the border was just a few miles further east. After that he called the Panola County sheriff's department and told them about the caretaker still in his chair.

A Louisiana state trooper found the Chevy abandoned by the railroad tracks just across the state line. Quarrie was asleep when a call came in on the radio the following morning. Parked out back of the supper club in Joaquin he had spent the night in his car. The rain had stopped and the sun was up and the wind had died to little more than a murmur now. Hanging up the radio, he drove thirty miles to a railroad siding where an old gray Chevrolet was parked. The driver's door was hanging open and it was a short hop from there to a bend in the rails where the pace of the trains would be slow.

The trooper was waiting for him, wearing a blue shirt and knee-high boots that were polished to a shine. In his twenties, he was sitting in his cruiser, a single red light on the roof and an outline of the state painted on the door. Climbing from the Ford, Quarrie felt a little weathered about the eyes. Taking a package of cigarettes from his pocket he peeled one out and stuck it in the corner of his mouth.

'Morning to you,' the trooper acknowledged him, with a smile. 'Got me a Thermos of coffee going and you look like you could use a cup.'

They sat in the cruiser; the trooper's flat-brimmed hat on the back seat, he had the Thermos on the dashboard and he poured out another cup. The coffee steamed and Quarrie blew on it, the trooper sitting next to him hunched against the window.

'So how long you been chasing this guy?'

'Coming up on a week.'

'Cop killer, huh?'

Quarrie nodded. 'Kicked off with a woman in Marion County and that's where he killed the cop. Stole him a cruiser and drowned another guy in the trunk. Since then it's been a colored girl from a mission cottage and an old caretaker as well.' He looked sideways at the trooper. 'Almost caught up with him last night down there in the Piney Woods but either he knows the roads better than I do or he just got lucky.'

The trooper whistled softly. 'I'm counting five there, Sergeant. That's quite a party. You got a motive for any of it yet?'

Quarrie made a face. 'He's looking for something. I just don't know what it is.'

Sinking the last of the coffee he handed the cup back to the trooper and they both got out. Fixing his hat, Quarrie crossed to the abandoned Chevy; the door wide open he considered the interior but there was nothing to tell him anything, at least not with the naked eye. He turned his attention to the dirt on the siding, looking for footmarks, and he spotted the same print as before.

'He's wearing a pair of jungle boots with a nick in the heel.' He indicated. 'You can see how it is right there.'

Dropping to his haunches the trooper took a good look at the handful of prints scattered next to the car. Then he followed as Quarrie picked out the trail to where the dirt gave out and the rocks around the rail ties began.

'I'd like to be able to tell you how those boots are pretty distinctive,' Quarrie said, 'but with what with the draft and all they're a dime a dozen right now.'

Twenty

Leaving the trooper to have the car towed Quarrie crossed the line back to Texas and pulled into a gas station. From the payphone he called Austin for Carla Simpson's address in Tulsa.

En route he made a stop at the Bowen house. When he turned into the driveway he could see the garage doors were open and both the pickup and sedan were parked in the yard. The hood of the truck was up and Isaac appeared wiping his hands on a rag. His uniform was gone and he wore a plaid shirt, a pair of jeans and some old work boots that looked as if they had belonged to his dad. His hair was slicked back and he peered across the driveway as Quarrie got out of his car.

Stuffing the rag into his back pocket, he smiled. 'Good to see you again, Sergeant. Do you have something for me? Anything about my dad?'

Quarrie shook his head. 'No sir, I don't. Not yet.'

Isaac made a face. 'But you still think somebody shot him, right? You don't hold anything by what that lieutenant from the sheriff's department said?'

'No, I don't. Somebody shot him all right and I can't believe the coroner's going to tell us any different when he finally gets round to the autopsy. Has anybody from his office been in touch?'

'No, they haven't, not yet.'

Quarrie followed him into the house and leaned against the arch that led from the kitchen to the living room.

'So the reason I swung by,' he said. 'I'm on my way to Tulsa right now and I just came from Trinity Hospital – the one where your brother was at.'

'You did?' Isaac reached for the coffee pot.

'Yes, I did. Isaac, that caretaker you talked to, the Mexican – he's dead. Somebody killed him not long after I left out.'

Isaac was trembling, coffee slopping from the pot as he tried to pour.

'You OK there?' Quarrie said.

Replacing the pot a little awkwardly on the side, Isaac made a fist and worked it with his other palm. 'Just nerves I reckon; everything that's been happening. I guess it's beginning to get to me.' Looking over his shoulder his eyes seemed a little hollow.

'You're doing OK,' Quarrie told him. 'You just hang tough and you'll be fine.' He paused for a moment then he said, 'The caretaker remembered your brother, who he was at least anyhow. Isaac, you told me how Ishmael had issues and everything but you never said that hospital was an asylum for the criminally insane.'

Isaac had stopped shaking. Shoulders hunched, he shrugged. 'You know what?' he said. 'I'm not sure I actually knew it myself. Now I think about it I don't know as anybody said.'

'Well, that's what it was, and Pablo told me that as far as he knew your brother was the only patient with no rap sheet, so I can't think why he was there.'

Isaac stared beyond him for a moment. Then he nodded. 'It's true,' he said. 'Ishmael might've had his problems but he'd never been in any trouble that I can remember; there were never any cops at the house.'

'So what was he doing in a place like that?' Quarrie spread a palm. 'The caretaker told me he'd only been there a few months. Where was he at before?'

Isaac pressed his palms together. 'A place in Houston,' he said. 'I don't know the name of it. He'd been in and out of lots of hospitals down the years and in-between times he would've been living here.'

Pouring a cup of coffee Quarrie took it through to the living room where he sat down on the couch. He considered the family photograph on the mantelpiece and Isaac echoed his gaze.

'That was taken when we were visiting a friend of my dad's in Oklahoma,' he said. 'Place called Lawton I think it was. Old army buddy from World War II, him and his wife; we stayed with them Memorial weekend.' He smiled then as if at the memory. 'I remember my mom saying how that guy and Dad sat up drinking whiskey and telling war stories after me and Ish were in bed. I guess they fought together in Africa when Dad was stabbed in the gut.'

Quarrie looked back at him. 'The bayonet you got downstairs?'

'Uh-huh.' Isaac nodded. 'Kept it as a souvenir and he was always working the blade, used to take a stone to it all the time.'

Quarrie returned his attention to the photograph. 'Lawton, Oklahoma,' he said. 'That ain't very far from where I live. Is that feller you were visiting still there?'

'I don't know. I'm sorry. I don't really remember him. I couldn't tell you his name.' Isaac gestured. 'It wasn't like we were around the house any. We were only there for the weekend, and it being a holiday and all me and Ish were off exploring most of the time.'

Crossing his ankle on his knee Quarrie sat back. 'Dr Beale,' he said. 'You told me how you saw him at Bellevue and then he came out here. So what did he tell you about Ishmael?'

Isaac made a face. 'Not much. When I was at Bellevue he just said how he'd been a patient at Trinity and he was one of the ones they couldn't account for.'

'What about when he was here?'

'We didn't talk about Ish. I'd only just got back and found out about my dad. Dr Beale thought the sheriff was right though, I mean about him killing himself. He told me that people do the most unexpected things and oftentimes it's most unexpected for the folk that are closest to them. He said that after a lifetime of dealing with Ishmael, it must've gotten too much.'

'The doctor said that?' Quarrie arched a brow.

'Yes he did.'

'But you still don't think so, right?'

'I didn't.' Isaac worked his shoulders into his neck. 'But he's a psychiatrist and he had a lot more to do with my dad than I did, at least he did these last couple of years. I guess he could be right. Maybe he is. Maybe the sheriff's department is right after all and he did take a gun to his head.'

'Is that what you're thinking now?' Quarrie lifted one eyebrow. 'You called me up remember, telling me you didn't believe there was any way he'd ever do that, and it was after you'd spoken to Beale.'

Isaac nodded. 'I know I did. The fact is I had a thing going on about the storm shelter and how somebody must've been casing the place. But you told me nobody could work out that panel unless they knew it was there, and I know my dad would never let a stranger in.'

Quarrie worked his tongue around the inside of his mouth. 'Well, anyway,' he said. 'I figure you need to find out why your brother was at Trinity. See if you can get hold of Dr Beale. Ask him what Ishmael was doing there and where he was at before.'

Driving the county road a thought occurred to him and he needed a phone so he headed for Mr Palmer's place. Catching the whistle of a freight train, he gazed across the flatland briefly as the box cars rumbled east, then pulled off the road into the yard and found the old man shovelling swill for a dozen or so blue shoats.

'Howdy, Mr Palmer,' Quarrie said. 'I'm sorry to bust in on you like this but I was hoping I could use your phone.'

The old man nodded towards the house. 'You ain't busting in. I like a bit of company. Go ahead and be my guest.'

Pushing open the screen door Quarrie found the kitchen a mess of unwashed pots and glasses with stains still lacing the sides. There were shavings of chewing tobacco littering the work surfaces and the place had the stale smell of a man too long on his own. Locating the phone Quarrie called the ranch and Eunice picked up. He waited while she went in search of Pious.

132

After a few minutes he came on the line. 'What's up, John Q? What can I do for you now?'

'Ike Bowen, he was a triple volunteer like us.'

'So?'

'So, I want you to do me a favor. Can you make some calls back to Georgia maybe? I figure there's got to be people still around who knew him. Isaac just told me about an old friend he had in Lawton, Oklahoma, they visited with but he couldn't remember his name. See what you can dig up for me, Pious, would you? Somebody killed this guy and right now all I know about him is how he was a stickler for cleanliness and never once wrote his boy.'

Hanging up the phone he looked round to find Mr Palmer kicking mud from his boots.

'Heard you talking about Ike Bowen,' the old man said. 'Cops round here think he shot hisself, but Isaac said how that ain't your opinion and it was you that found him, right?'

Quarrie gave a brief nod.

'What did the autopsy say?'

'It ain't been done yet, at least not as far as I know.'

Palmer made a face. 'Not gotten round to her, uh? Well, we had quite the road wreck out Bonham way just a few days back. Bunch of kids in some hot rod, and with them being so young and all I guess that's taken up most of his time. He's a busy man, the coroner. It ain't just Fannin County he works for, but Delta and Hunt, and sometimes Lamar as well.' Taking off his hat he dropped it on the table among the debris. 'Only met Bowen the one time and that was just to say hello to on account of he kept hisself to hisself.'

'But you did speak to him?' Quarrie said.

Again Palmer nodded. 'Yes sir, not long after he started the remodel on his place up there in the woods. No wife with him, no woman, and that bothered my wife at the time, but then she's gone herself now and they say it's the men that are taken first.' A little wistfully he arched his brows. 'Anyways, it was just Ike and his son living up there, though I never spoke to Isaac, not back then. I guess the other one was in the hospital.'

'Ishmael,' Quarrie said.

'That's right. Isaac told me about him, said he wasn't quite right in the head.' As if to emphasize the point Palmer worked the tip of his index finger against his temple. 'I guess they'd go visit with him from time to time, used to see them in a vehicle on the county road there now and again.'

'But you only spoke to Ike Bowen the once?'

Palmer nodded. 'Yes, sir, just that one time and I never been to the house.' He let go a sigh. 'I like Isaac. Been through a whole hell of a lot what with the war and everything, and he told me about that last firefight. Shit like that going down when it's just a couple of weeks left on your ticket, that's got to be the worst time.'

Twenty-one

Dr Beale was in his office listening to the tapes he had made in the Fannin County motel room when his secretary buzzed through. On the desk before him lay a stack of other tapes in cardboard cases that were numbered and inscribed *Trinity*. Ignoring the flashing light at the base of his phone, he rewound the spool, listened to the last part of the tape again then shut it off. Finally he picked up the phone.

'Yes, Alice, what is it?'

'Mr Briers, sir, and Nurse McClain. They want to see you, sir. They're out here in the office.'

For a moment Beale just sat there staring at the reels of tape. Then he asked his secretary to give him a minute before she showed them in. Removing the reels from the spools he put them in the bottom drawer of his desk then unplugged the tape recorder and placed it on top of the file cabinet. He was turning for his desk when there was a knock on the door and the nurse and orderly came in.

Beale gestured for Briers to close the door then he indicated the couch. He remained standing. Hands behind his back he stepped up to the window and looked out across the dividing wall to the women's section where another orderly followed Miss Annie as she pushed a metal stroller. For almost a minute Beale watched her, the way she walked with her head down, gnarled little fists bunched around the handle, glancing left and right as if she expected the other patients to try and snatch her baby from her.

'I see you're making sure Miss Annie gets plenty of fresh air, Nancy,' he said, without turning. 'That'll do her good, she's not happy when she's cooped up.'

'She's never happy,' Nancy said. 'None of them are happy. They don't know what happiness is.' Lifting a palm she gestured. 'It takes a lot of organizing to have her outside like that. She can't be there with anyone else around unless there's an orderly watching her every move, but that's what you wanted so that's what we've done.'

'And I'm grateful.' Beale looked round. 'Miss Annie needs to be among the other patients, she can't always be on her own. With the progress she's been making since she came here I think it's worth the extra manpower, don't you?' He took a seat across the coffee table. Young in the face with his hair oiled back from his forehead, he shifted his attention to Briers. 'So,' he said. 'What did you want to see me about?'

Briers seemed a little nervous. He sat on the edge of the couch with his heels tucked back and his hands clasped between his legs.

'Texas, Doc. The newspapers – I spoke to a friend of mine and…'

Lips pushed out Beale looked from him to Nancy and back. 'You're talking about Mary-Beth. I heard about that and I've been meaning to talk to both of you. It's a tragedy of course, but it's merely a coincidence. It's not connected with anything that happened at Trinity.'

For a long moment Nancy seemed to study him. Sitting back in the seat with her head resting against the wall she looked far from comfortable. Next to her Briers shifted his weight.

'It's all right,' Beale said. 'We can talk freely. This office is sound-proofed so nobody's going to overhear. If you have something to say then I'd rather you said it so it's out in the open and we can discuss it properly.' He turned to Briers again. 'What's on your mind, Charlie?'

Briers glanced sideways at Nancy.

'We're worried,' Nancy stated. 'Doctor, Mary-Beth was murdered. Strangled, the papers said. You talk about coincidence, but she took off right after the fire and she didn't tell any of us where she was going.' Pausing for a second her expression darkened. 'There's only one reason she would've done that and we all know what it is.'

Beale considered her with his fingers pressed together under his chin. 'All right,' he said. 'She was scared. I accept that. And it's a fact he was very threatening, but he has no history of violence and threats like that are almost always empty.' Smiling then he gestured. 'Look, it's a sad fact but lots of people get murdered in this country and an awful lot of them in Texas. You know how it is, the wrong kind of glance in the wrong place, a housebreak that turns into something else. It happens, and especially, I'm afraid, to women. We cannot assume this is anything to do with what happened at Trinity.'

'You really figure that's how it is?' Briers spoke with his eyebrows arched. 'Come on, Doc: what went on before the fire, the way he was and everything – hell of a coincidence, don't you think? And we still don't know how that fire started, do we?' His gaze drifted to the window. 'The way that night turned out, the treatment you were hoping would trigger whatever it was you wanted to trigger – it's not what you thought would happen. You were as shocked as the rest of us. I remember the look on your face when you hollered for me to come in.'

Features a little taut Beale's gaze drifted to the tape recorder on top of the file cabinet.

'You're right,' he said. 'His reaction was neither what I was hoping for nor what I was expecting.' Glancing at Nancy he sighed. 'I can't tell you exactly what I thought would happen because this is the coalface, right? There are no givens when it's the mind you're treating, and especially someone with his condition.'

'A condition very few other doctors even accept exists,' Nancy said.

'Nancy, just because someone doesn't accept something does not mean it doesn't exist. History is littered with examples. Pushing the boundaries is the very nature of what we do. He was upset, of course he was. I knew there would be a reaction, and if there had been even the slightest indication of violence in his past I would never have made the suggestion.' With an open palm he gestured. 'Look, I know how this appears but it's nothing more than a tragic coincidence. You've nothing to be concerned about. None of us do. Mary-Beth's death was nothing to do with what happened at Trinity.'

There was silence between them after that, the only sounds those that lifted from the grounds outside. Nancy was fidgeting a little where she sat. Next to her Briers was staring at the floor.

Finally Nancy spoke. 'Nothing to worry about, is that what you really think? I don't buy it. I don't buy it at all. Mary-Beth was murdered, and however you want to try and dress it up we all know who it was that killed her. You heard him that night. You heard what he said. He meant it, all of it, and he's making good on his promise.'

When they were gone Beale went back to his desk where he sat staring into space. Eventually he seemed to come to and retrieved his keys from the top drawer. Fetching the address book from the safe once more, he dialled the number he had called a couple of days previously. His eyes were hooded, brow cut in fine lines; he worked a hand through his hair.

'I'm sorry to call you again,' he said when she answered the phone. 'But I had to. Something's happened. There's something you need to know.'

*

It was a little less than two hundred miles from the Bowen house to Tulsa, Oklahoma, and the skies were dark by the time Quarrie hit the city. A little cooler than in Texas, he had the address Austin had given him written on a slip of paper posted in his wallet.

Leaving the highway, he drove the downtown area on North

Main Street and from there he was on the old part of the road coming up on Cain's Ballroom. Usually anybody driving this way could see the neon glittering from way back where, but for some reason the sign on the roof wasn't lighted.

He had been to Cain's once before, just after he got home from Korea when he and Mary-Clare had only recently started dating. The ballroom was world famous for swing and honky-tonk, and Mary-Clare could swing dance better than anyone. Not much more than a warehouse really, a facade constructed in adobe brick, inside it was one large room under a shallow pitch with a polished wooden floor and a bar. Driving all the way up from Amarillo one Saturday, they had danced into Sunday morning.

The old place had not changed. It looked no different now to how it had back then, only then the street had been heaving with people and that roof sign could be seen from a mile away. Tonight there was nobody on the street and only the red-and-white livery out front indicated that the place was open.

Quarrie pulled over just a couple of buildings south and he was weary after driving from Louisiana to the Bowen house and from the Bowen house all the way up here. On the sidewalk he stretched his legs, wearing his Carhartt with the Ranger's star still pinned on the breast. For old time's sake maybe, he pushed open the saloon style doors.

Only a handful of couples on the floor, the walls decked with old photos of jazzmen and country stars from the thirties. Two people were serving behind the bar, a younger guy in a black shirt with rhinestone stitching and a woman of around fifty with dark hair she had tied in a plait. A little lined around the eyes, there was something about her that felt familiar but Quarrie could not say what it was. With a smile he took a seat on a stool and indicated the coffee pot on the warmer.

'Been a long drive,' he said. 'How about pouring me some of that coffee?'

The woman wiped the patch of bar space in front of him and glanced at the star in a wheel on his breast. She did not say anything. She just fetched a cup for the coffee.

Taking a pack of cigarettes from his jacket pocket Quarrie shook one out, tamped the inscribed end against the heel of his thumb and the woman passed him an ashtray.

'Not so busy tonight?' he said, glancing over his shoulder. 'The last time I was here was fifteen years back and you couldn't move for people bopping.'

'Fifteen years is a long time.' The woman stated. 'A lot can happen in fifteen years, and that was before Elvis and Jerry Lee.' Looking beyond him to the all but empty floor she wagged her head little sadly. 'Nobody wants to dance like they used to anymore, not even in Oklahoma.'

Swivelling round on his stool Quarrie too gazed across the empty floor. And for a moment his wife was in his arms, back in the days when she had still been his girlfriend. He allowed the memory to cling as he sipped the coffee.

'They used to tell us that floor right there had springs under her, the way she seemed to move so much when we were dancing.'

The woman shook her head. 'That was just a rumor. The floor isn't sprung, it's regular hardwood; the way it moved was on account of the weight of the people.'

'That all it was? No kidding.' Lighting his cigarette, Quarrie snapped his Zippo closed then laid it on top of his package of Camels.

The woman indicated his badge as somehow he knew she was going to. 'You're from Texas and this is Oklahoma. Not that it's any of my business, but what're you doing up here?'

Quarrie held her eye. 'Actually I'm looking for someone.' He glanced down at the star. 'Guess I forgot to take this off when I crossed the state line.' Shifting his weight he sought the wallet in his jeans pocket and took out the slip of paper. 'I have an address right here and I don't think it's too far away so maybe you could help me find it?'

The woman considered the address and tugged her lip with her teeth. 'Yes,' she said. 'That's just a few blocks from here. Carry on up North Main and take a left at the light. Keep going and you'll come to it.'

She left him to his coffee, making her way down the bar to the guy in the rhinestone stitching. Quarrie saw them exchange a few words and the young man peered at him over the woman's shoulder. Spinning the slip of paper around with the tip of his finger, Quarrie slipped it back in his wallet.

Outside he turned up his collar, climbed into the car and drove the underpass on North Main as far as the red light where the woman had told him to make the turn. Locating the block, he switched off the engine and considered his surroundings. Small properties, single-story, they were built in fading clapboard and he was reminded of the street where Mary-Beth had been murdered.

1433 was set back from the road, not much more than a cottage really with a tiny yard out front and in close proximity to its neighbor. No lights in the house, though one was burning above the stoop. Checking the address against the slip of paper, he got out of the vehicle.

Crossing the pitted asphalt he walked the lawn to the stoop. A solid front door, there were curtains drawn across all the windows. He knocked but received no answer. Knocking again he still got no answer so he walked around to the back, found the kitchen door and knocked again. He could see no lights in any of the windows: the whole place was in darkness. Back at the car he scribbled a note then slipped it under the kitchen door.

*

With Cain's not busy enough for both bartenders, the woman left just a few minutes after Quarrie. Buttoning her coat, she went out the back way to her eleven-year-old VW Bug, pale blue with a vinyl section to the roof that folded to let the sun in. She drove home, taking the long route up North Main to the light and another block from there. When she got to her street she parked a few houses away. Sitting behind the wheel with her hands clasped in her lap, she watched the Ranger walk all the way around her place before going back to his car. Perched on the edge of the driver's seat with the door open, he seemed to be writing something down. She watched him walk around back of the house again, disappearing from view before he returned to the car. This time he started the engine. He drove right past the VW but she was lying across the front seats so he could not see her. She lay there until she could no longer hear the sound of his car and then she pulled into her driveway.

In the kitchen she saw the note he had left pushed half under the door. She stared at it, fingers stiff and her eyes puckered at the corners. She did not pick it up. Instead she opened the freezer compartment on her Frigidaire and took out a bottle of vodka. Collecting a tumbler from the closet above the sink, she poured a shot and drank it down and then she poured another. From her purse she took a pack of Lucky Strikes housed in a snap-to wallet and lit one. Finally she picked up his note and read how he needed to talk to her. He would try and call on the phone later and be back again in the morning.

Taking her glass through to the living room, she made sure the curtains were pulled all the way across so there was no gap at all before she switched on the lamps. Placing the note on the coffee table she sat down on the couch where a multi-colored throw was gathered. For an age she stared at the fireplace, the room adorned with Native American symbols, dream catchers and medicine wheels hung as if to ward off evil spirits.

Finishing the vodka, she fetched the bottle and poured another. She fetched her cigarettes and an ashtray and lit a couple of incense sticks. Reading the note again her gaze drifted to the telephone, then she considered the open door to the hallway and her bedroom. Switching on the lamp, she was on her hands and knees by the bed reaching for an old shoe box she kept underneath. Clasping the box to her breast, she moved to the window where she checked the street outside, but all was quiet.

Back in the living room she poured another shot from the vodka bottle and lit another cigarette before settling it in the ashtray. She opened the box, tissue paper covering a whole stack of photographs. Carefully she lifted the paper out.

With reverence almost, she cast her eye across the images. Dozens and dozens of them, she traced fingers over the topmost few, locating one of three young nurses in uniform together with another woman wearing a pale-colored dress. There was a sense of excitement, the exuberance of youth perhaps, illuminating their faces. Her hand shook as she placed the photograph on the coffee table and sought another: a nurse by herself this time, she was wearing the same crisp white uniform and folded cap, the picture taken on the steps of an old colonial mansion. Rummaging in the box once more she found another picture taken in the exact same spot, only this time it was of the three nurses.

Placing those two on the hearth she found one more and her hand was trembling again as she considered two of the three nurses. One of them was very slightly built, blonde and pale, the size of her eyes her most striking feature.

On her feet once more, she paced to the window where she stood close to the curtain. The sound of a car approaching lifted from outside and she listened with the vodka glass gripped in one hand and her other arm about her waist. She waited, ears pricked, but the car drove right past the house without slowing and carried on up the street. Eyes closed now, she stood there a minute longer and then she went back to her bedroom. Opening the nightstand drawer her gaze settled on a piece of brushed velvet. It was wrapped around another photograph, only this one was framed in gold, and for long time she just stared at it. Fingers brushing the glass, the tears that had gathered slipped onto her cheeks as she placed the photograph back in the drawer.

Twenty-two

He jumped off the freight train as it rolled towards the switching yard. A couple of hobos squatted in the box car with him, one keeping to the shadows wearing fatigues from Korea with the name *Venice* stitched above the pocket.

From the yard he made his way on foot, skirting the downtown district where skyscrapers were built in a mix of concrete and pale-colored stone. He walked right past the Holiday Inn where Sam Cooke had been arrested, and asked directions to Bellevue Sanatorium from a newspaper vendor working a stand on the corner of Moor Street.

A black man in his sixties, he looked down from his battered counter. 'Bellevue?' he said. 'What you want to go there for? That ain't a hospital, it's a prison for basket cases.'

'I'm visiting somebody.' His tone was as terse as the vendor's incredulous.

The black man lifted a palm. 'All right, all right, no need to get all jacked up. It ain't the kind place most folks ask for.'

'Well, I ain't most folks and I'm asking. Now do you know where it's at or not?'

'Sure I know where it's at and I hope you-all is driving. Mister, Bellevue's in Virginia Park and that's a distance if you be walking.'

Making his way around back of the news stand he went inside and clubbed the man over the head with the butt of his pistol.

Moments later a woman and her two children approached the stand. They asked for Hershey bars and bottles of soda and he served them. Taking their money he placed the dollar bill in the metal cashbox while the black man lay unconscious and bleeding.

Without a word he handed the woman her change, then reached for the latch that held the board up. Locking it from the inside, he emptied the cashbox before wiping the blood from his boots where it seeped from the vendor's skull. From a hook behind the cash box he grabbed a set of car keys with an Oldsmobile fob attached to them.

Outside he stuffed the pistol in his waistband and buttoned his jacket. The stains were much worse now though, and they were a lot fresher. Back inside the news stand, he hunted down a cloth and bottle of detergent the old guy probably used for his counter. No longer red, the stains were just dark and wet and he went in search of the Olds.

A station wagon with wood panels working both sides, it was parked around the corner between a Plymouth and a bull-nosed Ford. Automatic transmission with a shift on the column, pressing his foot on the brake, he worked the lever up and down. There was not much gas in the car but he had twenty-seven dollars and change from the cashbox, and when he tapped the gauge on the dashboard the level reached a little higher.

For a while he sat there staring through the windshield then he opened the glove box, rooted around for a moment before closing it again and searched the pocket in the door.

He found a faded, well-thumbed street map, laid it across the steering wheel and located the park the old man had mentioned, tracing his finger where Ockley Drive formed an S bend running east to west.

There were a few houses scattered here and there but it was not built-up. No boundary to the park itself but the brick buildings in the center were gathered inside a ten-foot wall. Carefully he scouted the area; driving Ockley first he made his way around the S bend and spotted what looked like a back entrance to the hospital. A dozen or so cars were parked in a small lot that opened just a few yards from an access track that was laid with pea gravel. Making a loop of the parking lot, he considered the handful of aging vehicles.

Heading onto Ockley again, he drove east from the park and about a mile further he pulled in and turned the car. Now he drove back, passing that access road and pulling around the loop at the northern section of parkland. He could see the wall. Beyond it the height of the building carried at least six floors and he stopped on the side of the road. Sitting there he ran his tongue across his lips and adjusted the barrel of the pistol where it dug into his groin.

He drove on, completing the loop, and made a left where Ockley met Fairfield Avenue. About a block south he came to a stand of thickly leafed poplars that bordered the entrance to a driveway. There was a signpost out front, though it said nothing about the inmates being criminally insane. It only read *Bellevue* just as the sign in the Piney Woods had said nothing but *Trinity*.

Again he pulled over. Then he backed up and drove between the trees all the way to where the walls grew up, broken by a set of iron gates. It was just like Trinity, only these gates were fronted by a red-and-white vehicle barrier with a guard sitting in a wooden hut. Beyond the hut he could see another parking lot that housed a much better class of vehicle. Before he got to the hut he swung the Olds around the turning circle and lifted a hand to acknowledge the guard.

Back on Fairfield, he considered the dashboard clock. It was early evening now and he made for the gravelled lot where the less salubrious-looking vehicles were parked. Sliding the Olds into a space he switched off the motor and sat staring at the banks of trees.

After a while he got out and went around to the back of the car. There was not much in the trunk: an old raincoat that was too big for him, the toolkit and spare wheel. There was also a heavy-duty tow rope and a long-handled shovel. He took a few moments to consider the contents then he closed the tailgate and made his way across the parking lot to another stand of poplars where he could see the back entrance to the hospital. A steel gate set in the stone wall. Chewing on a thumbnail, he leaned against the trunk of a tree.

He was still there when darkness enveloped the copse. Sitting cross-legged in the shadows with the Levi unbuttoned and the pistol in his hand, he watched as the gate in the wall opened and a few members of the hospital staff filtered through. A couple of orderlies, two young nurses walking side-by-side smoking cigarettes, he could smell the stench where it wafted.

The number of cars in the parking lot gradually dwindled and still he sat where he was. Then the gate opened and closed once more and this time he glimpsed the bulk of a big man shouldering his way through the trees. He gripped the pistol that bit more tightly, watching as the man shuffled down the path wearing a white housecoat and green T-shirt. On his feet he had a pair of tennis shoes.

Silently he got up. He stood beside the oak tree and looked on as the big man headed for the parking lot. There were only three cars left now and one of them was the newspaper vendor's Olds. Ten feet back he had the gun levelled at hip height as the orderly searched his pockets for keys. Another step and Briers stiffened. He stood very still. Then he turned and his gaze fixed on the gun. Neither of them spoke. He stood there peering at the big man through the gloom of the trees and Briers looked back, much taller, much bigger built, his eyes still fastened on the gun. Indicating where the Oldsmobile was parked he tossed Briers the keys.

'Right there,' he pointed with the pistol. 'The tailgate, open it for me.'

Briers did as he was told, swinging the rear door wide before he looked back. Gesturing with the pistol, he told him to fetch the long-handled shovel and Briers did that. He told him to fetch the tow rope as well. Briers hesitated, his gaze once more on the pistol before he turned and bent for the rope.

With the flat of the shovel he smashed the big man across the head. Briers buckled; a moan escaping his lips he toppled forward so he slumped over the lip of the trunk. Voices sounded from further down the path. Throwing the shovel into the car, he reached for Briers's legs and managed to lift him, heft his legs around and shove his bulk in the back. He just about had the door closed before two nurses appeared through the trees.

Side-by-side they walked up the path making for the last two cars and he heard their voices clearly.

'Charlie's car's still there,' one of them said. 'I thought I saw him leave.'

That voice: listening to that voice he stood absolutely still. He was peering through the darkness as the two women came alongside and there she was with her dark hair pinned back under her cap. Nurse Nancy and another much younger woman, they walked right past the Oldsmobile but they did not see him in the shadows and they did not spot the unconscious man in the back.

He watched them. He started after them. Two paces, three, then he stopped, with the gun gripped in one hand and the other bunched in a fist. Now he just stood there watching as they both got in one car and Nancy backed out of the parking spot. He watched as she pulled away. He watched till the tail lights were no more than a glow.

Briers remained slumped in the back of the station wagon and when he got behind the wheel he could hear his childlike moans. He drove south of the city into woodland and marsh. He drove asphalt till he found dirt, then he took that dirt deep into cypress and live oak where Spanish moss seemed to list in the breeze. Finally he came to a clearing on the edge of slack water where an old cabin jutted from the shadows. Pulling over, he allowed the car to idle for a moment as Briers let out another moan.

Shutting off the engine he left the headlights on and they coated the walls of the cabin in a whitened wash. Walking round to the back of the car he had the gun in his waistband as he opened the trunk. Briers looked up but his gaze was thick and he was breathing heavily. He could sit just about and he perched precariously on the tailgate. Then he tumbled. Like a tree being felled, he tried to save himself by throwing out a leg but it couldn't take his weight and he sprawled in the dirt.

Standing back from the car he looked down at Briers but did not reach for the gun. Instead he sought the shovel and held it loosely at his side. He sat on the tailgate with the door pressed wide, the shovel across his lap, one foot on the ground and the other swinging back and forth. He looked down on the big man where he lay with his back to him, bathed in the crimson glow of the tail lights.

'What do you want?' Somehow Briers was talking, his voice overloud, the sound bouncing off the trees. 'For pity's sake.' With another moan he managed to get one elbow underneath and rolled over so they faced each other.

Still cradling the shovel, he stared across the flattened marsh. 'Where is she?'

'Where is who? Who're you talking about?' Briers's breathing was ragged, a sucking sound in his chest.

'You know who I'm talking about. Where is she?' Still that one leg dangled, perched as he was on the tailgate, like a pendulum it drifted back and forth. 'Where did she run to?'

'I don't know. I don't know who you're talking about.'

Sliding off the tailgate he was on his feet. 'I asked you where she is.'

'And I told you I don't know.' Briers lifted a hand. 'I swear to God, I don't know who she is.'

Like a scythe he swung the shovel. It cut through the stillness and caught Briers's hand. Blood flew, two fingers sliced through the knuckle, like a child the big man screamed.

'For God's sake, none of this is my fault. I was only there to keep an eye on you.' Features contorted he was clutching his shattered hand. 'I wasn't the one brought you to Trinity. I wasn't the one sat you down. I didn't know anything about it. I followed orders. I only did what I was told.'

'Where is she?' he asked again.

'I don't know.' Briers was sobbing, clutching his hand under his arm, he lay on his side with his cheek in the dirt. 'I don't know who you're talking about.'

On his heels he had the gun in his hand and he worked the barrel across Briers's cheek.

'Sure you do. You were there, the three of you. I saw Ms Gavin and Nancy in the other room.'

Briers twisted his head to the side. 'It was nothing to do with us. We had no idea what Beale was planning or what he was going to do.'

He peered beyond Briers to the cabin wall. 'It was you who brought me to that room. It was you had me sit down and it was you who brought her in.' He leaned closer to Briers still. 'I told you what would happen. I swore I'd kill you all and I will.'

On his feet again he paced back and forth, criss-crossing the pale bands thrown out by the Oldsmobile's headlights. 'Tell me where she is. I'm not going to wait all night. I'm done here so tell me where she is.'

'I can't,' Briers whimpered. 'I can't tell you where she is because I don't know who she is.'

'You're lying.' He was on him again, legs astride he had him by the collar of his soiled white coat. 'Don't you lie to me. I'm sick of people lying to me. Don't lie to me, Briers. Not anymore.' He pressed his face very close. 'I saw Nancy walking by just now and if I didn't already have your ass in the trunk I'd have gone for her right then. I'm not going to stop. I'm not going to stop till I get what I want and I meant everything I said. If you don't tell me what I want to know I'll go ask Nancy.'

'She doesn't know,' Briers said. 'Nancy doesn't know and neither did Mary-Beth.'

'She knew all right. She had to know because she kept the records.' He bent close. 'Only she didn't tell me.' He lifted Briers by the collar before slamming his head in the dirt.

Briers cried out, teeth raking his lips, his eyes rolling right over so the whites were clearly visible.

'Did you hear what I said? I almost had it out of her but I was squeezing her throat so hard she was gone before she could say.'

'I can't help you,' Briers wailed. 'I don't know where she is. I don't know anything about her.'

With a sigh he rose to his full height. Weighing the pistol in a palm he dug it into his pants. Then he looked down at Briers again and he looked at the long-handled shovel. He seemed to consider for a moment. Then he picked up the shovel and as he swung the big man sobbed where he lay.

Twenty-three

When morning came she lay in her bed staring at the ceiling where a little gray spider had woven a web so fine it was all but invisible save where it caught in strands of sunlight. She lay with her arms at her sides and the blankets up to her chin, her hair no longer in a plait but splayed across the pillow. From the front door she could hear the sound of the bell ringing. She could hear the weight of boots on the wooden step and then the bell again followed by the sound of somebody knocking.

She did not move. She did not get up. Next to her on the nightstand were the photos she had dug out last night. She lay with her head to the side staring at those photos until the knocking ceased. She lay until the sound of footfall left the step. She lay until the sound came a second time, only at the back of the house where he knocked all over again. As if he did not believe the house was empty, he knocked again and again.

Sitting up finally, she threw off the bedclothes and crossed to the hall. No nightdress, no robe, she hovered for a moment and she could see his shadow, the shape of his hat through the frosted glass. He knocked again and she was reaching for a robe when she saw him walk away. Throwing the robe around her shoulders she made for the door then paused and crossed to the living-room window. She saw him walk to his car. She went to the front door but again she hesitated. She heard an engine fire and she fumbled with the dead bolt and safety chain. She had the door open finally and was out on the stoop in the cool of the morning but he was already driving away.

Inside the house she rested with her back to the door and the flat of her hands at the base of her spine. Eyes closed, she rocked back and forth. In the kitchen she switched on the coffee pot and squatted on a stool. Reaching for the telephone her hand shook a little as she dialled.

A woman's voice answered. 'Bellevue Sanatorium, can I help you?'

'I need to speak to Dr Beale.'

'I'll see if he's available. Who's calling please?'

'Clara – I mean Carla. Carla Simpson. Tell him it's very important.'

'All right,' the operator said. 'I'll see if I can connect you.' The line clicked then seemed to die for a moment before Beale's voice sounded.

'Carla, what is it? Has something happened?'

'I had to speak to you. That policeman was just here – the one I told you about, the Texas Ranger.'

'Did you talk to him?'

'No, I didn't. He showed up just now and I was still in bed and I didn't answer the door. I don't know why I did that. I should've spoken to him but yesterday you told me you were dealing with it and—'

'I *am* dealing with it,' Beale cut in. 'You did the right thing. There's no need for you to talk to anyone. There's no need for you to be involved. If you get involved now it will all come out, everything that happened; everything that went on back then.' He broke off for a moment then he said, 'You don't need that. You don't want that. It'll do nobody any good. Now, listen to me. It's as I said: there is nothing to worry about. Nobody is going ask you any questions. Just go on with your life, OK?'

Hanging up the phone, Beale peered across the desk to where Nancy was looking on with her shoulders hunched and her arms folded across her chest.

'Nothing to worry about? Are you kidding me?'

Beale held her gaze. 'Nancy, what I said to her applies to you too.

154

There's no need to speak to anyone and there is no need for panic. I can handle this and I will.'

'So you'll go to the police? You'll tell them what happened at Trinity, how this all got out of hand?'

'Didn't you hear me just now?' Beale said. 'The last thing we need is the police.' He let go a shortened breath. 'He won't let them take him. They'll kill him, Nancy, and he doesn't deserve that. We don't deserve it. Now, I said I'll deal with this and I will.'

'Are you sure? Are you sure you can? Are you sure it's not too late?' She stepped a few paces closer to the desk. 'If you want my opinion I think you've let your ego get in the way. I think . . .'

She broke off as color flushed through Beale's cheeks. On his feet he paced around the desk.

'I don't want your opinion,' he said. 'I don't need your opinion, and as for my ego – this is about science not ego. When all's said and done the only thing I did was have him brought to Trinity.'

'That may be, but he didn't belong there, did he? He'd committed no crime and he did not belong in a place like that. I swear to God, if I had my time again I would never have agreed.'

'*You* would never have agreed?' Beale's tone was suddenly derisory. 'It wasn't up to you. You're not in charge. I could've used any of the nurses I wanted.'

'But you didn't.' Nancy fixed her gaze on his. 'You used me because I knew her better than anyone else and you asked Charlie because he could handle both of them if it came to it. Shock treatment – well it shocked all right, only not in the way you thought.' The fear in her eyes was tangible. 'Doctor, no matter what you told her just now, you need to go to the police. Mary-Beth is dead and so is Ike. We both know why and we both know how this ends.'

She was trembling, a shudder in her shoulders, her hands knotted. 'Anyway, there's something else, something you need to know. It's why I came up here. Charlie Briers didn't show up for work this morning.'

Beale stared at her and his gaze was as troubled as hers now. Nancy glanced above his head at the clock on the wall.

'His shift started at seven and it's almost nine thirty. He's never late and he's never had a day off sick.'

Beale was open-mouthed. 'Have you called his house?'

'Of course I have. I did that as soon as I knew he wasn't here. I got no answer on the phone so I thought he might be on his way, but when I checked his car was still in the parking lot and it was there when I left last night.'

Twenty-four

Quarrie made his way back to the highway. Twice now he had called at Carla Simpson's house and twice nobody came to the door. She might not have been home last night, but a car was in the drive this morning and he was positive she had heard him knock. Why she didn't answer he had no idea, but he figured he'd have headquarters ask somebody in the Tulsa police department to call as soon as he got to a phone.

He drove south once more and stopped at the Bowen house where Isaac answered the door in a bathrobe, his hair still wet from the shower. Showing Quarrie into the kitchen he went to get dressed. A few minutes later he came back with his Army uniform on a coat hanger. Draping it over a ladder-backed chair he dug out the ironing board and plugged in the steam iron.

'I like to keep stuff neat,' he explained. 'Probably I get that from my dad – he was a stickler for neatness. I guess I told you already. Used to drive Mom crazy, like there was never anything for her to do, how he insisted on doing the dishes and pressing his own clothes. You know what I mean?'

Taking a cigarette from his pocket Quarrie rolled it across his palm. 'But you're discharged now, right?' He nodded to where the iron was heating up. 'You're no longer in the service.'

'That's right. I'm no longer in the service and I guess I don't need to be doing this anymore, but I've been in so long it's a habit already, and you never know when I might need the uniform again.'

Quarrie nodded. 'So what're you going to do then? For work I mean, now that you're a civilian? Have you got something figured out?'

Isaac shrugged. 'I haven't really thought about it. I've got more important things to worry about, like whether my dad killed himself or if someone came to the house. I have to find out whether my brother died in that fire.'

'Do you think he did?'

'I really don't know.' With a sigh then Isaac set the iron on its heel. 'I found some papers, some stuff my Dad signed. I need you to take a look.' Opening a drawer in the worktop he brought out a couple of sheets of paper. 'From the hospital, I found it in his desk last night when I was down in the study.'

Two parts of a medical discharge form from a sanatorium in Houston dated January 1967, Quarrie read them carefully.

'That's Dad's signature right there.' Isaac indicated the scribble at the bottom of the second page.

Quarrie looked up at him. 'Isaac, this form signs Ishmael out of Houston into Dr Beale's care.'

'Right,' Isaac said. 'And I don't get that. I mean, like you said, Trinity was an asylum for criminals and Ish never hurt a fly.'

Again Quarrie studied the papers. 'You need to make some phone calls. Houston first, this sanatorium right here.' He tapped the page. 'See if you can't get some answers. They won't talk to me on account of I'm a cop and unless I can prove that your brother is a danger to the public or himself, they'll just quote patient confidentiality. Right now I can't even tell them if he's alive.' He looked squarely at Isaac then. 'They have to talk to you, though. They might not do that on the phone. They might insist you be there in person. But you're next of kin now your dad is gone and that means you're responsible.'

'Responsible.' Isaac had his brows knit. 'Responsible for what?'

'For your brother, at least technically anyhow: that paper says he was committed to the hospital in Houston and it was your dad that had him certified. That meant Ishmael was unstable enough to not be responsible for his actions or wellbeing.

Isaac, if he is still alive then you're responsible now.'

Isaac called the sanatorium in Houston but there were no physicians available and the receptionist told him he would have to come down in person. Hanging up, he dialled the number for Bellevue but they told him only Dr Beale could give him the answers he wanted and he was away. Putting the phone down again, Isaac went outside to get some air and a few minutes later Quarrie followed. Overhead the sun was high and Isaac stood with his back to the house and his arms across his chest, gazing into the woodland that grew up ahead of the lake.

'I called you that day because I wanted to know who it was that shot my father.' He gestured towards the garage. 'I showed you that passageway because that's how I figured they got in.'

'They didn't.' Quarrie assured him. 'I've told you already. And you've said it yourself: nobody could get in there unless they knew how that panel worked. Whoever it was must've rung the bell and your dad opened the door. I figure they had a gun on him and he had no choice but to let them in.'

Isaac turned from the yard to face him. 'So if they had a gun on him, why kill him with one of his?'

'Guns can be traced, Isaac, bullets matched. The perp used his own weapon to get in the house but after that why not use one of your dad's? Suicide,' he said. 'Any trail ends there and it worked already: the sheriff's detectives went for it.'

Together they went downstairs and Isaac switched on the lamp on his father's desk. Standing in the doorway Quarrie watched him, conscious of the way the darkened panels on the walls seemed to make the room feel smaller than it actually was. Sitting in his father's chair, Isaac opened a desk drawer and brought out a sheaf of old letters minus their envelopes and bound by a couple of rubber bands. Rolling the bands clear, he spread the letters on the desk.

'All of what I wrote him,' he said, picking up the topmost page. 'Crow's Foot valley, the Fishhook, no matter where I was, I never once got anything back.' He indicated the pile. 'So why keep them? If they don't mean enough to him that he can't write back why bother to hold on to the letters?'

Quarrie had no answer.

'It doesn't make any sense. Just like some stranger coming in the house and killing him doesn't make any sense. I'm sorry, John Q. I figure I wasted your time. A man who never writes his son, maybe that's the kind of man that kills himself.' Gathering up the letters again he fixed them with the rubber bands before dumping the whole lot in the trash.

Quarrie could see where tears pricked his eyes and he perched on the edge of the desk. 'Isaac,' he said, 'I need to ask you something. You told me that after you left Trinity you went to Shreveport and spoke to Dr Beale?'

Isaac nodded.

'Because the caretaker told you that's where your brother might be?'

'That's right.'

'So how did you know to go to Trinity in the first place?'

Isaac looked puzzled.

'How did you know Ishmael was there if your father never wrote?'

Isaac got up from the chair. 'I spoke to him on the phone, called from Saigon just before they shipped me out. I never said I was on my way home. I wanted that to be a surprise. I asked him how Ish was and he told me he was in a different sanatorium. He never said why and he didn't say what kind of a place it was, just told me he'd been transferred to the Piney Woods. It was no great shock. I said to you how Ish was always being sent to different institutions. It's been that way for years, Started when Mom left, I guess.'

'And that was when you were how old?'

'Ten or eleven I suppose.'

'And you've no idea where she is?'

'My mom? No, we haven't heard from her since.'

'So what's her name? Tell me who she is and I'll have the Feds try and track her down.'

Isaac furrowed his brow. 'Why would you want to do that?'

With a shrug of his shoulders Quarrie gestured. 'You don't think she'd want to know that her ex-husband was dead and might've been murdered?'

'If she gave a shit, why take off in the first place? Why leave him with two kids to bring up on his own and why not ever contact me or Ish?' Isaac was on his feet, his eyes dark. 'If she gave a damn about any of us she wouldn't have left when she did.'

'Even so,' Quarrie said. 'She's your mother and it's never too late. Besides, she might be able to throw some light on what was wrong with Ishmael that your father had him sent to Trinity.'

Isaac seemed to think about that. Then he ushered a mouthful of air from his cheeks.

'OK,' he said. 'I suppose you're right: family is family and right now she's all I got left. Her name's Clara. Before she married Dad she would've been Clara Symonds.'

Upstairs the phone was ringing and Isaac went to answer it. Quarrie retrieved the pile of letters he had dumped in the trash and leafed through them, trying to imagine how he would've felt in Korea if none of his letters had been answered. He wondered what it must be like watching all your friends get mail when there was never anything for you. With a shake of his head he re-wrapped the bands and put the letters back in the drawer.

In the kitchen he found Isaac still on the phone. 'OK,' he was saying. 'If that's what the coroner believes . . .' He looked round at Quarrie. 'No, he still thinks the same as he did. He's here right now as a matter of fact. Do you want to speak to him?'

He held out the phone and Quarrie looked at him with an eyebrow stretched.

'Deputy Collins from the sheriff's department,' Isaac explained.

'The coroner has examined Dad's body and he concurs with their lieutenant.'

'You're kidding me.' Quarrie lifted the receiver to his ear. 'This is Sergeant Quarrie.'

'Hello, sir, this is Deputy Collins speaking. I was the one come down there when you found Mr Bowen's body.'

'I remember you, Deputy. I told you he'd been shot and you were to secure the scene.'

'That's right, sir. And I did that but my lieutenant said how he shot himself. The coroner agrees with him, sir: he told me just now that the fact blood had gathered at the base of his throat was on account of the way he was set in the chair. He told me that bodies can move, sir; on their own I mean, especially if they're in a sitting position. He's done the autopsy now and he's sure that's how it happened. The only prints on the gun were Mr Bowen's and in the coroner's opinion – in the opinion of the sheriff's department – he used that gun himself.'

'What about the powder burns?'

'He dismissed those, sir, on account of the fact Mr Bowen had been a soldier and wouldn't have needed to be holding the gun against his head because of all his training. He said the fact that there were those powder burns wasn't proof of anything.'

'OK, Deputy,' Quarrie said. 'If that's what he said that's what he said and it ain't the first time I've disagreed with the coroner.' With a shake of his head he handed the phone back to Isaac.

Late that afternoon Pious landed the Piper Cherokee in Mr Palmer's field where Quarrie was leaning on the top rail of the fence with Isaac standing next to him. The Ford he had borrowed was parked in Palmer's yard and Quarrie had been on the phone to Marion County for someone to come and collect it.

'Isaac,' he said, 'regardless of whether the coroner's right or wrong you need to get a-hold of Dr Beale.' Loosely he gripped him by the shoulder. 'Don't let him stall you. Remember you're next of kin now and nobody can keep anything from you. He has to tell you everything there is to know about your brother and he can't soft-soap or bullshit either.'

'All right.' Isaac looked grateful. 'And thank you. I don't know what I'd be doing right now if you hadn't come around when you did.'

'Well, I have to tell you, if the coroner's writing your dad's death down as suicide there ain't a whole lot more I can do. Let me know what happens with your brother though, OK? Let me know when you've spoken to Beale.'

They flew back to the ranch, Pious glancing across the cockpit as Quarrie sat in the co-pilot's seat working his eyes with the tips of his fingers.

'Thank God for Mrs Feeley and this plane. I'm tired, bud. Could do with a hot shower, my own bed and a couple of days hanging out with my son.' He looked sideways then at Pious. 'How is he anyway?'

'He's just fine. Working hard on that project his teacher wants written up.'

'Is he now?' Quarrie smiled. 'Well I'll be. James never was much of a one for his lessons; guess this thing's really gotten hold of him.'

'Sure has,' Pious glanced at him again. 'Listen, I had to tell him about them bones. I know how I said I'd leave that up to you, but Sheriff Dayton had a couple of his boys come out to the ranch and I took them to that bend in the river. I guess they drug what was left of that poor kid out of the wreck, and when we got back James was home from school. According to the newspapers me and him been looking at, there weren't many children on that train so it's possible we might come up with a name.'

They flew low across the state with the sun in their eyes, Quarrie sitting in silence, thinking about Fannin County and the coroner and how Tom Dakin, the medical examiner from Wichita Falls, would not have discounted the powder burns.

'So, are you making any progress with what-alls going on?' Pious asked as the ranch lands came into view. 'Marion County I'm talking about, that sumbitch you been trying to tree.'

Quarrie drew a stiff breath. 'Got close to him, Pious, down in Panola County.' He told him about the old Mexican and what had happened during the rainstorm.

'Old Mex and a black girl, huh?' Pious shook his head. 'Wrong place at the wrong time, always the way it goes.'

Quarrie nodded. 'ME going to take a look at those bones, is he? That what the sheriff said?'

'That's what he said.'

'Well, maybe I'll call by before I drive back.'

'So, you're going over there again then, are you?'

'Have to, bud. More's the pity. I'd kindly like to spend some time at home right now but I got this sleazeball to scoop up and there's a woman in Tulsa, Oklahoma, who I need to talk to, only she doesn't want to talk to me.'

The following morning he was sitting on his back porch, watching the sun come up as he and his wife used to when they lived on the banks of the Snake. Smoking a cigarette and drinking hot, sweet coffee with cream, he heard the phone ring inside the house. James was still asleep, but for all he'd said to Pious about his own bed, Quarrie had tossed and turned all night. Twice he'd been up for a smoke and once for a shot of bourbon to see if that would knock him out. In the end he gave up and got dressed.

The phone was still ringing, and at this time of day that could only mean one thing.

'Morning, Captain,' he said.

'Morning, John Q. How did you know it was me?'

'Well sir, you're the only sumbitch in Texas would call a Ranger at home this time of day.'

'Is that right?' Van Hanigan said. 'So if it's that early, how come you're up and about?'

'Don't sleep so well anymore, probably the same as you.'

'That's a fact,' Van Hanigan said. 'I haven't had a full night's sleep since before World War II.'

'So what can I do for you?' Quarrie swirled the dregs in the bottom of his cup.

'The fingerprints you asked about from Marion County – had us a teletype from the NCIC.'

'You telling me we got an ID?'

'Not quite, they can't give us his name right now but whoever it was, his dabs match those from the motel room in Fairview as well as the sawn-off barrel from that shotgun.'

'Well, I kind of figured that,' Quarrie said.

'I ain't done, John Q. There's something else you need to know.'

Twenty-five

Dr Beale drove his Fairlane west. A steady sixty-five miles an hour, he had one hand on the wheel and now and again he would glance in the rear-view mirror only not at the upcoming traffic but at the expression in his eyes where they were reflected. The tape recorder lay across the back seat, microphone clipped on the side, and his briefcase with the catches unfastened. On the dashboard was a letter addressed to him postmarked *Fannin County*.

He twiddled with the radio, picking up some country music he listened to that. After a while, though, he twisted the dial to where a newscaster was discussing a speech made to Congress by President Johnson. Letting that play out, Beale found himself hunting his gaze once more in the mirror before shifting station and catching some Buddy Holly. As he crossed the state line into Texas he switched the radio off.

*

Back at the hospital Nancy had watched him go. She had been in the records office on the top floor, checking over some papers when she saw Beale pace the length of the drive.

She went back to the women's wing, passing through the common room and twin sets of doors. In the corridor all was still, but as she got closer to her desk she could hear Miss Annie's voice lifting from inside her cell. She was crooning, singing a lullaby to her porcelain doll. As Nancy came alongside she glanced through the panel on the door and spotted a fresh batch of scribbled etchings on the only patch of wall space that had remained unblemished.

She paused with one hand pressed to the glass and the keys on a chain at her side. Miss Annie was sitting on her bed cradling the doll in her arms and singing more softly now, as if her baby had fallen asleep. She did not look up; if she sensed the presence outside in the corridor it was not apparent. Still Nancy stood there; sweat on the palms of her hands, she wiped them on the front of her uniform.

The movement sparking something perhaps, Miss Annie twisted around where she sat. For a moment they stared at each other; the same age roughly, though, skeletal as she was, Miss Annie looked much older. The dullness in her eyes, the darkness; Nancy could hardly bear to look at her yet she couldn't peel her gaze away.

*

Fetching the canvas duffel bag from the closet in his room, Isaac laid it on the bed then dressed in the uniform he had recently cleaned and pressed. Downstairs in the kitchen he looked under the sink for the box containing boot polish and brushes and set about working the toes of his shoes. Only when he could almost see his face in them did he put the brushes aside.

Silent in his father's study, he stood in the half-darkness where the smell of death seemed to permeate still. He stared at the cabinet housing the array of weapons and the blade of the German bayonet seemed burnished in the half-light that bled from the corridor.

Settling in his father's chair, Isaac glanced at those tiny stains he had yet to scrape from the floor. Then he looked sideways, as if somebody was standing next to him. Bunching his eyes he made the shape of a pistol with his right hand and held it to his head. Index finger pressed against the soft spot of his temple he eased the finger back a couple of inches then worked his thumb like it was a hammer falling.

Hands in his lap he swivelled left and right. Like a child he wheeled the chair all the way around. He considered the desktop and the papers his father had signed. With a shake of his head he spun the chair once more and faced the panels behind. On his feet he slid his hand down the left-hand side, heard the click, then the panel opened.

Beyond it was the darkness of the passage; the only sound that of his shoes on the concrete floor. He had no need of a light. Exactly thirty feet and he came to the storm shelter and there he did switch on the light. Various bulbs set into the ceiling showed him the camp beds, sleeping bags and the shelves stacked with food enough to survive any tornado, hurricane or nuclear attack.

Tracing fingers across the labels he studied the assortment of cans: Campbell's soup, meatballs, haricot beans in tomato sauce, peaches and plums, apricots in syrup, sliced apple, and can after can of condensed milk. The lowest shelf formed part of the wall. Moulded in concrete like a prison bunk, the space underneath was deep enough for someone to lie down comfortably, a final vestige of safety if the rest of the shelter failed.

Water coolers like they had in offices, there were at least a dozen of them. Sleeping bags from Army/Navy stores all neatly rolled. On the wall next to the door that led to the garage was a metal box that housed first aid. For a moment Isaac stood there with his head slightly to one side as if lost in some distant memory. Then he crossed to the wall, opened the box by popping the catch on the top, and the lid fell forward to form a tray that sat at ninety degrees. The body of the box remained in the vertical, the contents neatly packed on plastic shelves, and metal clips where bandages were rolled, along with bottles of antiseptic. There was everything anyone could ever need, including syringes and antibiotics, hydrocodone tablets, as well as needles, dressings and suture thread. He ran his eye across a pack of steri-strips and next to that a polythene bag containing a flat, metal key about an inch in length.

Switching off the light he walked the passage back to his father's study. The wood panelling closed, he tossed the key in the air and caught it, his gaze drifting to the desk and the discharge papers from Houston. Sitting down in the chair once more, he laid the key on top of the papers and went through each of the drawers. He found nothing: no box, no pouch or satchel that might fit the key. Standing tall once more, he tossed the key in the air and caught it again then placed it on the shelf next to his father's photo.

Outside, he opened the garage doors. The ignition keys to both the pickup and the Pontiac were on their hooks and he started both engines and checked each gauge for gas. The Pontiac was half full so he backed that out and left the motor running, then he backed the pickup out too. Shutting off the engine he hung the keys back on the hook and closed the garage doors. He stood there looking at the pickup and then the house as if making sure it appeared some-body was home.

He trundled the length of the drive and, hitting dirt, he headed south. When he got to the county road he made for the junction that would take him to Paris. Close to the turn he spotted an Olds-mobile station wagon with wood panels on the doors that someone had left by the side of the road. Four miles later he was in Paris. As he came to the H-E-B grocery store he pulled off the road and in-to the parking lot where he locked the car and crossed to the men's room.

*

Walking the aisle in his jeans and jungle boots, he selected a bag of potato chips and a hunk of Monterrey Jack cheese. At the checkout he hunted his pockets for some money then grabbed a Hershey bar and an ice-cold bottle of Coke. Stepping out to the parking lot, he jerked the cap off the bottle using the opener fixed to the wall by a chain. He drank. From the corner of his eye he glimpsed a vehicle parked close to the perimeter wall, a midnight-blue Pontiac sedan;

he stared hard as sweat seemed to scatter his brow.

From the store it was a short walk to the gas station where he asked the girl at the counter if he could borrow a jerry jug. As he was pumping a young man in mechanic's coveralls came out of the workshop working his hands with a rag.

'So you ran out then, did you?' he said. 'How far away is it you left your vehicle?'

He looked sideways briefly then returned his attention to the clock-face dial on the pump. 'Little piece up the road there. Had to hike me all the way back.'

Hands in his pockets the mechanic tossed him a smile. 'I guess you swung right through town without thinking you was needing gas. Easily done, things on your mind like that. Been caught that way myself.'

The needle on the pump clicked back to the top of the dial and he shut it off. Shaking the last few drops from the nozzle he returned it to its housing and fished in his pocket for a dollar. The mechanic took the money, went into the office and came out with a quarter and pennies.

'So if it's the county road you need, I guess that's a couple of miles.'

He looked at him. He looked once more at the can of gas. 'I'll bring it right back, soon as I get to the vehicle.'

'I tell you what,' the mechanic said. 'How about I whistle you up there and fetch that jerry jug back myself? Ain't as if we're run off our feet right now, and Josie can hold the fort.'

The mechanic drove a wrecking truck with a heavyweight winch on the back. Across the bench seat he sat against the window with the Model 10 Colt hidden under the skirts of his sleeveless jacket.

'You a veteran then?' The mechanic indicated the jungle boots.

He shook his head.

'The draft and all – failed your physical, did you? I know how that feels.' The mechanic indicated the pedals on the floor.

'Flat-foot apparently, though I never knowed it till the doc from the Army told me.'

A few minutes later they came up on the Oldsmobile where the mechanic eased off the gas. 'That her?' he said, nodding through the windshield.

'That's her. I'm obliged to you for the ride.'

Stopping behind the car the mechanic got down and fetched the jerry jug from the bed of the truck and removed the top. Dispensing the gasoline, he gave the jug a waggle to make sure it was empty and then re-fixed the fuel cap on the car. 'You best fire her up just in case.'

As he fished the car keys from his pocket the skirt of his jacket popped up to reveal the grips of the pistol. The mechanic spotted it and the color drained from his face. For a moment they just looked at one another, then he got behind the wheel of the Olds.

'I don't want any trouble,' the mechanic said softly. 'Whatever business you got going on it ain't anything to do with me.'

He was no longer looking the mechanic's way. He was staring the length of the quiet road.

'Like I said just now, I'm obliged.' Closing the door he started the engine, slipped the transmission and pulled away with dust rising from the rear tires. In the mirror he could see the pale young man with the jerry jug scuttling back to his rig.

He drove the county road as far as the T junction and waited there. Nothing coming either way, he pulled out to the middle of the road and sat behind the wheel with the engine idling and scrutinized the landscape both north and south. Swivelling round in the driver's seat he rested the flat of his arm and checked the way he had come. Nothing there either, he turned for the house in the woods.

He drove slowly, eyes on the road ahead as the sun dipped behind clouds that seemed to be gathering off to the east. Signposts for the lake and fishing ahead, as well as the camp ground, he got to the point where the road forked and there he stopped. Leaving the engine idling he got out of the car and opened the tailgate where the boards were still stained with Briers's blood. Hidden under the raincoat he had the sawn-off shotgun with silver tape pasted over the grips. Back down the road a little way he could hear the sound of another car approaching and he got back into the Olds. Instead of making the turn for the house, he drove deeper into the woods.

Pulling into a glade he sat with the shotgun across his knees and his gaze fixed on the door mirror. No car appeared. He remained where he was, staring into the mirror, but nothing came up the dirt road and he hunched around in the seat. Opening the door he listened but could hear no sound now and gathered his brows in a frown. Starting the engine he closed the door, turned the Olds around and rolled back the way he had come.

He did not see any car and he stopped at the turning that led to the house. There he waited, the Oldsmobile squatting with the wind brushing the trees and the windows rolled down both on the driver and passenger's side. He fished the pistol from his waistband and laid it on the seat next to the shotgun. Making the turn he crawled along, keeping his eyes on the road until he came to where the driveway peeled off and the mailbox was fixed on its post.

His eyes were cold, brows still knit and again he stopped the car. For a full sixty seconds he stared at the driveway and the mailbox then he guided the Olds a little further up the road. On the right-hand side the trees thinned out enough to form a turnout where a car could spin all the way around. Pulling in there he switched off the engine then reached across the passenger seat and rolled the window up.

He approached the house through the trees. Cutting north from the dirt road he picked his way carefully, following foot trails and watching for snakes. He found no snakes and as he got closer the woodland grew less dense and the day a little brighter and he could see the edge of the lawn.

He came out of the trees in the lee of the garage. Head cocked, he listened to the sound of someone walking the pea gravel on the other side. He had the pistol in his waistband, the stain-spattered sleeveless Levi undone and the shotgun gripped by the breech. Moving soundlessly he peered around the corner and picked out a Ford and a man in a business suit who was knocking on the front door. The man waited, knocked again and waited but nobody came. A quiver in his muscles, he saw who it was and shrank back. Dr Beale. He listened intently as he crossed the driveway and stopped. He listened as the car door was opened then he heard it close and waited for the engine to start. But it did not start and he peered around the corner once more.

On the far side of the car Beale was facing him but not looking his way. He had a sheet of paper in his hand and he seemed to be reading what was written as if it were some instruction. Turning around he studied the facade of the house before striding across to the garage.

Again he stepped back; saliva in his mouth, he sent his tongue across his lips like a snake. On the other side of the garage the footsteps were suddenly silent and it was fifteen seconds before he heard them again. Releasing a trapped breath, he raised the shotgun so he held it broadside across his chest. He waited for Beale to appear around the corner but instead the garage doors were opened and he heard the doctor go inside. Eyes closed, he leaned with his back to the wall, the sun casting shadows across his face though sweat still cloaked his brow. From inside the garage he heard the grating sound of the trapdoor as it was raised and the clatter as it fell again.

Back to the wall, he waited for silence to descend. Then he made his way around the side of the garage and stood staring at the hole in the floor. Shotgun yoked across his shoulders he stood above the ladder and looked down. Jungle boots on metal rungs, he was in the darkness of the walkway and a moment later in the storm shelter itself. Shelves lined the walls, moulded concrete forming the lowest bank where a man could make doubly sure.

Something on the wall caught his eye: the first aid kit lying open with the tray fixed in the horizontal. For a moment he studied the contents, bottles of antibiotics and painkillers, syringes sealed in polythene bags. He noticed one polythene bag was empty and lying across the top of the fold-down tray. He stared at it for a moment then moved across the room, listening intently as he passed into the passage through the open door.

No sound, nothing at all, and yet he could feel a hint of movement like the faintest of breezes disturbing the otherwise stagnant air. Sweat worked his brow. Shifting the weight of the shotgun his hands were clammy and he wiped them on the legs of his jeans.

He was halfway down the passage before his eyes grew accustomed and he could see that the wooden panel was standing open and that's why he could feel movement in the atmosphere. He stopped; he was trembling, swallowing hard as if there was some blockage in his throat. He could hear no sound from the study beyond.

Inside, he had to wipe perspiration where it burned his eyes. He stared at the desk and chair, his gaze attracted by a few dark spots on the floor. Footfall above his head, he cast a short glance at the ceiling and closed the panel in the wall. Then he moved to the door.

There he paused. He could hear Beale moving around above him and he stepped into the passage walking on his toes. At the bottom of the stairs he checked. Still he could hear Beale up there and he stood very still. Slowly, inexorably almost, he climbed to the top of the stairs. Again he paused. The hallway a little dim, he could see one of the bedroom doors was ajar.

Beale did not hear him approach. He was in the living room with a metal box before him on the coffee table and the lid open; he was leafing through a stack of documents inside.

Fifteen seconds, thirty maybe, then, as if Beale felt his presence rather than heard anything, he swung round. Panic in his gaze, the pallor of his skin was wax as he took in the twelve-gauge pump and the pistol grips and the look in the young man's eyes.

Twenty-six

Pious caught up with Quarrie before he left the ranch. The Riviera fully gassed up and ticking over, he was letting the engine warm up.

'Wanted to get a-hold of you before you-all took off,' Pious said as he came over from the cottage he shared with his mother and sister. 'Georgia, Ike Bowen – I made those calls like you wanted and a buddy of mine from the old 2nd Company called me back last night.'

'What did he say?' Quarrie was adjusting the straps on his shoulder holsters.

'Not a whole lot as it goes,' Pious stated. 'Not much to say about Ike Bowen except he was a pretty good soldier.'

'Yeah, well, that part I figured already.'

Pious made an open-handed gesture. 'That shelter he's got going underneath the garage: all that stuff backed up in case of a hurricane or whatnot, they reckon he was always one of those survivalist types. As far as the service goes he had something of a reputation as a point man, never missed a booby trap once. A little paranoid maybe, but they said he was pretty tough.'

'Pious, all tough guys are paranoid. You ought to know that by now.'

Pious cracked a smile. 'Anyways, there is one thing struck me as a little odd maybe. Back in the day Ike was something of a lady's man apparently. It wasn't as if he had a girl in every port or anything, but he did like to fool around.'

At that Quarrie raised an eyebrow. 'Lady's man, uh? That don't seem to square with him living way up there in the grassland all on his lonesome.'

'No, it don't,' Pious agreed. 'But it might account for his wife leaving out when she did. That feller you mentioned from Oklahoma, he was 82nd with Ike when the Japs hit Pearl Harbor.' Pious fished in his back pocket for a slip of paper. 'Sergeant name of Morley. They gave me this address. Came through that little town myself, John Q, after I got out of Leavenworth and found me that grabbling spot.'

Walking around the car he checked the tailpipes where a little moisture was leaking out.

'Sounds like she's running OK.'

'Sweet as a nut; you know how she always is.'

Lifting the hood, Pious checked underneath. 'So you're headed back to East Texas again then, are you? What's up with that? Don't you have any Rangers over there?'

'Sure we do, but they're tied up with all the protests right now.' Opening the driver's door Quarrie slipped behind the wheel as Pious settled the hood. 'Blame it on the students, bud – them or LBJ.'

'You sure you don't want me to fly you back over there?' Pious said. 'It'd be no trouble.'

Quarrie shook his head. 'No sir, thank you. I'm going to need wheels when I get there and I already gave Marion County theirs back.' He cast a glance towards his cottage. 'What I need is to get quit of the Rangers and find me a sheriff's job.'

'James is it you're thinking about?'

'No momma around all these years and his dad on the road all the time. You know that can't be good.'

'John Q,' Pious said, 'if we laid you down and cut you open we'd find the word *Ranger* stamped right through your marrow. James knows that. He's always known it and he's just fine. Got him a black man to learn life's lessons from, and in this day and age that ain't any bad thing. You might not be around as much as you'd like but they's plenty good folks looking out for him – Mama and Eunice,

177

Mrs Feeley and Nolo, not to mention all the other hands. Think on her this way: your son's got a whole bunch of different influences to study on, and I never knew Mary-Clare, but from all of what you told me, I reckon she'd settle for that.'

Quarrie drove back to Fannin County and the Bowen house. When he got there he found both the Pontiac and the pickup truck parked in the driveway and the trapdoor open in the garage. As he parked the Riviera he saw Isaac peer out the front door. He did not say anything but the expression in his eyes was hollow.

'You OK?' Quarrie called. 'Isaac, are you all right?'

Isaac did not speak. He just stood in the doorway, dressed in his uniform with his tie loose at the collar.

Inside the house Quarrie could see that the furniture had been shunted around, marks in the carpet where the couch had been, the coffee table was standing askew as well as one of the armchairs. The card table was on two legs where it leaned against the bar. The fire was burning, though it was warm outside, and he could see the family photograph lying on the mantelpiece with its glass smashed.

'What happened here?' he said. 'Looks like there's been a fight.'

Squatting down beside the fire Isaac stared. 'My brother happened,' he said.

'What do you mean?'

Isaac did not look at him.

'Isaac, what do you mean *your brother happened*?' Quarrie indicated the uniform. 'You told me you're done with the service. Why are you dressed like that?'

Getting up, Isaac set the card table back on its legs. 'I was going to Shreveport,' he said, 'on my way to see Dr Beale. He didn't call, so I thought I'd go over there anyway and figured I'd feel more confident if I was dressed like this. I've been in so long I still can't get my head around being a civilian.' He looked back. 'Dad had to have a soldier in the family – did I ever tell you that? It was a given right from when me and Ishmael were kids. There's always been a

178

Bowen serving, firstborn usually, and I guess with this generation that should've been Ish.'

'Isaac,' Quarrie looked at the fragments of broken glass that seemed to float in the strings of the rug. 'You said you went to Shreveport. What happened?'

'Nothing, I never made it.' Isaac shook his head. 'Fact is I only got as far as the H-E-B in Paris. Went in to take a leak and I swear . . .' His voice seemed to fail him suddenly.

'What?' Quarrie said.

Isaac stared into space. 'I thought I saw my brother. I thought I caught sight of Ishmael standing at the door, but when I looked I couldn't find him, not inside the store or out in the parking lot.' He worked the heel of a hand through his hair. 'Gave me one hell of a shock because I'd already resigned myself to the fact he was killed in that fire. But he wasn't. Ishmael didn't die in the fire; he was there at the grocery store.'

Arms folded, Quarrie stared.

'I figured he'd come here so I drove on back.' Isaac gestured to the way the furniture had been shifted. 'He must've made it ahead of me though, because this is how I found the place. Like you said just now, it looks for all the world like someone had a fight, and Ishmael fights with himself.'

He sat down heavily in a chair. In the kitchen doorway Quarrie stood with his arms still folded. Isaac not looking at him, he was staring into the fire. Warm in the room, Quarrie slipped off his jacket and sat on the couch with his holsters pouched against the walls of his chest.

'Isaac,' he said. 'Why I'm here – there's something I have to tell you, something you're not going to like.'

Isaac snorted. 'I swear to God, there's nothing you can say that'll piss me off any more than I am right now.'

'I wouldn't bet on it,' Quarrie said.

Taking a moment, he drew a breath. 'I've been working down in

Marion County. I told you, on account of a couple of murders?'

Isaac nodded.

'One of them was a woman called Mary-Beth Gavin and she used to work at Trinity Hospital. She ran the office down there but took off right after the fire.' Quarrie was quiet for a moment before he went on. 'The thing of it is the National Crime Information Center has picked up on a set of fingerprints. That's the forensics department the FBI put together, and they discovered that the prints found in Mary-Beth's house match a set from a motel room in Fairview, as well the sawn-off barrel of a shotgun. The same prints were also found at a Baptist mission cottage in Marshall, Texas, where a young maid was murdered. I'm sorry, bud, but another set were recovered from right here at your daddy's house.'

As if he couldn't quite comprehend what he was being told, Isaac stared out of half-closed eyes.

'The lab team from the sheriff's department,' Quarrie went on. 'They sent all the prints they recovered back east, but they didn't know about Marion County. The NCIC picked up the match and sent a teletype to my captain in Amarillo.'

Isaac lifted a palm. 'So what're you telling me? What does all that mean?'

'It means that the coroner got it wrong. Isaac, whoever it was killed those other folk, they murdered your dad as well.'

Isaac was trembling where he sat. Eyes closed tightly, his lips no more than a scar against the pallid shades of his face. He did not say anything; he just sat there with his hands clasped in his lap. And then he looked up.

'John Q,' he said. 'You remember how I told you that whoever it was killed him they came in through the garage?'

Quarrie nodded.

'You told me that wasn't possible.'

'It isn't, not unless they knew how to open that panel.'

Together they went downstairs to the study where Isaac sat in his father's chair. His expression haunted, he studied the confines of the room then swivelled the chair all the way around. For a moment he stared at Quarrie then turned back to the wall where he opened the panel.

'That is how they got in,' he said. 'And they didn't need to have a gun because there were plenty already here. Nobody came knocking on the door, John Q. Nobody forced Dad down the stairs.'

Closing the panel again he cast a glance towards the study door. 'There.' He pointed. 'He was standing behind the door. He had the twenty-two from the cabinet and Dad didn't know he was there. He came down to do some paperwork or something and he didn't turn on the overhead light. He hated that light, always said it was way too bright, couldn't figure why he ever put it in.' Reaching across the desk he switched on the lamp. 'He wouldn't have known that anyone was there, not till he was sat right here.'

He got to his feet and hovered for a second then paced the width of the room. Features taut, he opened the door to the basement passage and stood in the shadows it cast. 'He was right here.' Again he pointed. 'Dad was at the desk and he stepped out from behind the door.' Crossing the floor once more he walked around the desk and paused by the side of the chair. Briefly he looked at Quarrie. Then he formed the shape of a pistol with his thumb and index finger and pointed at the empty chair.

Quarrie considered him carefully. 'Isaac,' he said. 'What're you telling me?'

He saw Isaac swallow. His saw his Adam's apple working up and down.

'Ishmael,' Isaac said. 'It was my brother with the gun down here.'

Twenty-seven

A couple of hours later they turned off Fairfield Avenue in Shreveport, Louisiana, and drove up to the checkered barrier ahead of the hospital gates. In the passenger seat Isaac had half a smile on his face.

'Man,' he said, 'that didn't take hardly any time at all.'

Quarrie winked at him. 'Perk of the job, that red light. Means nobody's going to pull you over and under that hood is a 425. Pious hooked her up to a supercharger and replaced the old tailpipes with 2.5s. Get a kick every time I drive her, bud. Be a liar if I to said otherwise.'

Despite being out of state, he carried his badge on his jacket and Isaac still wore his uniform. A young guard with a crew cut waved them into the parking lot and the two men got out of the car. They had to wait for the hospital Jeep to come down from the main building and pick them up because patients were roaming the grounds.

Inside the building they were greeted by an orderly who ushered them into an elevator. On the third floor they found another orderly who walked them to Dr Beale's office where his secretary greeted them with a slightly nervous expression on her face. She came around from behind her desk and considered Isaac first and then Quarrie.

'Gentlemen, I am so sorry,' she said. 'Somebody should've told you at the gate. Dr Beale isn't here.'

Quarrie furrowed his brow. 'Probably we should've called ahead of time, mam. I guess we figured he'd be back.'

'Well, I'm afraid he's not.' In her forties with short bobbed hair, the secretary shook her head. 'The fact is I don't know where he is.

I wasn't here when he left and he didn't write me a note. Normally he writes a note but he didn't leave one this time so I can't tell you when he'll be back.'

Quarrie nodded. 'This is Isaac Bowen, mam. He's next of kin to Ishmael Bowen who was a patient of Dr Beale's at Trinity Hospital. I'm not sure if Dr Beale mentioned Ishmael at all. Would you know anything about him?'

Gesturing for them to take a seat, the secretary went back to her desk. 'I don't know anything about any of the patients I'm afraid, though I remember Mr Bowen from the other day.'

Isaac sat forward. 'After I left here Dr Beale came to my father's house.'

'Did he? He never said. But then he doesn't always tell me where he's going and that's due to patient confidentiality. Not all his patients are in sanatoriums, he has people he treats in their homes.'

'Ms Barker,' Quarrie said, glancing at the name plate on her desk, 'this isn't actually a sanatorium as such, is it? Technically, I mean: it's an asylum for the criminally insane.'

The secretary looked a little puzzled.

'As was Trinity,' Quarrie went on. 'A secure facility. You know about Trinity I imagine, back in Texas?'

'Of course I know about Trinity.' The quizzical expression hadn't left her face. 'As you say, it was one of the other hospitals where Dr Beale's expertise was required.'

'So what exactly is his expertise?'

'Well, he's a psychiatrist; he helps people with mental conditions.'

'I understand that, mam, but what kind of conditions are we talking about?'

'I'm sorry, I can't explain that to you. I'm not a doctor, Sergeant. You'd have to ask him.'

'We'd like to,' he said. 'But he's not here and you can't tell us when he'll be back.'

She lifted her shoulders then a little helplessly. 'I don't know what else I can say. I wish I could tell you where he is because it's not just you who wants to know, it's the trustees. Normally he checks in every day but so far he hasn't been in touch.'

Quarrie was holding her gaze. 'And you have no idea where he might've gone?'

'No sir, it's as I already said.'

Quarrie got to his feet. 'Ms Barker,' he said, 'it's the fire at Trinity we want to talk about. I spoke to the caretaker down there and he told me that some members of staff were relocated here to Bellevue as well as a few of the patients.'

'That's correct,' she said. 'But, I can't disclose anything about any patient. Even if I knew anything, I'm only a secretary.'

'I get that, mam,' Quarrie said. 'But what about the staff? How many came up here? If we can't speak to Dr Beale, maybe we could speak to one of them?'

Taking off her glasses now the secretary wiped them on a tissue she plucked from a box on her desk. 'Once more I have to apologize,' she said. 'But only two members of staff were actually relocated, a nurse and an orderly, and neither of them are here.'

'Not here?' Quarrie said. 'Can you tell us where they are?'

'Nurse McClain called in sick this morning and Mr Briers . . .' She faltered. 'Mr Briers – well it's a fact his car is in the parking lot but he's not been seen for a couple of days.'

Quarrie exchanged a glance with Isaac and then he turned back to the secretary. She was looking really flustered now, shifting awkwardly in the seat.

'Look, I'm sorry,' she said. 'This is really nothing to do with me. Dr Beale is in charge of this hospital and—'

'That's all right, Ms Barker. Don't worry.' Getting to his feet Quarrie crossed to the window where he looked the length of the narrow road. 'You say the orderly's car is here but he didn't show up for work.'

'That's right; he's not been seen in a couple of days.' Leaving her desk, she came over to the window. 'His car isn't down there,' she said. 'That parking lot is only for the doctors, visitors and trustees. There's another one across the way.' She pointed beyond the dividing wall and Quarrie could see women on their own or in small groups, wearing the same loose pajamas as their male counterparts. 'The other side of the perimeter wall,' Ms Barker explained, 'there's a parking lot for the staff that's accessed from Ockley Drive.'

Five minutes later Quarrie and Isaac were pacing a pathway through the grounds where women were gathered and the sight of two strangers caused quite a stir. En masse they tried to crowd around them but the orderlies ushered them away. Isaac walked alongside Quarrie with an orderly in front and another behind. The age of the women seemed to range from those in their twenties with sad faces and even sadder eyes to well beyond middle age.

Quarrie noticed one woman walking by herself. She had an orderly right behind her, mirroring her steps as she made her way across the lawn. Her downcast face was skeletal, lips pinched; hair so thin he could see her scalp like a ball of wax. She was pushing a pre-war metal baby stroller, and every time she passed another patient she would cast a savage glance their way.

The orderlies led them through the outside gate and into a copse of poplar trees. They were younger men and neither of them seemed to know a great deal about Briers.

'He came over from Texas though, right?' Quarrie asked as they approached the parking lot.

'Yes, sir,' the first orderly said. 'Along with Nancy McClain.'

'The nurse off sick right now?'

'Is she?' the man glanced back at him. 'I didn't know that.'

'So what's Briers like?'

The orderly shook his shoulders. 'We didn't see him much. Big guy, real meaty – which helps when you're doing this job. Looked after the male patients mostly, the only time we'd see him on our side of the fence was when they sent him over to walk Miss Annie.'

'Who's Miss Annie?' Isaac asked.

'That old crone you saw just now pushing the stroller.' The orderly glanced at him. 'Normally it would be Briers watching her. She came up from Trinity at the same time he did. Pushes a doll around in that stroller, and the way she is, you'd think it was a regular baby.'

Hand on his arm Quarrie made him pause. 'That woman we saw on the path just now?'

The orderly nodded. 'She's one of the meanest we've ever had here. Don't know much about her but she's been in isolation ever since she arrived.' Looking from Quarrie to Isaac he gestured. 'She's only just now been allowed outside. For the first few weeks she was kept locked up in her room.' He glanced back the way they had come. 'You saw that orderly walking right behind her? Well, if he was here right now that'd be Charlie Briers. It's the only way Miss Annie is allowed outside, and she's not allowed to mix with the other patients, she has to keep well away. She might be skin and bone but one wrong word and she'll kill you.' He glanced to his compatriot for support. 'Or at least that's what they say.'

The orderlies led them to the parking lot and a 1961 Chrysler with an oval-shaped windshield and squared-off steering wheel. Quarrie walked all the way around the vehicle, studying the door locks, the trunk lid and hood. Nothing struck him as odd though, and he turned his attention to the parking lot itself where a mishmash of tire treads and various different footprints broke up the dust.

Taking his pocket knife he jacked the lock on the trunk lid. There was nothing in there however but an aged-looking tire and a pile of old newspapers.

The trunk lid fastened again, they walked back to the perimeter wall, but halfway along the path Quarrie stopped. Something caught his eye, a patch of dirt off to his left, a piece of open ground at the bole of a tree. He moved closer and Isaac made to follow, but Quarrie lifted a hand indicating for him to stay where he was. A partial print, no heel, just the ball of the foot, but it was flatter than it should be. He recognized the pattern on the sole and moved around to the other side of the tree. There he spotted a second print, full this time; the earth much softer, he could see a nick in the heel.

Back on the path he exchanged a glance with Isaac and spoke to the orderlies.

'Boys,' he said, 'as soon as you get to a telephone I want you call the police. Not the city but the state. Tell them your orderly has been abducted.' He turned to Isaac. 'He's wearing a pair of jungle boots, Isaac, they—'

'I know the boot.' Isaac was staring at the bole of the tree. 'I've worn it plenty. Steel shank in the sole on account of the sharpened bamboo.'

Upstairs in the office Quarrie spoke to Beale's secretary. 'Ms Barker,' he said, 'the Louisiana State Police are on their way up here and they're going to want to speak to everyone who came into contact with Mr Briers. I'd like to speak to those people myself, but I don't have the jurisdiction. This nurse, though – the one you talked about earlier, the one from Trinity?'

'Nurse McClain,' she said. 'Nancy.'

'Nancy, right. Mam, jurisdiction or not, I really do need to speak to her.'

'She's off sick, Sergeant. I already told you.'

'Did she know about Briers?'

'Of course. She was the one who reported it. She told Dr Beale and he had me call Mr Briers at home.'

Sitting on the edge of the desk Quarrie smiled at her. 'Ms Barker,' he said, 'I'm reaching out here because I think Mr Briers has been abducted, and if Nancy called in sick it's because she's very afraid. I believe she's hiding from the man who abducted Briers and I can't afford to wait for the state police. I need to get to her now. I know all about policy and how you're supposed to act and everything, but you have to tell me where Nancy lives.'

She lived in the suburbs well away from the hospital, an apartment block overlooking the highway as it trailed south from the city. There was no answer at her door when they knocked and Isaac considered Quarrie as they stood in the silent hallway.

'We could break it down,' he suggested.

'We could.' Quarrie knocked again and still there was no answer. 'I've been known to do that before, but I reckon there's another way.'

He waited on the stairs while Isaac went back to the lobby and the building manager's office. Five minutes later he stepped out of the elevator with the manager and Quarrie watched them walk the hallway through the glass panel in the door.

'Just back from over there then, are you?' The manager looked old enough to be a veteran. 'Good to see you in uniform, son. Landed on Omaha Beach myself and I can't be doing with how things are. This is America, for Christ's sake. Those kids waving placards on the street right now, they ought to be ashamed of themselves, I swear.'

'Yes, sir,' Isaac nodded.

Quarrie looked on as the manager hunted down a pass key and fit it in the lock. 'Well,' he said, 'when your mom gets home no doubt she'll be happy to see you.' Patting Isaac on the back he left him in the open doorway.

There was no sign of Nancy McClain. A bedroom and bathroom, a living room with a kitchenette, there was no evidence of an occupant at all. The closet in the bedroom was empty, hangers on the floor, hangers on the rail and the doors standing wide. The drawers in the bureau had been pulled out and emptied. The bed was unmade; no clothes, no jewellery, and nothing in the bathroom either. A moonlight flit, Quarrie stood there with his thumb hooked in his belt and considered how swiftly the place seemed to have been vacated.

He told Isaac he was putting him on a train. By the end of the day he was pale in the face, dark circles crawling beneath his eyes; he looked as if he hadn't slept in weeks.

'I'm going to take this from here on out,' Quarrie said as they walked back to the car. 'I'll need you when Dr Beale shows up though, so I'll call you at the house later on.'

They split a pitcher in the station bar. Perched on a pair of stools they drank beer and Quarrie smoked a cigarette.

'I really am sorry about all this,' he said. 'Real shitty how you came home to find what you did and how things have turned out since.'

Isaac did not say anything. He sat there toying with his glass. 'I'm OK,' he muttered finally. 'What matters now is that we find Ishmael. If he's been killing people, then any other cop that comes up on him will be so twitchy they'll probably just shoot.'

'We'll find him,' Quarrie stated. 'We'll get there before anybody else does, and nobody is going to shoot him. But listen to me: don't start beating up on yourself, OK? Don't start asking what you could've done different because the answer is *nothing*. When something like this goes down people start in on themselves with all kinds of questions they could never begin to try and answer. None of that does any good. You understand, Isaac? It ain't your fault how your brother turned out and that's something you have to remember.'

'But how come he did?' Isaac looked sideways at him. 'Turn out like this, I mean. I don't get it. I don't understand it at all.' Lifting a palm he let it fall. 'When we were kids he wasn't like that. He . . . Me and him . . . What the hell am I going on about that for? We're all grown up now. We're not kids anymore.'

'Like I said,' Quarrie looked squarely at him, 'don't be beating up on yourself. It ain't going to do any good.'

Finishing his beer Isaac poured another half-glass. He toyed with it. He seemed to study the amber liquid. 'By the way,' he said, 'I've been meaning to ask you. My mom and all – did you come up with anything on where she might be? I know what I said before, but now we got this going on I wouldn't mind talking to her, if she'll talk to me.'

Twenty-eight

Seeing him onto the train Quarrie went back to his car. Behind the wheel he picked up the radio and put a call in to the state police to see if there was any news on the missing orderly. They told him they had nothing so far, but mentioned a newspaper vendor who'd been found locked in his news stand with a fractured skull.

Quarrie left the station and headed south. Something was bugging him, and he took the back roads to Funston and Logansport before crossing into Texas where the Sabine River formed the neck of the lake. From there it was a short hop to Joaquin and he was into the woods again.

He drove with darkness swallowing the trees. He drove with the heel of his hand on top of the wheel and all manner of thoughts picking at him. No wind tonight, no rain. Above the trees a crescent moon cast a little light as he made the dirt road and narrow causeway. Beyond the iron gates the grounds took shape and the main building loomed just ahead. Coming to a halt thirty feet from the steps he shut off the engine. It wasn't cold tonight, but as he climbed out of the car a shiver worked his bones just the same. For a moment he stared at the grisly facade where scorch marks tainted the rotting wood. He considered the bank of darkness where the doors had been. He considered the pillars, the broken glass and vertical bars that split them like piano keys. He looked up to where the roof was all but gone and from there to the second-floor windows.

Opening the trunk of his car he rooted around for his flashlight, a heavy-duty triple cell he had picked up at the mercantile in Wichita Falls. When he switched it on the beam reached all the

way to the trees and he worked it across the far wall, thinking about
Pablo's cabin. That old Mexican. Like Pious had said, wrong place
at the wrong time; it felt like a kick in the gut. The worst thing
about this job was the plight of those that inadvertently got in the
way. Nothing to say to their relatives: no reason, no explanation;
nothing that could begin to assuage their pain.

He kept thinking about what that old man had said about
Sonora and how he used to drive a fluorspar truck from Coahuila
to Oklahoma City. Why it should bother him so much he could
not say, but an image of his face seemed to cloy like that skull from
the Red River.

Jaw a little tight now, he eased the pistol from his right-hand
holster and checked the cartridges. Closing the loading gate he
spun the chamber all the way around then cocked the gun and
slowly lowered the hammer. A few of his contemporaries were using automatics these days, but he'd had magazines jam on him and
that didn't happen with a single-action. Gun back in its holster, he
started for the doors. The second time he had done this, only with
no wind blowing the isolation seemed strangely more intense. He
thought about what Isaac had said about his brother having been
in the house with a gun in his hand, a gun he'd used on his father. Pausing on the steps Quarrie looked up at those windows again,
wondering what could have prompted him to do that.

Inside the lobby he felt the hairs gather on the nape of his neck.
There wasn't much he hadn't seen in his life and it was a fact not
a whole lot bothered him. Years ago his Uncle Frank had told him
to trust nothing that he could not see, and he'd made a practise of
only ever being cautious of the living. That said, it was eerie as hell
out here, and he was conscious of an almost sickening sensation in
the pit of his stomach.

He climbed the stairs, keeping close to the wall with the boards
being so weak in the middle. Moving slowly he worked the flashlight from the steps at his feet to the landing above where the

plaster was missing from the walls. Passing beyond the fire doors he was in the corridor again. A narrow tunnel of darkness only breached when he swung the light from one wall to the other.

Almost subconsciously he counted the doorways until he came to the fifth. The walls inside that room were covered with images of stick-like children that lived and died by the beam from his flashlight. Sweeping the light from the walls to the floor he studied the boards closest to the far wall. It had been raining hard the other night, the ground muddy underfoot, and just as he had seen the mark of those boots in the caretaker's cabin, he saw them under that second-floor window.

*

Mr Palmer picked Isaac up from the railroad station in Paris, Texas, and gave him a ride home. Quarrie had made the call after Isaac got on the train.

The depth of the night spread across the flattened landscape as the two of them drove the county road. Mr Palmer chewed with his window cracked so he could expel tobacco juice every now and then. Hunched against the passenger window, Isaac sat with his arms folded.

'So, I saw you the other day,' Palmer said at length. 'And that Ranger seemed kind of worried when he spoke to me on the telephone. Is everything OK?'

Staring through the windshield Isaac seemed intent on the weakness of the pickup's headlights.

'Figure this whole business been a real shock to you. I read in the newspaper how the coroner decided your daddy took that gun to hisself.'

Isaac did not say anything.

'Hard on anybody, that kind of thing. My heart goes out to you.'

Isaac closed his eyes.

'You got any idea why he'd want to do that? I never really met the man, but they say he was a decent feller.'

'Mr Palmer, my dad didn't shoot himself.'

Palmer stopped chewing and tossed a glance the width of the cab. 'What d'you mean?'

'I mean the coroner's got it wrong.'

'You sure?'

'Positive. I told the sheriff's department but they didn't want to listen, and they made their report now anyway. But this isn't their deal anymore so it doesn't matter.'

'The Rangers took over then, did they?'

'Yes, they did.'

'And they take no account of the coroner?'

'No, they don't. Look, I don't mean to be rude, but I'm beat already, and if it's all the same to you I'd rather not talk about it.'

Palmer took him as far as the mailbox at the head of the road leading up to the driveway. 'Listen, son,' he said. 'I'm your nearest neighbor, and it might be a couple of miles but I got a telephone, so holler if there's anything you need.'

From the side of the road Isaac watched him go. With clouds beginning to mass overhead he walked the dirt to where gravel took over. The early hours, his connection from Texarkana had been the last train out, and the fatigue almost made him totter. Under the glare of the security lights he fumbled in his pockets for keys, the whole yard illuminated in an alien glow. Inside the house he worked his shoulders into his neck and in the living room he put a match to the fire.

The gas caught and he sat down cross-legged in front of the flames where they licked at the stack of fake logs. Tunic unbuttoned, he stripped the tie from his collar and wrapped it around his fist. For a long time he sat like that and then his gaze drifted to the coffee table on the other side of the room and the couch where it was back in its proper place.

Finally he got to his feet. Downstairs he stood in the open doorway to his father's study and looked at the desk and the chair before his gaze wandered to the shelf where he had left the key. It was no longer there.

He checked the other shelves but could not see it. He checked the drawers in his father's desk. Upstairs he stood in the kitchen and considered the work surfaces, cupboards and closets. Back in the living room he looked all along the mantelpiece and the window ledge. Dropping to one knee, he checked underneath the green felt table where an alcove had been fashioned to hold spare decks of cards. He walked around the back of the bar area and looked there too, but he could find no trace of the key.

Heading for the basement stairs once more he paused at his father's bedroom. The door was ajar and, as he considered the gap between the edge and the jamb, he was frowning deeply. From the doorway he took in the neatly made bed, the nightstand with the white-faced alarm clock that had long since stopped, and the chair in the corner where some of his father's clothes were still folded as if he had only just laid them out. His gaze shifted to the closet where again the door wasn't shut properly.

He trailed fingers over the rack of shirts and jackets, the old uniform wrapped in cellophane. On the floor were his father's shoes and work boots and next to them was a discarded sweater. Isaac cocked an eyebrow at the sweater and at the pile of clothes on the chair. Then he scooped up the sweater. He stared. A metal box, long and thin like a safety-deposit box, he worked a hand over the nape of his neck and his palm came away a little clammy.

He carried the box through to the living room and laid it down on the card table. Eyes sharp suddenly, he headed back down the basement stairs. Opening the panel in the study he went through to the storm shelter. The lid of the first aid kit was closed and when he opened it and the tray dropped forward, he saw the key back in the polythene bag. For a few moments he stood and stared. Then he took the key from the bag and went back upstairs.

The key fit the lock and inside the box he found a stack of official-looking papers, including his father's discharge order from the Army and a handful of bank statements that were stapled together. Underneath those were the deeds to the house. Laying them to one side he saw an address book. Slim and black, it was bound in leather and he flicked through the pages where a few names had been written in his father's scrawling hand. At the letter *S* one of the pages had been torn out, the edge at the binder ragged. Isaac looked closely at the page beneath: an indentation, though it was only slight, and he could not quite make out the pen strokes. Setting the little book aside he rifled through the rest of the box and at the bottom he found some insurance documents and some more letters he had written to his dad, only those were still in their envelopes. Then he found something else. A single document, a piece of parchment, he stared at it with his mouth open.

He was shaking. He was trembling, gaze flitting from that sheet of paper to the metal box and from the box to the address book where the page was missing. On his feet he grabbed both the book and the document. In the kitchen he picked up the telephone and hunted down the business card Quarrie had given him. Hands still shaking he dialled the number and was connected to Ranger Headquarters in Austin.

'This is Isaac Bowen from Fannin County,' he said to the woman on the end of the line. 'I need you to get a message to Sergeant Quarrie. Tell him I know what's going on. Tell him I know what happened. Tell him I know what happened with Ishmael.'

Twenty-nine

Quarrie spent the night in a motel. He didn't get much sleep, and when he did doze off his dreams were plagued by images of stick-like children. It was barely 6 a.m. when he called his son at home, and Eunice answered in a voice that was thick with sleep.

'It's me, Eunice,' Quarrie said. 'Sorry to wake you, it's early still I reckon.'

'Time I was up, John Q; got to be getting James ready for school.'

'Can I talk to him? Is he awake?'

'If he's not he will be. Just hold on a sec and I'll fetch him.'

Sitting on the edge of the bed Quarrie tapped stiff fingers against the crown of his hat. He waited a couple of minutes and then his son's voice yawned in his ear.

'Hey, kiddo. Sounds like I woke you up.'

'Good job you did, Dad. I've got to get ready for school.'

'So Eunice said. So what's going on over there? What's up?'

'Not much. I guess me and Pious are still looking at the newspapers.'

'Getting what you need then, are you?'

'Yes, sir. There was a bunch of names we found, people who never made it out of that train wreck.' James sounded a little plaintive. 'Dad,' he said, 'I can't stop thinking about how it must've been, coming up on a bridge like that nobody knew was out. I mean, they get on that train thinking they were going some-place, meeting family or something like that, but the ones in the paper they never got to where it was they were going. I keep thinking about them other folks waiting on them to show up and how it must've been when someone told them the train wrecked.'

'Whoa,' his father said gently. 'Are you OK, son? I don't think I ever you heard you like this. Sounds like it's really gotten to you.'

He heard James sniff. 'That's what Miss Munro said. At school yesterday she said how it can get you like that when it's regular folk you're discovering about. But I like it, Dad. I mean history. I like trying to find stuff out. I really enjoy it.'

'Do you? Well, that's great: maybe you can do something with that?'

'At school you mean?'

'Sure. If you put together a good project then maybe Miss Munro will decide history is what you're best at.'

'That'd be good,' James said, 'because I sure ain't any good at math.'

'Your mom was pretty good. It's a pity you take after me.'

'So you were no good then neither?'

'Couldn't get my head around her, son; no matter what I tried. Don't worry about it. From the way you're talking I get the impression this project is going to be real good and Miss Munro is going to see James Quarrie in a whole different light altogether.'

'I hope so,' James said. 'I'll show you the stuff we got as soon as you get home.'

'I'll look forward to that, bud. I'm sorry it was so short the last time. No sooner was I there I was gone.'

'So where are you at right now?'

'Shreveport, Louisiana. Give me a day or so and I'll be home.'

When he got back to Bellevue Quarrie found a couple of uniformed patrolmen from the state police talking to the staff about the missing orderly. They had been to his house but found no trace of him and his car had already been towed. One of them was the young guy who had discovered the Chevrolet stolen from the Baptist mission cottage. Taking him to one side Quarrie asked him if they had come up with anything.

'Not much so far,' the trooper admitted. 'It seems this orderly was pretty new, had only been renting his apartment for a couple of months.'

'What about Nancy McClain? I swung by her place last night but she'd quit the building.'

The trooper nodded. 'We spoke to the manager and he said something about her son showing up to see her – soldier from Vietnam?'

'That wasn't her son,' Quarrie told him. 'That was just a ruse to get into the apartment.'

The trooper nodded. 'Well sir, nobody here has heard from her, at least they haven't this morning.'

Quarrie took the elevator up to Dr Beale's floor where he found Alice Barker in her office working away at her typewriter, and she looked up in surprise.

'Sergeant,' she said. 'We weren't expecting you back, not with the state police being camped out like they are.'

Quarrie echoed her smile. 'Yes mam, I guess that's what it must feel like. But we have to find Mr Briers so their questions have to be asked.'

She offered him a cup of coffee and he took a seat on her couch.

'Your first name's Alice, right?' Do you mind if I call you Alice?'

A little color bruised her cheeks. 'No, I don't mind. That would be fine.'

'People call me John Q. Not just John so much as John Q. I reckon it was the same with my dad.'

Alice passed him a cup of coffee then poured one for herself and sat down behind her desk. 'So what brings you back then? Yesterday you reminded me how you have no jurisdiction here in Louisiana.'

'That's a fact.' He smiled at her again. 'But there's something I need you to do.'

'Oh,' she said. 'What's that?'

'I need you to show me the women's wing.'

Cup halfway to her mouth, Alice gawped at him over the rim. 'Are you kidding me?' she said. 'The women's wing?'

'There's something I have to see, Alice; something I need to find out.'

Alice seemed to think about that. Setting her cup down on the desk she glanced towards Dr Beale's door.

'I need you to do this,' Quarrie insisted. 'It's real important.'

Pushing back her chair Alice got to her feet. Hesitating for a moment she unlocked the door to Dr Beale's office. At his desk she opened the top drawer and withdrew a set of keys. 'I really should not be in here,' she said. 'And I certainly should not be handling his keys.'

'He's not around,' Quarrie reminded her. 'It's all right. He's not going to find out.'

Closing the drawer she palmed the keys but still looked hesitant. 'I'm not sure I have the authority. I'm just a secretary, and I know if Dr Beale found out I'd probably lose my job.'

'No.' Quarrie took her free hand and held it. 'You wouldn't. I'd explain it to him, Alice, and given the circumstances I'm sure he would understand.'

Her eyebrows shot up. 'You've never met Dr Beale, have you?'

'No, I haven't.' Quarrie smiled. 'So tell me about him. What's he like?'

Before she answered Alice took a moment to glance around the office. Nodding to the couch she said that Beale liked to lie on his back, stare at the ceiling and think.

'Think about what?' Quarrie asked her. 'The different cases he's working?'

She nodded. 'I suppose. He's a pioneer, always trying to push the boundaries, always trying to stay ahead. He takes ideas under consideration that other doctors shy away from, and for the last few years he's been working on trying to prove a theory that nobody else accepts. I've asked him what that is, but he just tells me to wait till I read his book.'

'He's writing a book?' Quarrie said.

'He plans to once he's proven his case, once he can show his contemporaries that whatever it is he's working on actually exists. His thesis he calls it, his opus; something that will put him right at the top of his profession. Anyway,' she flapped a hand, 'he's very ambitious. I've had conversations with Nancy about it and I know that some of his passion – his zeal, she called it – used to bother her back in Texas.'

'Nancy McClain you're talking about?

'That's right. She came up here to the office the morning Charlie Briers didn't show up and I know she had things on her mind.'

'What kind of things, Alice?'

'I don't know. I can't tell you, but it looked like there were things she needed to talk about.'

'With Dr Beale you mean?'

Alice made a face. 'I don't know. I guess so; although I got the impression she would've quite liked to talk to me. I can't tell you for certain because she never actually got around to saying anything.' With a shake of her head she pressed a hand to her breast. 'There I go running my mouth again. What on earth must you think?'

Back in her office, she stared at the set of keys where she still cupped them in her palm.

'I really don't know about this,' she said. 'What about the other staff?'

'What about them?' Quarrie's tone was reassuring. 'They know the police have been asking questions.' Producing the star in a wheel from his pocket, he fastened it to his jacket. 'They'll just figure me for another one.'

Still Alice looked doubtful.

'You were talking about Nancy,' he reminded her gently. 'How you thought there were things she wanted to say?'

Placing the keys on her desk Alice nodded. 'Nancy and Mr

Briers – they worked at Trinity of course, but after the fire Dr Beale made sure they were given jobs here.'

'Why them in particular?'

Alice shrugged. 'I don't know. There were cases that only they dealt with and I suppose he wanted the continuity.'

'What cases, Alice?'

'Well,' she said, 'I suppose it was Miss Annie mostly.' She gave a nervous little laugh. 'A woman in her fifties, skinny little thing, she's been here since the fire. She was kept in isolation at first, though these past few weeks she's been allowed outside, but only under strict supervision. She's not allowed to mix with the other women and Mr Briers used to watch her closely.' Looking up at him then she gestured. 'Miss Annie's a special case, one that the three of them worked on together: Dr Beale, the nurse and that orderly. They used to come up to his office. Sometimes it would be just Nancy, sometimes just Briers and sometimes it would be the two of them.'

Brows knit, she looked a little puzzled. 'They'd have meetings with Dr Beale – a lot of meetings, and especially just recently. I always found that odd because when he wasn't with patients Dr Beale was so busy with his tapes he tried to avoid meetings as much as possible.'

'Tapes?' Quarrie said. 'What tapes, Alice?'

'The reels he made when he was researching: the notes for his book. He usually had me type stuff up but not those tapes, those he keeps locked in the safe.' She colored at the neck once more. 'Would you listen to me – blabbermouth. I really shouldn't be telling you this.'

Again Quarrie took her hand. He was smiling, his eyes kindly. 'Alice, right now Briers is missing and Nancy McClain has vacated her apartment. If Dr Beale were here I'd be asking him why she might've done that. You can't give me the answer to that question, but everything you can tell me has a bearing on what's happening.

If it wasn't me asking, it would be a Louisiana cop.'

'Even so, 'I—'

'Miss Annie,' he said. 'Why is she a special case?'

'I don't know.' Alice shook her head. 'All I can tell you is that she tried to murder her husband. She stabbed him three times and it was a miracle he survived. Twenty-five years ago Miss Annie was deemed mentally unfit for trial. She was certified and committed to Trinity Hospital.'

Head to one side Quarrie studied her. 'Alice,' he said, 'does the name Mary-Beth Gavin mean anything to you?'

'Of course,' Alice said. 'I never met her, but when Dr Beale was dividing his time between here and Texas, I spoke to her sometimes on the phone.'

'What did you talk about?'

'Just business stuff. She ran the office down there, in charge of the paperwork; you know, the hospital records and everything.'

Quarrie nodded. 'When was the last time you spoke to her?'

Alice's eyes clouded a little. 'It was just before the fire. She phoned here wanting Dr Beale urgently and she sounded pretty worked up.'

'Why? What was bothering her?'

Alice shook her head. 'I can't say. She never told me.'

'But she spoke to Dr Beale?'

She nodded.

'And afterwards?'

'He told me there was an emergency and he had to go down there right away.'

Together they rode the elevator to the ground floor. There they passed through two locked doors into the women's common room where the patients were sitting out. Some of the older women were knitting and Quarrie was reminded of what Pablo had said.

Another pair of locked doors and they were deep in the heart of the building. Quarrie could sense Alice's nervousness and got the feeling it was not just that she was breaking hospital rules that was worrying her. When they came to the next set of doors she peered through the glass panel and told him this was as far as she would go.

'The nurse is on her break so if you're going to do this it has to be now.'

She unlocked the door and Quarrie passed into a narrow corridor that seemed to burn with the scent of disinfectant. Linoleum tiles on the floor and fluorescent strips flickering above his head, yet for all its light and modernity this hallway reminded him of Trinity.

Slowly he paced the corridor. Room after room, the doors staggered down both sides so no patient could see into any other. He could hear something, a woman's voice, it was thin and nasal; singing, someone was singing a song though the words were muffled and all he could make out was the tone. Macabre that sound: he was conscious of sweat where it crept on his scalp.

Finally he came to a door on his right; weighted and wooden, it was punctured by a panel of wired glass. When he looked inside he stared. Every inch of wall space was covered by scribblings of the same stick-children he had witnessed in that room at the burned-down hospital.

Miss Annie was sitting on the bed. Bug-eyed and hair scant, she looked up from where she was singing to the porcelain doll she nursed at her naked breast.

Thirty

Isaac found the street he was looking for not far from Cain's world-famous ballroom. A quiet suburb, a little rundown, it was nothing like his father's place. Single-bedroom homes built side-by-side on quarter-lots with driveways that were overgrown with weed.

He drove slowly, gaze switching from the road itself to the houses on either side as well as the cars parked against the curb. He drove the entire street, looking back the way he had come and at the end of each block he considered the side streets before he went on. He drove all the way to where the road petered into salt brush and scrub and there he turned the car.

1433 was about halfway along with a pale blue VW Bug parked just ahead of the garage. Pulling up he switched off the engine and sat where he was with his palms sweating. Adjusting the mirror on the dashboard he took in his reflection where he was pale in the face. He checked his necktie and the collar of his tunic. He had hung the uniform on a coat hanger last night and had worked the toes of his shoes with polish and brush.

No movement from where the VW was parked. Nobody in the yard, though the sun was still out and no wind disturbed the trees. He could see nobody at any of the windows and still he sat with his hands clasped in his lap. Another minute passed before he opened the door and got out.

Hesitating for a moment on the sidewalk, he flattened the skirts of his tunic and pasted a hand through his hair. He looked up and down the street but no cars were on the move, nobody was walking, there was not so much as a dog. Making his way up the drive he glanced at the VW where a plastic flower was fixed underneath the windshield.

On the stoop his palms were sweating even more than they had been just now and he worked one hand against his thigh. Lightly he knocked but nobody came to the door. He knocked again and still nobody came. Concentrating hard, he eased his tongue across his lips and knocked on the door once more.

He was about to try one last time when he heard the clack of shears coming from the other side of the house. Sweat on his brow, he walked around the yard to the back and there she was, clipping dead heads off some weary-looking flowers. The kitchen door stood open and she was on her knees at the stoop wearing a pair of slacks and a loose fitting top. Her hair was dark and long and it hung in a single plait.

She stiffened as his shadow fell across the grass. She remained like that for a few seconds then she looked up, eyes wide and her mouth open as she took in the uniform. The look on her face, the expression in her eyes, it was as if for a moment she thought he might be his father. Isaac opened his mouth to tell her she was mistaken but no words seemed to come and when finally they did his voice sounded as if it might crack.

'It's me, Mom,' he said. 'It's Isaac.'

For a long time she still seemed to stare. Then she was on her feet, and making for the kitchen she tried to slam the door. Instinctively Isaac stuck out a foot and it caught between the edge and the jamb. Tears glassed. He swallowed hard.

'Mom, please,' he said. 'Mom.' He peered at her through the crack. 'What's going on? Why're you calling yourself Carla Simpson?'

He eased his shoulder against the door and with no choice but to step back, his mother let go and pressed herself against the kitchen wall. Palms flattened at her sides she stared at him. Isaac went in and closed the door. Then he turned to face her and leaned with his back to the door.

'It's all right,' he told her. 'I know this is a hell of a shock after all these years. It's not exactly easy for me.' He tried to smile. 'Coming up here like this, it was just about all I could muster. The fact is I drove right past the house just now and when I got to the end of the street I almost gave up and went back.'

Still she stood flat to the wall and her eyes were fixed on his.

'But I couldn't do that,' Isaac went on. 'I couldn't just turn around and go back. I had to see you, Mom. It's not as if I had any choice.' His expression had darkened a little and he cast a glance towards the window. 'I had to make sure I got to you before Ishmael.'

*

Quarrie was sitting on the couch in Alice Barker's office, hat upturned on the cushions next to him he had his elbows on his knees. At her desk Alice looked a little pensive.

'Why does she do that?' Quarrie said. 'A woman her age: why does she do that with a child's doll?'

Alice shuddered visibly. 'I have no idea. I'm just a secretary. No matter how well I might get on with Dr Beale, he's a professional and does not divulge anything about his patients.'

'You haven't heard from him this morning?'

'No, I haven't.'

'Have you heard anything since he left at all?'

She shook her head.

'How long has he been gone?'

'I guess it's a couple of days.'

Quarrie nodded. 'And he never spoke to you about Miss Annie?'

Alice shook her head.

'But you know he considered her to be a special case.'

With a sigh Alice got to her feet. Hugging her arms about her she walked to the window and gazed across the grounds as if she hoped to see her boss striding up from the gate.

'It was Mary-Beth who told me,' she stated. 'Trinity had burned and she was just about to leave. She told me that Miss Annie would be coming up here and she was one of Dr Beale's special cases.'

Quarrie frowned. 'What did she mean exactly?'

Shaking her head, Alice spoke without turning to look at him. 'I don't know. All she said was that Dr Beale wanted her brought here.' She paused for a moment and then she added, 'There is one other thing though: Mary-Beth told me that before she was a patient, Miss Annie used to be a nurse at Trinity.'

Quarrie was on his feet. Crossing to the window he took her by the arm and turned her around so she faced him.

Alice looked into his eyes. 'We talked – it was the last time I spoke to her and I remember how Mary-Beth sounded agitated, a little upset. She told me that once upon a time Miss Annie had been a nurse down there working with Nancy McClain.' Stepping around him she went back to her desk. 'It must've been twenty-five years ago. Mary-Beth said she wasn't known as Miss Annie then though, she was whoever she used to be before she got sick.'

'So Annie's not her real name?'

'I don't know. I don't think so. Nobody ever said.'

'But it will be listed in the hospital records?'

'Her full name, yes, of course. But I have no access to that.' Catching the look in his eye she went on. 'There's no point asking anyone else because they won't show you any of the files, not without written permission from Dr Beale.'

Quarrie turned to the window and gazed across the grounds to the women's wing but all he could see was that wizened-looking woman from behind a panel of reinforced glass.

'I need to talk to her,' he said almost to himself. 'Alice, I have to speak to Miss Annie.'

*

Isaac sat in a cane chair in his mother's living room. She was perched on the edge of the sofa, her gaze like that of a bird, eyes darting from his features to the window and from the window back. Isaac was more composed now, the tears that had threatened when he first arrived were not there anymore and his palms were no longer sweating.

'I'm sorry this is such a shock,' he said. 'I'm sorry I didn't call but I had to know you were all right. I had to know he hadn't gotten here ahead of me.'

Lips hollowed into an oval, Clara looked at him but did not speak. She peered beyond him again to the door.

'Why would Ishmael come here?' she asked finally.

Isaac twisted his lip. 'He's looking for you. He's angry. He's in some kind of rage, and you know he's crazy, don't you?'

On his feet he crossed to the window and eased aside the drape. It was getting dark outside and he peered up and down the street. Clara remained where she was on the lip of the couch with her legs crossed at the ankle.

Isaac spoke without looking round. 'He killed Dad and I have to protect you. I couldn't figure why he'd go after Dad at first, but as soon as I found those papers I understood. You're not safe here, Mom. Ishmael had the key and he found those papers before I did. He knows where you are, and for all we know, he's watching the house right now.'

Sitting down next to her he tried to smile. 'Look, it's all right. It's OK. I know this is a bolt from the blue. It was for me too. But so much has happened since you left. It was so long ago. We're all grown up, me and Ish. We're men now and when you left we were boys.' Leaning back in the chair he sighed. 'Ishmael's problems, they've been going on for a long time.'

The way she stared at his uniform, his mother seemed transfixed.

'Something, isn't it?' Isaac said. 'One of us had to join though, us being Bowen's and all and I guess the Army wouldn't take Ish.'

He looked her in the eye. 'I bet you wouldn't have guessed it, would you? Three tours in Nam, Mom: I did three full tours in Nam.'

Sweat on his brow, he spread his palms. 'There was only one time I was ever really scared and that's when I knew I was coming home. One last firefight, thirty-one of us already dead and they had us really pinned down. But the CP sent in air support and we got out of there without taking any more hits. Back at camp I phoned Dad and he told me Ish was at a hospital called Trinity.' He looked beyond her then with his brow deeply lined and his eyes gathered into wrinkles. 'You know, in the three years I was over there I wrote Dad every week and not once did he ever write back.'

Listening to him Clara was sitting very upright, rigid almost, her hands balled into fists. Reaching over, Isaac smoothed out those fists and entwined her fingers in his.

'Mom, that hospital where Ish was at was an asylum for criminals. I never knew that till I got down there. What was the old man thinking?'

'He didn't tell you?' she said.

He shook his head. 'No, he didn't. The truth is Dad never talked to me hardly at all. Since you left out he's kept himself to himself, and in all those years he's rarely spoken two words to me about anything other than what it was that had to be said.'

Once again he got to his feet. 'It's weird,' he said, 'but ever since I found out he got shot, it's like it was back when we were kids. Ishmael, I'm talking about. Twins and all, I can sense him the way I used to, and the craziest thing happened at the grocery store.' His eyes dulled a little. 'Actually, given what I found out since I guess it wasn't so crazy after all.' Turning again he smiled. 'But it's OK. There's nothing for you to worry about. Not now. It's why I came. I know what Ishmael wants and he's not going to get anywhere near you. But we can't stay here, Mom. It's not safe.'

*

Quarrie bought Alice an early dinner at a restaurant about a mile from Bellevue while they waited for things to settle down at the hospital. Ordering their entrées he poured her a glass of wine and explained what he wanted to do.

'You understand, Alice,' he said, 'every minute that goes by is a minute lost. So far the state police have come up with nothing on Briers and nothing on Nancy either.'

'But I don't understand,' Alice said. 'You told me Mary-Beth was murdered and Charlie Briers too most probably, and now he's going after Nancy. Why would someone do that and what's it got to do with Miss Annie?'

Sitting back with his hands flat on the table Quarrie let go a sigh. 'The fact is I don't understand it myself. But Ishmael Bowen wants something. He's looking for something only I don't know what it is. I think he tried to get it from his father back in Fannin County but either he didn't have it or he would not give it up and Ishmael shot him. He wiped his prints from the gun and put it in his father's hand to make it look as if he'd killed himself. I don't know why he'd do that, guilt with it being his father perhaps, but whatever the reason it's a fact the Fannin County coroner has gone for it.' Sitting back he spread his fingers. 'Patricide, Alice; that's a hell of a thing and very few people are capable of it. What it was made him do it I can't tell you. But I saw him in Miss Annie's old room down at Trinity. For some reason he was up there and I have to find out why.'

Taking a sip of wine he glanced beyond the counter towards the kitchen. 'Those steaks will be here in a piece, but if you'll excuse me I need to call my son before he goes to bed.' Pushing back his chair he got up. 'He's been doing a school project about an old train wreck and the whole thing seems to have upset him.'

He found a payphone in the hallway next to the restrooms and, with no quarters in his pocket, he called collect. Eunice picked up and told him James was in the shower.

'He's been working that calf-roping horse with Nolo,' she said. 'The two of them been in the big corral ever since he got home from school.'

'OK then, I tell you what,' Quarrie said. 'I'm still in Shreveport right now so don't go getting him out of the shower. Tell him I'll talk to him tomorrow. There's a chance I might even make it home but don't tell him that in case it doesn't happen.'

'Whatever you want,' she said. 'Listen, while I've got you on the phone, your captain called here this afternoon wanting to get a-hold of you. Told me you don't check in with him nearly as often as you should.'

Quarrie chuckled. 'That what he said?'

'Yes, he did. Said for you to call him just as soon as I gave you the message.'

Hanging up, Quarrie called Van Hanigan's number and again he had to call collect.

'Knew it'd be you, John Q,' the captain said when he picked up. 'Nobody else would phone me at home and make sure it's me that paid for the phone call.'

'I'm in Louisiana,' Quarrie told him.

'Yeah, the operator said as much. So what you doing over there?'

'Hanging out with a real nice lady, a secretary at Bellevue Hospital. I'm coercing her, Captain; persuading her into doing something that she shouldn't.'

'You think I want to hear about that?'

Quarrie worked a hand through his hair. 'So anyway, Eunice said how you were looking for me?'

'Yeah, I was. Austin took a message from Isaac Bowen. His brother and all, he called to tell you he's figured out what's going on.'

Quarrie stood straighter where he was leaning against the wall. 'Isaac said that?'

'Yes, he did, yesterday; last night in fact: early hours of this morning.'

Again he dialled the operator and this time asked her to connect him to the Bowen house in Fannin County. The phone rang and rang but Isaac did not pick up. Settling the receiver back on the hook, Quarrie returned to the table where his steak was waiting.

Back at the hospital a couple of hours later he and Alice walked from the gate to the main entrance where all was quiet. With the patients locked in their rooms for the night there was only a minimal number of staff on duty. Using Beale's keys again, Alice took him into the women's wing where this time the common room was empty. Formica tables and chairs neatly stacked, the floor had been freshly polished and there was no light at the nurses' station. They passed beyond the next locked door and the one after that, and then they were outside the door to the isolation corridor.

On the other side of the glass panel Quarrie could see that the hall was only dimly lit and no nurse occupied the desk.

'That station isn't staffed at night.' Alice repeated what she had told him earlier. 'There's no need, the patients are checked by an orderly every couple of hours but usually things are pretty quiet.' She looked doubtful all over again, weighing the keys in her hand then clutching them tightly. 'I'll have to come with you,' she said. 'And I hate going down there. You know this could cost me my job.' She peered back the way they had come. 'Look, I'm not sure anymore. I'm really worried. This is Miss Annie we're talking about. Just about anything could happen.'

Taking her hand Quarrie held it tightly. 'All you have to do is get me the key from the nurse's desk. I can do the rest.'

She snorted. 'How do you think she's going to react to some stranger in her room in the dead of night, a woman as unbalanced as that? She'll think you're there for her baby. She thinks everyone wants to take her baby away from her and she might try and hurt you. She's capable of just about anything, you know. In Texas she put out the eye of an orderly.'

He nodded. 'I know, Alice. I'm aware of that. But I've got an idea how I can deal with her.'

'I'm sure you can handle her physically,' Alice went on, 'but that's not the point. No matter what you tell me, if we're found down here I will lose my job.'

Again Quarrie peered through the panel. 'Alice,' he said, 'you're not going to lose your job. Look, I understand how you feel but I have to do this and we're here already. Miss Annie won't attack me. And if she does I can deal with it.' He tapped the weight of the door. 'These are fire-proof. Any noise she makes won't be enough to disturb anybody.'

Inside the corridor Alice re-locked the door behind them and together they walked the floor all the way past Miss Annie's room to the nurse's workstation. Locating the keys, Alice worked them around the ring until she came to the one she wanted. Prising it loose she handed it to him and Quarrie stripped off his jacket. Unbuckling his shoulder holsters, he placed his weapons on the desk and was about to leave his hat as well, but then he remembered Miss Annie had seen him wearing it.

Alice took a seat at the desk. 'Try not to let her make too much noise because fire doors or not, if the other patients start up you'll be able to hear the racket clear across to Texas.'

Quarrie glanced at her. He could feel his heart beating a little bit faster than he would've liked, and he could not help but be reminded of two dark nights at the ruin in the Piney Woods. 'Wish me luck, Alice,' he said.

'I've already done that.' She wasn't smiling. 'On account of how badly I figure you're going to need it.'

Quarrie walked back the way they had come with the key in his palm and his palm sweating. When he got to the door he looked the length of the corridor but could no longer see Alice's face where she was hidden deep in the shadows.

Through the reinforced glass panel he could see the bed and the frail-looking figure of its occupant under the glow of a nightlight. Alice had told him that Dr Beale agreed to humor Miss Annie with the light for the sake of her baby. Apparently she'd had one like it at Trinity.

Inside the room she did not stir. With the door closed, Quarrie stood with his back to it and listened to the sound of her breathing. It was even and regular, coming in little whistles from deep in her throat. Quarrie could not quite believe he was there, and now that he was, he wasn't sure if his plan would work. He wondered what he would do if she attacked him.

'Miss Annie,' he said softly. 'My name's John Q and I'm a Texas Ranger. I'm the guy in the hat who came by this afternoon and I'm here to protect you and your baby.'

Her breathing stilled, the whistle died to nothing. Still he remained with his back to the door and she lay exactly where she was, only he could no longer hear any sound.

And then she sat up.

Hunched against the wall where stick children played she peered through the darkness and he could just about make out those bulbous blue eyes that, once upon a time, might have been her best feature.

She did not speak. She just stared at him, but he noted how she did not clutch the doll to her breast like he'd thought she would, it remained on the pillow.

'I'm on guard, Miss Annie,' he told her. 'I know they try and take your baby away from you, but I'm on guard tonight to make sure nobody does.'

Still she remained silent and Quarrie indicated the chair by the side of the door. 'If it's all right with you I'm going to set down here so I can keep a better watch on the corridor.'

Slowly, he lowered himself onto the chair. Hat on his head and hands on his knees he was barely two feet from the bed. Still Miss Annie sat there. She was absolutely silent and Quarrie was close enough that he could see her face, pinched and bitter and looking so much older than it ought to.

She lay down. He could hardly believe what he was seeing but Miss Annie lay down again and curled up next to her porcelain doll. Quarrie peered through the gloom where the emerald-colored nightlight cast a ghoulish glow across her face.

'All right then,' he said. 'I'm here to protect the two of you, so if you want to go back to sleep you-all go ahead.' He waited a moment before he added. 'On the other hand I know how you don't get a lot of company, so if you want to chat awhile that'd be just fine too.'

Thirty-one

Isaac watched as his mother packed an overnight bag, her movements a little stiff as if she had not yet recovered from the shock of seeing him. Leaning in the doorway he had his arms folded across his chest.

'Fifteen years is a long time, Mom,' he said. 'I know how you feel because it's as difficult for me as it is for you. It was all I could do to summon the courage to drive up here.'

Taking fresh clothes from her dressing-table drawer Clara placed the garments in the bag.

'Make sure you pack plenty,' Isaac said. 'I don't know how long it'll be before you can come back here so make sure you have enough.'

'Why don't we just stay here? If you think you have to protect me, why can't you do that here?'

Isaac shook his head. 'I told you, it's not safe. You have to trust me. I'm good at this. I know what I'm doing. I was long-range recon just like Dad. Escape and evasion, extraction; we'd go in after American prisoners and get them out without the enemy knowing we'd ever been there.' He nodded towards the window. 'This position cannot be properly defended. He could come from any number of different directions and I can't cover them all. No,' he said. 'I know where we'll be safe, and even if he figures it out it's somewhere I'll be able to deal with him.'

Expelling an audible breath his mother sat down heavily on the bed. Head bowed, she seemed to be thinking.

'It'll be all right,' Isaac assured her. 'It's difficult to get a handle on it all, I know. But it's been hard on me too. Dad dead and Ish missing, then this Ranger shows up and tells me Dad didn't kill himself when the other cops are saying he did.' He threw out a hand. 'I didn't know what hit me. I mean, I figured it couldn't get any shittier than it was over there in Nam, but it sure did, I can promise you.' His eyes had darkened slightly. 'Fifteen years without a single word. Why didn't you call? Why didn't you get in touch?'

Clara was trembling. She opened her mouth as if she wanted to explain it to him but she closed it again and sat there staring at her bag.

'It's OK,' Isaac said more gently. 'It's been too long and this is too much of a shock. We don't have to do this now. We can talk about it later. We can talk about it as much as we want.' He nodded as if to himself. 'I got so many questions. After all this time you have no idea how much I want to talk. I tell you what though, when that Ranger first suggested they try and get a-hold of you I couldn't see the point. I mean, you'd taken off and I figured you wouldn't want to see me. But that was before I knew about Ishmael. We've got a lot of time to make up,' he said. 'Now I'm here and we're talking like this all I want to do is make up for the time we lost.'

*

Quarrie was sitting just feet from a woman who had stabbed her husband three times and jammed a knitting needle through the eye of an orderly. A woman who had been locked up for twenty-five years, she was sleeping with a porcelain doll, and despite how macabre the whole thing was, he felt nothing but a deep-seated sense of sadness.

'You like to draw, Miss Annie, don't you? The walls of this room are the same as the walls of your old one back at Trinity.'

She sat up again and he could see her eyes where they were almost too big for her emaciated face. She seemed to consider him very carefully, resting on the palm of her hand she was hunched over the doll now as if to make sure he could not grab it.

'You must really love children,' Quarrie went on. 'I understand that. I got a boy of my own. His mother passed away back when he was a baby. Not quite a year old, it's been him and me since then, and I guess we're similar you and me. I mean both of us being sort of single parents. His name's James by the way. Did I tell you that? My boy's called James. What do you call your baby?'

Miss Annie did not answer. She just looked at him and then swung her legs from underneath her and sat on the edge of the bed. If she reached out now she could touch him.

'What are you doing in my room?' Her voice sounded chill and she peered at him, her bone-thin arms reminiscent of those in the drawings where the sleeves of her pajamas swamped them.

'I told you,' Quarrie's tone was gentle still but he could feel the way a chill was working through him. 'I'm here to protect you. I'm here because I know everyone wants to take your baby away and I'm not going to let that happen. I'm a policeman, Miss Annie, a Texas Ranger, and protecting people is what I do. I'm not a doctor or a nurse or an orderly. That means we could be friends. It means you can talk to me if you want to. What's your real name by the way? I know it's not Miss Annie.'

Miss Annie lay down again only on her back this time and she drew the doll very close. She soothed it, stroking its hair where it was thin as hers and making little cooing sounds in her throat.

'You had a room like this at Trinity,' Quarrie said. 'I saw that room, Miss Annie: on the second floor it had a window that over-looked the grounds. That was a nice room, really nice, overlooking the garden like that. This room doesn't have a window.'

'They moved me,' her voice came as a crackle, rasping a little where she lay. 'They took me away from Trinity.'

'You used to be a nurse there, didn't you?'

The silence that followed seemed to hold the tiny room in its grasp and the images on the walls crowded around them ever more closely. Quarrie sat where he was with his gaze fixed on the bed. 'Do you remember that? Do you remember working at the hospital?'

She did not reply. She was cradling the doll and he could hear the whistle again of her breathing.

'Can you remember anything about that time?' he asked. 'Do you remember working with Nurse Nancy?'

She sat up. A sudden movement, she was cupping the doll in one arm and blinking at him through the half-light cast by the lamp.

'Nancy.' She tasted the word, as if she knew the name but could not remember where or why she had heard it.

'Nancy McClain,' he said. 'Nurse Nancy; she works here now. She looks after you just as she did at Trinity.'

Slowly, as if finally she remembered, Miss Annie nodded. 'She follows me. She follows me everywhere I go. She walks where I walk because she wants to steal my baby.'

'Why would she want to do that?'

She worked her jaws; he could hear the way her teeth were grinding.

'That's what she wants. She always wants to take my baby. Nurse Nancy wants to take my baby away from me.'

'Why would she want to do that?'

'Because he's special, a special case; they told me my baby was special.'

'Who told you, do you remember? Was it Nancy that told you?'

She did not answer.

'Dr Beale perhaps? Was it Dr Beale who said your baby was special?'

Again she did not answer.

'What's your real name?' Quarrie asked. 'Who were you before you were Miss Annie?'

Still she did not speak. She hunched forward now, the globes of her eyes fixed steadfastly on his.

'When you were a nurse at the hospital,' he prompted, 'what did they call you?'

He heard her sucking a breath. 'When I was a nurse,' she echoed. 'What did they call me?'

'You used to be a nurse at Trinity. Do you remember that? Do you remember what they called you when you were a nurse at the other hospital?'

For a long time she looked at him and then those massive eyes seemed to light up, only the light was a little brittle. 'Peggy,' she murmured. 'They used to call me Peggy.'

*

Half an hour later Quarrie was back in the car, driving as fast as he could with the red light flashing under the clamshell grille. Isaac had left a message telling him he understood what was going on and now Quarrie thought he too might just have an idea. In his mind's eye he could see Miss Annie as he had left her, a wretched creature hunched on the end of the bed with that porcelain doll clutched once more to her breast.

It was 2 a.m. when he got to the Bowen house. The pickup was in the yard and the garage doors were closed but not locked and when Quarrie opened them he saw the sedan was gone. The security lights were on but all the windows in the house were dark, and those lights were bright enough to wake the dead.

For a moment he stood by the garage doors and considered the weight of the metal trapdoor. With another glance across the driveway, he lifted the trap to reveal the deeper darkness below. Backwards he made his way down the ladder, scrabbling for the light switch he was not able to find it, and it was the same in the storm shelter. Using the flame from his Zippo to see his way, he crossed the room to the second passage and walked to the door that opened onto the wooden panelling.

It took him a few minutes to locate the hidden switch but he did so eventually and the panel swung open. Inside the study it was coal black just as it had been in the passage. He could make out the desk by the flickering flame from his lighter and he fumbled for the switch on the lamp. Finally the shadows were banished and he slipped the overheated lighter back in his pocket. He was thinking about Miss Annie. He was thinking about what Alice had told him about the poor woman having been a nurse at Trinity before she was admitted as a patient.

Stripping his hat from his head he worked a hand across his scalp then sat down at Ike Bowen's desk. Opening the top drawer he considered the sheaf of letters Isaac had sent home from Vietnam, then he put them to one side and concentrated on the rest of the drawers. He did not know what he was looking for but he did know he would recognize it if he found it. He didn't find it. He could see nothing in any of the drawers that gave him a clue as to what Isaac might have discovered and he got up from the desk again.

Upstairs in the kitchen he considered the work surfaces and closets, thinking how everything was just as spotlessly clean now as when he had been here the first time. Isaac had the same sense of detail, the same fastidiousness as his father – he had seen that in the way he pressed his uniform.

In the living room he found the family photograph upright once more and in its proper place on the mantelpiece, though the glass was smashed. Quarrie took a good long look: Ike and his wife, the two boys who were alike but not identical, though Isaac had said they'd been born with only fifteen minutes between them.

Moving to the little bar area he searched the shelves but there was nothing that caught his eye. He was stumped. No clue as to what Isaac had discovered and yet he had left that message in Austin. He walked the hallway to the stairs once more, conscious that he must have missed something down in the study. He noticed one of the bedroom doors was ajar and he paused. For a moment he stood there and then stepped inside and fumbled on the wall for the light.

The bed was neatly made, a nightstand and chair alongside it. On that chair a set of Ike Bowen's clothes still folded. A clock beside the bed, no book, no photograph, this was where a soldier slept and that space was entirely functional. Reaching for the light once more, Quarrie was about to go back downstairs when he noticed the open closet.

Inside he found two rails of jackets, shirts and trousers, one fixed below the other, and underneath those a pair of work boots he had seen Isaac wearing. Next to them a sweater lay discarded. Lifting that he found a small wooden shelf with a space underneath, but the space was empty.

He checked the nightstand drawers and the other half of the closet, but found nothing there either. Back in the hallway he went downstairs and searched Ike's study a second time without any luck, and again he climbed the stairs. In the living room he stood in the middle of the floor trying not to let the frustration get the better of him. He considered the bar area and the coffee table then he stared at the green felt card table. Crossing to it, he dropped to one knee and sought the alcove Isaac had mentioned. He stared. No deck of cards, no chips. What he saw was a slim, metal box.

It reminded him of something from a safety-deposit vault in a bank. He could see no trace of a key, however. He hunted for it, felt around in the alcove then looked behind the bar again. Carrying the box to the kitchen, he searched the drawers and cupboards but still there was no sign of any key, so he took his knife to the lid instead. It took him a couple of minutes and he was cursing under his breath, but finally he got the box open.

Papers, insurances, the deeds to the house and an aged-looking address book. He flicked through that and came to where a page had been torn out, but on the page after that an indentation had been left and somebody had shaded it with a pencil.

Quarrie stared: Clara Bowen née Symonds who had left the family fifteen years ago, she was living in Tulsa as Carla Simpson. Taking a moment to consider what that actually meant he leafed through the rest of the papers and found yet another letter that Isaac had written to his father. This one was still in its envelope however, unlike those in the desk. Another mission, a marine captured by the Vietcong in the Crow's Foot, Isaac had been part of a two-man insertion team sent in to get him back. The boy had seen some action, that was for sure. Quarrie slipped the letter back inside the envelope and as he returned it to the box he noticed the postmark stamped on the front.

*

Clara was sitting in the passenger seat as Isaac propelled his father's car south. The road not lit, a median separating the four lanes of blacktop, she sat with her knees drawn up, her heels pressed to the floor and her hands together in her lap. Next to her Isaac drove with both hands on the wheel and his gaze intent on the road. He didn't speak. She didn't speak. Every now and then, however, he would look round at her as if he still couldn't quite believe it was her.

'You've changed,' he said, finally. 'I know it's been fifteen years already, but you're not how I remember. You're not how I thought you'd look.'

'I'm older,' she said. 'We're all much older. You were only a boy when I left.'

He nodded; eyes on the road once more, he pushed out his lips. 'So why did you leave us anyway?'

Clara did not answer.

'You need to tell me,' Isaac said. 'You need to explain. Fifteen years is a long time. Me and Ish were only kids and we never could get our heads around why you took off.'

Clara just gazed ahead.

'Was it to do with my dad? Did he hurt you? Was he fooling around?'

Clara glanced at him but did not speak.

'Tough to talk about, huh? I get that. I understand.' He offered a smile. 'Look, we got plenty of time, maybe now's not good, maybe right now we just need to get where we're going and you can tell me all about it then.' Again he looked sideways. 'Things weren't the same after that vacation though, were they? Lawton, Mom: you changed after we got home. I remember. I watched you and you weren't the same. It was like you were somebody else.'

Still she sat there, fists clenched where her arms were folded across her chest.

'It's OK,' Isaac told her. 'I understand, or at least I'm trying to. I *have* tried to, all these years I've been trying to make sense of you leaving out on us when you did. Me and Ishmael, we had a great time over in Lawton but I remember how it was with Dad. Memorial weekend, he and his army buddy hanging out together talking about the old days and drinking all day and all night. That must've been hard on you, Mom. I could never remember that guy's name.'

'Morley, his name was Morley,' she said.

'That's right, Morley.' Isaac lifted a hand from the wheel. 'Well, anyway, on the Saturday night they were setting out on the porch sharing another bottle and talking about all sorts of stuff. I know because though Ish was asleep, I was awake, and I heard every word they said.'

A car swept past in the outside lane and Clara stared at the tail lights where they gathered in red.

'I always figured it was something to do with that weekend.' Isaac was nodding as if to himself. 'You taking off I mean. It had to be because it wasn't so long afterwards that you left.'

'It was fifteen months,' she said.

'Was that how long it was?' Isaac looked at her with a glaze to his eye. 'Really, I never figured that. I guess time's different when you're a kid and I guess that was right around the time Ish started having his difficulties. I remember that pretty well. I just don't remember if he started having those difficulties before you left, or was it on account of how you did?'

They drove in silence. Isaac's gaze had darkened a little, as if talking about those times had really bothered him. Clara sat where she was, still upright, still very tense; she kept her gaze fixed straight ahead. A couple of miles further down the road she turned to him. 'So, where are we going?' she said.

'I told you, somewhere safe.'

She looked ahead once more as another car came tearing past, only this time it was on the other side of the median and she could see a red light flashing at the grille.

Isaac drove on. Head cocked to one side, he pushed out his cheek with his tongue.

'Dad had your address,' he said. 'I never thought about that till just now, but you were only just up the road and he knew where you were all the time. When we were growing up I mean, so he must've been in touch.' He frowned. 'Why would he still be in touch? And if he was in touch then why did you change your name? You're either Clara Symonds or Clara Bowen. Why did you change your name?'

She did not answer. She stared ahead.

'It's not so different to your real name,' Isaac went on. 'I mean Carla for Clara and Simpson for Symonds, but why change it at all?' Lifting a hand from the wheel he gestured. 'I don't understand. I mean, if you wanted to leave the old man and get a divorce, that's OK I suppose, but when a woman does that she goes back to what she was called before.'

'I wanted a fresh start,' she told him.

'Sure you did.' He stared at her. 'Otherwise why would you leave when you did?'

*

It was dawn by the time Quarrie drove North Main Street in Tulsa. A glance at the sign outside the ballroom, he was thinking about Clara and why she hadn't told him who she really was. Why had she not answered the door? And why did she tell him on the phone that she didn't know who Mary-Beth Gavin was?

When he got to the house he could see the pale blue VW Bug. Another car was bumped up against the curb a little further up the road and he could see a woman in the driver's seat, fishing around in her purse. Pulling across the bottom of the drive, Quarrie shut off the engine.

On the sidewalk he considered the little house where the curtains were drawn across the windows. At the front door he knocked, but nobody answered. Expelling a breath, he lifted a fist and knocked again. He was thinking about how Isaac must've felt after he discovered that his mother was only a couple of hundred miles away. He was thinking about the message he had left in Austin and that last letter he had seen in the box.

He knocked a third time but still nobody answered. He didn't think anybody was in there but he walked around back just the same. There he knocked one last time but nobody came to the door. When he turned he saw a middle-aged woman watching him from the path.

'Morning,' he said, conscious of the way she was staring. 'It's all right, I'm not a housebreaker, I'm a cop.' Reaching in his jacket pocket he showed her his star.

Around five feet five, she had dark hair pinned with a wooden clip and she seemed to stare as if transfixed.

'Are you a neighbor, mam?' Quarrie said. 'Do you know where Ms Simpson is?'

She looked up sharply as if suddenly snapped from a trance. 'Her name is Symonds not Simpson. You should know that if you're a cop.'

For a second or so Quarrie stared. 'Are you OK, mam? Is everything all right?'

She did not reply. She remained where she was: her body stiff, he noticed she was standing on the balls of her feet. She looked like a frightened child, and in some macabre kind of way he was reminded of the etchings on the walls of Miss Annie's cell.

'My name's Quarrie,' he said. 'I'm a Texas Ranger. Is everything all right?'

'I know who you are.' Visibly gathering herself, the woman started towards him. 'I talked to Clara on the phone and she said how you showed up here at the house.'

Quarrie raised one eyebrow. 'Did she tell you why she didn't come to the door?'

The woman bit down hard on her lip. 'She was frightened. She was scared. That's why she didn't come to the door. She was confused. She told me she'd been going through her old photos and it was all coming back. She told me she couldn't deal with it.'

'Mam,' Quarrie said. 'I'm not sure I know what you're talking about.'

'She knows she should've spoken to you,' the woman said. 'She told me that. She knows she should've just come to the door regardless.'

'Regardless of what?'

'Of Dr Beale: what he said to her, what he said to all of us.'

Quarrie peered at her now. 'Who are you, mam? How do you know Dr Beale?'

'He told her he was taking care of it,' the woman went on. 'I told him we had to talk to the police but he didn't want to do that. He said all the police would do is gun him down and he wasn't going to let that happen.'

There were tears in her eyes now and she was sounding very confused. Taking her hand, Quarrie led her to his car where she sat down in the passenger seat. He stood before her, resting an elbow on top of the door. 'Who are you?' he asked again. 'How do you know about this?'

'I'm sorry,' she said. 'My name is Nancy McClain. I'm a nurse at Bellevue Hospital.' She looked him hard in the eye. 'I called there yesterday looking for Dr Beale, but he's still not back so I spoke to Alice instead. She told me what happened. She told me what you did. She told me how you were in Miss Annie's room.'

She was quiet again and she seemed to be fighting her emotions. 'I nursed her – Miss Annie. For twenty-five years I nursed her and before that I worked with her, back when she was still Peggy-Anne. She only became Miss Annie later, after. It was much later that Miss Annie turned up and we never saw Peggy again.'

'Mam, I—'

'She'd been having problems.' Nancy was staring beyond him now as if he wasn't there. 'We all knew that but we just thought it was a hazard of working with mental patients. It happens to some nurses; psychiatric stuff, it can take its toll and we all suffered a little I suppose. It's hard on the nerves working with people who're so unpredictable, and that's all we thought it was. We had no idea how serious things had gotten, not till much later on.' She lifted a hand to gesture. 'When she was working she seemed just fine, or at least she did until she found out.' Her eyes darkened as she focused on Quarrie's face. 'That's when things changed, that's when Miss Annie showed up and she's been there pretty much ever since.'

'Nancy,' Quarrie said. 'I'm not following you. What're you talking about?'

Eyes downcast, Nancy chewed her lip. 'So much has happened. So much happened back then and so much since. Four years ago Dr Beale took over from Dr Sievers down in the Piney Woods, and he was much younger, he was much more modern. He had different ideas about the patients; his was a completely different approach. He was keen to make his mark. He was always so keen to make his mark I think he let his ambition get the better of him. I told him as much just the other day.' She turned to look at Quarrie again. 'What he tried to do, how he brought Ishmael to the hospital and what happened when he did . . .'

Quarrie squatted on his haunches. 'Nancy, why did Dr Beale bring him to the hospital? I know he wasn't violent. Not then. Ishmael wasn't a criminal. Why bring him to a secure facility?'

Nancy didn't answer. Again she bit her lip.

'You need to tell me,' Quarrie insisted. 'You need to tell me why Ishmael was brought to Trinity.'

'Dr Beale,' she said. 'He was treating Miss Annie and he found out that Ishmael was in a sanatorium in Houston. He heard what his symptoms were and as far as he was concerned they weren't treating him properly. It was his area of expertise, his forte; and he had a particular theory. He thought he could help. What he saw in Ishmael was exactly what he'd been working on, but the symptoms – most doctors don't accept they exist.'

She took a moment to catch her breath. 'Dr Beale went to visit Ishmael's father. He told him what he wanted to do and what he thought it would achieve, and Ike agreed to it right off the bat. He came to the hospital and Dr Beale had me in on that initial consultation.' Tears seemed to burgeon again as she continued. 'Ike said he would try anything – anything at all that might help. So Dr Beale had Ishmael brought to Trinity and we gave him three months to settle in. We were told he wasn't dangerous, had never hurt anyone or been in any trouble. We gave him plenty of freedom. He was allowed to mingle pretty freely. Dr Beale wanted him to mingle as freely with the other patients as was safe. His intentions were sound. Dr Beale, I mean – you have to understand his intentions were medically sound and he was doing what he believed was for the patient's good.'

'But what was he doing?' Quarrie said.

She did not seem to be listening. She seemed to be recounting a series of events as if to convince herself. 'He thought that if we sat him down, if they were able to talk, it might help Ishmael break out of his trap.' She nodded then, she nodded as if to herself. 'We were all there: Mary-Beth and me on the other side of the mirror, with Dr Beale in the room and Charlie outside just in case.'

Taking her hand Quarrie squeezed until she looked up. 'You just said "trap". You said Ishmael was trapped. What do you mean, Nancy? Where was Ishmael trapped?'

Nancy did not answer right away. She sat staring across the road. '"Trapped" was how Dr Beale described it,' she said finally. 'He thought if we brought him in, if he knew what'd happened then perhaps the spell might break and we'd be able to find out what it was that locked him in.'

'Locked him in?' Quarrie said. 'What do you mean, Nancy? What're you talking about?'

Still she peered beyond him. 'But that's not what happened. The spell wasn't broken. Ishmael was broken instead. What we did, what Dr Beale thought might help – it sent him clear over the edge.'

She was trembling. Hands in her lap, she was shaking. 'He went after Mary-Beth because she held the records and she called Dr Beale asking for help. When he couldn't get what he wanted Ishmael broke into the kerosene store and set that fire and the whole place went up.' She was crying now as she spoke. 'We thought he was dead. We thought he'd burned in his own inferno. But he hadn't. He escaped that fire and he knew what had happened and he knew who he thought was to blame.'

Thirty-two

With the darkness finally beginning to dissipate Isaac pulled into his father's house. He had left the pickup parked on the drive but the garage doors were open. Stepping hard on the brakes he brought the car to a stop and sat with his hands white-knuckled around the steering wheel.

He remained like that for a moment, his gaze darting left and right. 'Somebody's been here,' he said. 'Somebody opened those doors. Wait here while I check it out.' Opening the driver's door he had one foot in the gravel before he stopped. 'No,' he said, as if he'd had second thoughts. 'That's a stupid idea. You can't stay in the car, it's not safe.'

Clara looked over at him. She laid a hand on his arm. 'I'll be fine. It's all right.'

He seemed to consider that for a moment then sat back in the seat. 'Mom, I think it's Ishmael that might've been here and he means to kill you like he killed our dad.' He took her hand. 'Do you understand? That's what he plans to do, but I'm not going to let him do that. I lost Dad already. I'll lose Ish too if the cops catch up to him. I only just found you, Mom. I'm not about to lose you again.' He lifted his hand to her cheek. 'You have to trust me. You have to come with me. You're not safe in the car by yourself.'

Clara sat there for a moment longer and then she got out. Taking her hand Isaac led her across the gravelled drive.

'Where are we going?' she said. 'Why the garage and not the house?'

Isaac spoke without looking round. 'It's all right. I know what I'm doing. You just have to trust me, OK?'

Inside the garage he considered the floor where the trapdoor was closed and seemed to take a few moments to think. Again he looked back the way they had come and then he shut the garage doors before he dropped to his haunches and hoisted the metal hatch.

'Down there is a storm shelter,' he explained. 'This part of Texas is hurricane alley, or at least that's what Dad used to say. He built the shelter himself and told me you could last six months.' He gestured to the hole in the floor. 'Go on,' he said. 'Use the ladder; I'll be with you in a little bit.'

Clara stared at the hole in the floor then she looked back and Isaac gave her an encouraging smile. Reluctantly she turned around then began to climb down to the passage below. When she got to the bottom of the ladder she looked up.

'Are you coming?'

'I'll be with you in a minute. Don't worry. There's a switch for the light right there.' He pointed to the darkened wall.

'But why?' She spoke sharply now. 'Why aren't you coming too?'

'I'll be there in a bit. Switch that light on and you'll see how the passage leads to the room Dad built. There's another light switch behind the door.'

Still she looked up. Still she looked unsure.

'Mom, it's all right. You have to trust me. I know what I'm doing. I'm a soldier, remember – same as Dad.' He nodded now. 'I'm going to close this door because that's the way Ish got in before. Just go to the shelter and wait for me. I promise you everything will be OK.'

He let the trapdoor fall then fetched the keys to the pickup, opened the garage doors and went outside. He drove the truck inside and parked right over the trap. After that he closed the doors a second time before crossing to the house.

In the storm shelter Clara found the light. Halogen spots in the ceiling, they created an almost bluish glow. About fifteen feet square, an artificial space, she saw the array of water coolers and a first aid kit fixed to the wall. She took in the racks of metal shelving, the folding chairs and table and the propane-fired stove. She considered the cans of food and camp beds ready to be assembled, then her attention fixed on the opposing side. The lowest shelf, it was made of concrete as if it had been fashioned as part of the wall. There was something underneath: a sleeping bag, all bulked up as if somebody was inside.

For a long moment she stared. Then she crossed to the shelf. Trembling a little she looked down at the sleeping bag and sucked an audible breath. On one knee she reached out. She hesitated, fingers curling, the trembling so acute suddenly she had to make a fist. Then she spread her palm once more and finally gripped the bag. The weight shifted, the bag rolled over and she could not contain her scream.

In his father's study Isaac stood stock still. His mother's voice, like a dim and terrified echo, it lifted from beyond the wall. Wrenching the door to the gun cabinet open, he grabbed a Colt 45 and the bayonet. Then he cut behind the desk to the panelled wall. Working his fingers over the wood, he was in the darkness of the passage on the other side.

He could no longer hear her voice, that one scream then nothing. He was at the door to the storm shelter where the seal was so tight no light crept from inside. Still he could hear no sound and he threw open the door. He stood there with the Colt in one hand and the bayonet in the other and saw his mother crouched among several cans of food that had spilled to the floor. He was halfway to her when he stopped: her face pale, eyes like orbs, she stared at a sleeping bag pressed against the other wall.

*

Quarrie drove south; right foot flat to the floor, he had the siren wailing and the red light flashing under the Riviera's clamshell grille. He had sent Nancy McClain back to Bellevue with instructions to get the safe in Beale's office open and find out what was on his tapes. He was pretty sure he knew where Isaac would have taken his mother; somewhere he could secure one entrance and guard the other. He would do his best, he would try to keep his brother at bay, but eventually Ishmael would show.

Late morning, he drove up to the Bowen house where he could see no sign of the pickup truck that had been there earlier and the garage doors were closed. Leaving his car Quarrie made his way around the house to the kitchen door. Sliding one of his pistols from its holster he used the butt to knock out a pane of glass.

In the kitchen he stood with the pistol in his hand aware of no sound but the wind blowing hard outside. Moving to the living room he paused. No sign of any disturbance, no furniture out of place. In the hallway he noticed the door to Ike Bowen's bedroom was closed and he couldn't remember if he had shut it when he left or not. He could hear nothing from below and he started down the stairs to the basement passage. At the bottom he stopped. The study door was wide open and he listened again but still he could hear no sound. Inside the study he paused. The door to the gun cabinet hung at right angles and he noticed two more empty hooks.

A little more cautiously he moved behind the desk to the panel and there he listened once more. Still nothing, no sound, no hint that anyone was back there. He worked fingers down the lip of wood, feeling for the spot where the lever was housed. Locating it finally he heard the faint click and the panel swung in. Darkness in the passage beyond, no light from the storm shelter, he gripped his gun a little more tightly and made his way to the door.

'Isaac,' he called. 'Are you in there? It's John Q.'

No reply. Nobody answered. When he pushed open the door blue light flooded the room. There was nobody there. He could see nothing but a few cans of soup where they rolled on the floor. Gathering them up he put them back on the shelves and when he turned he froze. Slumped under the lowest shelf a dead man was zipped into a sleeping bag. His head encased in a mummy-shaped hood, his eyes were open and his features bruised and bloody.

Quarrie holstered his gun. On one knee he reached for the drawstring that bound the hood and the dead man's head lolled back, telling him that rigor mortis had already been and gone. That meant this guy had been in here when he came through in the darkness last night. Carefully he worked the zipper all the way down and folded back the flap. No sign of any bullet wounds, the man wore a business suit and tie. His mouth was open and a sheet of paper had been screwed up and forced inside. Pinching with his index finger and thumb Quarrie drew the paper out and saw it was the missing page from the address book he had found in the banker's box.

A savage-looking purple mark blotted the base of the dead man's throat, the skin stretched and swollen; a protrusion of bone creating the kind of lump that would be there if he'd been hanged and his neck broken, only he had not been hanged, but his neck was broken just the same. Searching the dead man's jacket he came up with a wallet containing a driver's license in the name of Dr Mason Beale.

Upstairs in the kitchen he found the keys to the garage on the drainer. He called the Fannin County sheriff's department then crossed the drive and unlocked the garage doors. The pickup was parked right over the trapdoor so it could not be raised and he figured it would've been Isaac who had done that. He had been back here clearly, he'd been down in the storm shelter with his mother and found Beale's body, and that was what scared them off. Time was short and as he stood there he wracked his brains trying to figure out where they might have gone.

He was still trying to work it out when a sheriff's cruiser pulled into the yard driven by the same young deputy he had met before. The guy looked a little sheepish when he saw it was Quarrie and he shifted the weight of the sidearm buckled on his hip.

'The body's in the storm shelter,' Quarrie told him, 'Dr Beale out of Shreveport, Louisiana. You'll find a wall panel open in the study down where you were at before. I figure his car must be somewhere in the woods.' He gestured to the far side of the house then looked the young man up and down. 'Your name's Collins, right?'

The deputy nodded.

'What we talked about on the phone – I guess Ike Bowen ain't in the ground just yet so best give the coroner a call.'

*

Isaac was a few miles north of Marshall, Texas, with Clara in the passenger seat. They had stopped for gas and he had bought her some coffee and a muffin to eat but it lay on the dashboard untouched. He was sipping coffee and telling her she really ought to put something in her stomach.

'Even if it's only a mouthful, it's been a long night and you've had one hell of a shock. You need your strength, Mom because where we're going it won't be as easy to protect you as it would've been in the storm shelter.'

Clara stared at the road ahead.

'That was Dr Beale by the way,' Isaac went on. 'The dead guy in the sleeping bag. I recognized him, Ishmael's doctor. He'd already been to the house.'

South of Marshall he didn't take Route 59. Instead he zigzagged, driving a little further east and hit the county road from there. Tiny little hamlets; De Berry, Deadwood and finally Logansport after crossing the state line briefly, before cutting back to Joaquin where they were into the woods.

Next to him Clara peered out of the window. 'Trinity,' she said. 'You're taking us to the hospital. Why?'

Lights and siren going on the Riviera again, Quarrie drove back
to Bellevue with his foot to the floor. Before he'd left the Bowen
place he called Alice Barker and told her that Dr Beale was dead.
He called the FBI and he called the Louisiana State Police. Then
he called Van Hanigan back in Amarillo and gave him the heads
up too. Right now every cop in Texas and Louisiana was on the
lookout for a blue Pontiac sedan.

Quarrie was trying to stay ahead of this and figure out where
Isaac had gone. The truth was it could be just about anywhere,
some motel somewhere, some out of the way hidey-hole that he
didn't think Ishmael would find.

It was mid-afternoon by the time he pulled into the main gates
of the hospital. Instead of parking where he had before, however,
he drove all the way to the main building. Inside the lobby he took
the elevator to the third floor.

Alice met him in the corridor and he could see she had been
crying from the redness around her eyes. She told him that Nancy
McClain had been back for a while and she was in Beale's office
waiting for him. She told him that the police had found Briers's
body in a clump of reeds by an old fishing camp after the owner
showed up with his dogs.

Inside Beale's office Quarrie found Nancy sitting on the couch.
Her face was pale and Quarrie gazed beyond her to where the reel-
to-reel was plugged into an outlet and a stack of tapes lay on the
table marked with Ishmael's name.

Thirty-three

Rolling the length of the causeway, Isaac put the Pontiac between the pair of iron gates. Next to him Clara's gaze seemed fixed on the wall where moss and lichen scattered the bricks. Inside the grounds she saw the burned-out mansion and an audible breath broke from her lips.

'Something, isn't it?' Isaac said. 'Saw it myself when I first hit back in the world.' He let a breath go of his own. 'This is his handiwork, Mom. What you see there, all that's left of the building, that's what Ishmael did.'

Next to him Clara was sitting bolt upright, no color in her face and her hands knotted between her thighs. 'Why have you brought us here?'

He did not reply. Pulling up out front of the main building he sat for a moment holding the wheel and looked sideways to where she twitched a little in her seat.

'Relax,' he told her. 'It's all right. I know what I'm doing. This is my kind of country. We'll be fine.'

Getting out of the car he flipped the seat forward and reached to the foot well behind. When he stood up again he had his father's Colt 45 in one hand and in the other the bayonet.

'Recognize this?' he said. 'North Africa, the Sbiba Pass, or that's what he told us at least.' His eyes had glazed a little and from where she sat in the car, Clara's voice was sharp.

'What's the matter? Are you OK?'

He did not reply.

'What is it?' She spoke louder now. 'Are you all right? Is everything OK?'

239

He did not answer. He seemed to concentrate on the blade in his hand. His lips parted but he didn't speak.

Clara got out of the car and stood watching him, her face pale, hands almost pasted to her sides. As if noticing her for the first time, Isaac looked up. He squinted. He looked at the blade again then slipped it into his belt.

'Ish sure set this place alight.' He strode towards her now with the tunic of his uniform undone and the bayonet hooked at his side. 'Can you imagine all the buildings going up? They must've really pissed him off.'

His mother did not say anything. She was standing by the car still, her gaze shifting from the ruined walls to the barred, glassless windows and back. Isaac stood beside her, the gun in his hand and his hand hanging at his thigh.

'I don't get it,' he said. 'Before Dr Beale got a-hold of him my brother never hurt a fly.'

His mother looked into his face.

'It's OK,' he said. 'There's no need to be worried. Look at this place: if he shows up there's a million different spots we can hide.' He took her hand. 'But the fact is I don't think we need to. I figure I can talk to Ishmael because he used to listen to me.' He looked a little wistful then. 'Back when we were kids I'm talking about. He always used to listen to me. And the games we'd play, the adventures we'd get up to, whatever it was, always it was me made the suggestion, not him.' Slowly he shook his head. 'Ish never came up with anything, not a swimming tank or a camp spot or where to dip a fishing pole.'

Gazing towards the woodland he threw out a hand. 'That vacation, the one in Lawton before you took off. You pretty much left us to ourselves. Do you remember that? Me and Ish would be gone from the house right after breakfast and only just back ahead of suppertime. What we'd do, the stuff we'd get up to, that wasn't anything to do with Ishmael, Mom: it was always down to me.'

Sliding the gun into his belt now his hand hung loose at his side. He stared back up the causeway to the gates. 'Anyway, what I'm saying to you: probably there's no need to hide from my brother, but we best not be taking the chance.' He worked his hand a little absently through his hair. 'He'll go back to the house for sure. He'll figure we went back there but I doubt he'll think to come here.' Breaking off for a moment he frowned. 'But then Ishmael's got a habit of surprising me so we ought to hole up just in case.'

*

When Nancy switched off the tape Quarrie just stared at the floor. Sitting on the arm of the chair his mouth was dry and he could still hear the voices ringing out. A man and a woman, what had started as a stilted conversation had descended into screams and shouts. After that there had only been one voice, Ishmael's voice, rising in an animal howl.

'You were there,' he said quietly. 'You and Mary-Beth helped set that up?'

Nancy nodded. 'We were in the next room. I had to supervise the meds so Mary-Beth worked the tape. Dr Beale had to be in the room with them and Briers was in the corridor outside. Someone had to work the tape so Beale asked Mary-Beth if she would do it and for Ike's sake, she agreed.'

Quarrie looked at her now. 'She knew Ike from before?'

'Of course, we all knew Ike from before.'

'And the three of you – Ishmael knew you were there?'

Again she nodded. 'The door to the corridor was open. He saw us when Briers walked him past.'

Quarrie considered the tape recorder on the coffee table. 'Mary-Beth there for Ike's sake,' he murmured, 'so Ike wasn't there himself?'

Nancy shook her head. 'He couldn't deal with it. And besides, Dr Beale didn't think it was a good idea.'

Quarrie blew out his cheeks. 'Given what I just heard he was probably right.' He looked back at her. 'Nancy, Beale was killed because he showed up at the Bowen house to try and stop Ishmael finding Clara, only he left it too late. Ishmael killed him and stuffed that page from the address book in his mouth. Beale should've spoken to us. He should have called the police right off.'

'He was convinced he could deal with it.' Nancy lifted a palm. 'He told me he thought the police would shoot Ishmael and nobody would be able help him after that. Sergeant, you have to understand that, in the beginning at least, he had no idea about Mary-Beth.'

Moving to the window Quarrie gazed across the grounds where some of the male patients were gathered in their oversized robes. Still he could hear that howl. Not a scream or a cry so much as a deep primordial wail.

'It didn't work,' he said, almost to himself. 'That experiment. Like you told me back in Tulsa, far from snapping him out of anything it only served to lock him in.' His gaze carried the dividing wall to the women's wing. 'I don't see it,' he said. 'I don't see the reasoning. What was Beale thinking about?'

Nancy gave a helpless shrug. 'I don't know, I'm no psychiatrist, but I told you how he wanted to prove to his colleagues that his theory was right. I think he wanted that so badly he didn't quite think it through. He told us that something had happened to lock Ishmael into his prison and nobody knew what it was. When he explained his reasoning to Ike, he agreed it was worth a try.'

Quarrie looked sideways at her then. 'And both of them paid with their lives. Nancy, you did the right thing when you took off. If you'd stuck around your apartment we wouldn't be having this conversation now. You did the right thing driving to Tulsa. You did the right thing trying to warn Clara. But she should've told me who she was when I saw her in Cain's Ballroom, and she should've answered her door when I knocked.'

Nancy did not say anything, she just stood there gazing out of the window with her arms folded about her as if she was cold. Quarrie looked on as the side doors opened and a male orderly came out. Behind him Miss Annie seemed to stumble into the grounds, pushing that old metal stroller ahead of her with the breeze catching wisps of her wasted hair. They both watched as she guided the wheels down the series of stone steps with the orderly falling in behind.

Aware of a chill working through him Quarrie turned from the window once more.

'Nancy,' he said, 'I got a question for you. Where was Ishmael born?'

*

Isaac woke to the light from a single, flickering candle. Blinking slowly he peered left and right, taking in the shadows of a room. Brow furrowed deeply, he seemed to contemplate the way the ceiling hung as if the walls labored under the weight. He was sitting in a worn-out chair in front of an empty fire where aged ashes gathered in flakes of gray. A plethora of unlit candles coating the hearth with strings of calcified wax, he sat very still, aware of the sound of rain falling on the roof.

Turning round in the chair he considered the rest of the room, all in shadow, some darker, some lighter; an old woodstove and beyond it opaque-looking panes of glass.

On his feet he could see something staining the floor. Unable to make it out, he reached for the lighted candle and held it aloft. Marks leading from the door to the chairs then all the way back to the door. Boot prints; he recognized the tread from the patch of earth Quarrie had shown him outside the Bellevue wall.

From the doorway he could barely pick out where the woodland stopped and the perimeter of the hospital began. Rain was falling and the wind seemed to skate through the trees.

'Mom?' he called. 'Are you out there, Mother? Are you there?' No answer. Nobody returned his call.

Hurriedly, he made his way along the path with one arm outstretched like a blind man until he came to the gap in the wall. On the other side he could just about see where the ruin was squatting against the partially clouded sky. Rain still fell but with the way the wind was blowing those clouds were moving away. 'Mom?' he yelled. 'Where are you? Where are you, Mother? Are you there?'

Still she did not reply. No voice lifting through the darkness, he hesitated for a moment, his already faded uniform soaking up water as his eyes grew more accustomed to the darkness. Halfway to the building he scanned the facade as far as the night would allow. He called out again but still there was no reply. He was about to go on when he heard a sound on the path behind.

*

Ishmael studied the shadow that was his father's sedan. At the corner of the building he rested a shoulder against the burned and rotten boards. From there he scanned the grounds very carefully before he crossed to the car. Rooting around in the glove box he located a flashlight but did not switch it on. He just crouched by the door and stared at the building where the roof was gone and the upper stories were supported by the pillars below. His gaze travelled from those pillars to the second floor and the fifth window out from the door. For a little while longer he remained where he was, then shot a glance back along the path. Finally, with rain beginning to fade now, he started for the entrance once more.

At the top step he halted, taking in the darkness of the wood where it had burned. A hint of kerosene still lacing the air, he peered into the deeper shadow left by the missing doors. Inside the lobby he flicked on the flashlight, though only for a moment so he could pick out the flight of stairs.

His back to the wall he kept to the right of each step as he made his way up to the second floor. On the landing he paused, the broken-down wall ahead of him and the twin sets of doors either side. Again he cast a little light, the doors intact as if the fire hadn't bothered them at all. He listened, hearing nothing at first, but then he caught the sound of her voice, a sort of mewling cry that only became recognizable as a human sob when he pushed open the door.

Gaze fixed on the corridor, he hovered where the hallway seemed to drip with shadow. He could hear her crying clearly and the sound was pathetic and lost. It was even more fearful now. At the empty doorway he paused. She was at the window, hands half lifted above her head where he had bound them to the bars. When she realised he was there the crying stopped.

Switching on the flashlight Ishmael cast the beam across all four walls. Every inch of space covered in faded scribblings of stick children, he stared for a minute or more. He did not say anything. Clara did not say anything; she just hunched where she was. His gaze falling on her finally, Ishmael worked his elbow across the grips of the Colt in his jeans and hefted the shotgun in his palm where the duct tape was beginning to wear.

He shut off the flashlight and darkness settled the room. Deliberately he picked his way past the broken-down frame of the bed and Clara shrank back. He could not pick out her features, the white of her face hidden by the weight of her hair.

'What do you want from me?' she said.

Ishmael did not reply. Rain fell on the world outside and he just stood there looking down. Then he stepped away. Standing a few paces back he cocked his head to one side.

'You know I killed my dad.' His voice seemed to echo in the confines of the room. 'I guess Isaac figured it out otherwise why else would you be here? I know he's home. I saw him. I knew he was back from the war.' His voice seemed to fade into the darkness for a moment, then he spoke again. 'He shouldn't have done what he did. The old man, he had me brought down here and he knew what would happen and he should never have done what he did.'

He stood over Clara for a moment then he sat down heavily on the floor. Shotgun over his knees he looked across the room where stick-children gathered to stare.

'I asked him where you were. I asked him but he wouldn't tell me. I asked Ms Gavin but she wouldn't tell me either and I got so mad I started the fire.' He shook his head. 'Didn't mean to do that, or at least I never meant for the records to burn. Ms Gavin, she took off right after but I followed her. I knew where it was she went. I left her alone. I let her be and went home. I went to see Dad to ask him where you were, but he wouldn't tell me so I had no choice but to go back for her.'

'Ishmael,' Clara cut in, 'why're you telling me this? What do you want?'

He looked coldly at her then. 'I'm telling you so you know how it's been. What do I want? I want you, Clara. That's what I want.'

Through the gloom he stared. 'Ms Gavin it was who admitted me.' He spoke now as if to himself. 'She was the one did the paperwork, though Nurse Nancy was with her and Mr Briers, the orderly who looked after the dogs. Nice to me he was to begin with, had him those three or four hound dogs, told me how he'd let them loose if any of the inmates broke out. He said there was no better trail dog than a Walker hound, not a Blackmouth or Catahoula Cur.' He fell silent again then he said, 'I never got to Nurse Nancy. I saw her, wanted to get to her, but she was with another nurse and I had Briers already in the car. I guess talking to her would've been a whole lot easier than talking to him but when your mind is set on a thing . . .' In the darkness he shrugged. 'Anyway, Briers didn't know where you were at; he said he didn't know who you were.'

'Did you kill him too?'

'Yes, I did.'

Clara started to sob.

'Knock that off.'

Another cry broke from her in a half-labored sort of cough.

'Quit that, woman, I said.'

Sitting there with his heels scraping the floor and his back against the wall Ishmael was just a few paces from where Clara was tied.

'I planned on bringing you down here myself, but Isaac got there ahead of me and I don't know why he'd think to do that. Double-bluff or something I suppose. I'll bet he didn't figure on me coming down here as well though, did he? Second guessing him like that. He forgets how it used to be when we were kids. I always knew what he was thinking, no matter what.' He shifted his weight where he sat. 'Isaac doesn't know what this place means though, does he? Not unless Dad told him and I doubt he would've done that. He has no idea what's been going on. He joined the army; a Bowen in the service because that's how it's always been.' His voice died for a moment before he went on. 'It should've been me though, right? On account of I was a Bowen long before him.'

No more sobs now, Clara had gone very still.

'It wasn't just him though, was it, Clara? I was a Bowen long before you.'

'Where is he?' Clara cried. 'Isaac – what happened to him?'

He did not answer. Chin on his chest and the shotgun still on his knees he stared at the walls and the frame of the bed. 'I was a Bowen before any of you, though the old man had no account of me.'

'Is that what you think? Is that what you really believe?'

'You weren't there. When he'd had a few drinks, you didn't hear the things he said.'

'What happened to you, Ishmael? You have to tell me. I can help you. What happened to you back then?'

Still he sat. Gaze peeling across the walls, perspiration ran on his brow. 'Do you know what they did to me here?'

Clara did not reply.

'Dad's idea it was.'

'No, it wasn't,' she said. 'Dr Beale told me what happened. After the fire he called and told me what'd happened and it was not your father's idea.' Her tone was almost angry now. 'I'm sorry. I didn't know about it. I had no idea. If I had I'd have told them you weren't ready for that.'

'Dad thought I was,' Ishmael said. 'Maybe it wasn't his idea but he knew what Beale planned to do and he was happy to let him go ahead. I've seen the papers: how he signed me out of Houston and let them bring me down here.' He wrinkled his lip. 'Well, now Beale is dead and for all his talk he didn't know what he was dealing with.'

He sat for a while working the points of his fingers into his eyes. 'I'm not bad,' he said. 'Not a bad man. I'm not a killer; at least not on purpose anyway.'

'I know that, Ish.' Her voice came to him gently through the darkness then.

'Do you?' He looked over to where she crouched. 'Do you really?'

'Yes, I do.'

'So why leave out? Why take off on us when you did?'

'You know why. You know what happened. You're the only one who does.'

'What're you talking about?'

'You know what I'm talking about. If you think about it you can remember. You were there, Ishmael: you're the only one who was.'

Ishmael shook his head. 'That's what Beale kept telling me. That's what he'd say when we'd sit down and he'd try and get me to talk. But I couldn't get my head around it. I didn't know what it was he wanted me to say.'

Breaking off for a breath, he went on. 'They never should've brought me here. They never should've done what they did. OK, so Dad didn't want to deal with me and you were gone, but I was all right. I was doing all right. In Houston I was doing OK.'

'No,' Clara said. 'You weren't. You were getting worse and worse, you were just like . . .'

'Just like what?'

She was silent.

'Come on, say it. Just like what, Clara? Or is the word I'm looking for *who*?'

With an effort he got to his feet. Working the grips of the pistol around in his waistband again, he unbuttoned his jacket and let it hang loose. 'When I think about it I should've let Briers be and squeezed the life out of Nancy instead. You and the old man, Nurse Nancy, the three of you conspiring the way you did.'

'Ishmael,' she said. 'You have to believe me, darling. It's not how you think it was.'

'Don't call me that,' he snapped. 'Don't you call me that; I'm not your darling. Isaac's your darling. I'm nothing to do with you.'

'Where is he?' she cried. 'What happened to Isaac? For heaven's sake, what did you do?'

Pacing the floor he had his head down and she could not make out his face. 'You haven't seen her, have you? In all these years you haven't seen her once.' Dropping to one knee he reached out and gripped her chin. 'I hadn't seen her till they brought me down here. I had no idea who she was.' He stared right into her eyes. 'So imagine this. Dad tells me that Dr Beale is going to help me now because all those other doctors in Houston have got their diagnosis wrong. He swings by the sanatorium to tell me and that's something he's never done. Visit with me, I'm talking about. You know the old man, Clara: he likes to hole up in that big old house by himself. Have you seen it? Have you been there, right up in the grassland all on its own? Everything is just so. Everything is shipshape like he's in the service still. He did the remodel himself. He even made a storm shelter all stacked with food and water in case of a hurricane or something, I saw the plans before he put it in. You should see the place, a room under the garage with a passage that leads to the house.' Breaking off suddenly he cocked his head. 'You hear that?' he said. 'I thought I heard something. Did you hear that?'

Moving to the door he stepped out into the corridor to take a look and then he came back. Again the silence took him and he sat cross-legged against the wall.

'So anyway, there I am in Houston and here's Dad and this young doctor I've never seen before. Told me his name was Beale and he worked a bunch of hospitals and he knew how to help me once and for all.' He threw out a hand. 'I don't know what they think is wrong with me. There isn't anything wrong with me. I tried to tell you that before you left. I tried to tell Dad but neither of you would listen. Only Isaac ever listened. It was always him and me.'

Clara was weeping. Working her hands across the bars she shifted her position so she could see him where he was hunched against the wall. Outside the rain had stopped and the moon was out and a pale glimmer spread across the half-burned floor. Blinking through tears she could see the scribblings, the bed frame and the corridor beyond the door.

'Dr Beale,' Ishmael went on. 'He brought me down here and I talked to Ms Gavin and I had no idea Dad knew her from before. I talked to Nurse Nancy and Briers let me play with the dogs.' Lifting a hand he gestured. 'I had my own room and they didn't even lock me in. It wasn't a bad deal actually, what with the dogs and the woods and all.' His voice had dropped an octave. 'The patients were all right too, some of them anyway: they worked the garden and a couple of them helped the caretaker with his chores.' Lifting a hand he bent his little finger at the knuckle and held it to the moonlight so it looked as though part of it was gone. 'I'd seen him before. He never knew it and I never told him, but I'd seen that old man before.'

He fell silent again, sitting with his chin on his chest. From the window Clara peered at him, trying to penetrate the gloom.

'What was I talking about?' Ishmael said. 'Oh yeah: how they brought me down here, the patients and everything.' Switching on the flashlight he panned it across the walls.

*

Quarrie saw the light from the hospital gates. A few moments earlier he had driven the length of the causeway with no headlamps burning and made it as far as the drive. As he opened the car door he picked out that snatch of brightness coming from the second floor. He reached for his gunbelt where it lay on the passenger seat. Buckling it around his waist he slipped the hammer clips off and eased both pistols halfway out of their holsters before allowing them to settle once more.

*

Ishmael stared at Clara where she cowered, her gaze shifting from his shadow to the drawings on the walls.

'This was her room,' he said as he turned off the torch. 'This was where she slept and this was where Nurse Nancy showed up one night with a couple of orderlies all those years ago.' He fell silent, ears pricked as if he heard something from outside again. On his feet he went to the window and peered through the bars.

'It's remote here, miles from anywhere. They told me this used to be a rich man's place. He died though, he died and it was a hospital after, and far enough away from anybody else for it not to be a problem if any of the nut-jobs escaped.' Turning from the window he looked down. 'Well, one of them did, Clara. One of them got away.'

*

Quarrie thought he caught a glimpse of a shadow as it appeared at the window above. Fleeting, no more than a whisper, moonlight breaking the clouds, he was working his way across the lawn.

*

Upstairs Ishmael dropped to his haunches in front of Clara. She twisted her head away but he gripped her chin a second time.

'The old man's idea,' he said, 'or maybe it was Dr Beale; but who-ever it was they brought me down here and let me settle in. They let me wander around, but always with Briers there to keep an eye on me. He showed me those dogs; let me fuss over them. Between him and Beale, Nurse Nancy, they let me settle in.

'Then one night they came to my room. I don't know what's going on because nobody's telling me, but they walk me around back of this building right past the office and kerosene store. Briers, he brings me into this corridor and as I pass this one room I see the door is open and there's Ms Gavin from the office along with Nancy McClain. I see Nurse Nancy has a tray of meds and Ms Gav-in's got a tape recorder all set up and I don't think anything of it till Briers brings me into the next room.' Breaking off then he curled his lip. 'That orderly, he sits me down at a table with two chairs and another under a mirror against the wall. On the table there's a pack of playing cards like the old man used to keep but never play.'

Still he held Clara by the chin, keeping her eyes fixed on his. 'Dad wasn't there but he knew what was going on. He told me that much when I asked him and that was just before I shot him on ac-count of how he wouldn't tell me any more.' Taking the pistol from his belt he pressed the barrel against Clara's skull. She gave a squeal, a little whimper, and he could feel her shaking where he pinched her skin.

'He didn't squirm. He didn't cry out. He didn't do anything at all. He just stared into nothing like he didn't give a shit. His own gun, I squeezed that trigger. I squeezed that trigger then I sat him up where he flopped in the chair.'

*

Quarrie was inside the building. Taking great care with the front steps, he crossed the ruined lobby floor. A glimmer from the moon through the empty doorway, he could see the staircase where it scaled the wall.

*

Rocking back on his heels, Ishmael let go of Clara's chin. Lifting the pistol he waved the barrel in front of her nose.

'So I'm sat there waiting and not knowing what's going on. Then Dr Beale comes in and I'm at the table and he sits down in the chair underneath the mirror.' He nodded then as if to himself. 'He doesn't sit across the table from me but in that other chair and he starts on about some goddamn cornfield and a game of hide-and-seek. I tell him I don't know what the fuck he's talking about, but then the door opens and there's Briers with this old witch of a wo-man everyone avoids like the plague. Thin hair and bug eyes, she looks about a hundred years old.' He pressed his face close to Clara's now. 'Only she's not a hundred years old, is she? She's not much older than you.'

Shifting the Colt to his other hand he wiped his palm on his thigh. 'I'm going to kill you, Clara, just like I killed my dad.'

'Ishmael, please—'

'Before I do that I'm going to tell you what I asked that old wo-man and what it was she said to me.' In the shadows he clicked his jaw. 'I had no idea. I had no idea this was what Dad had been talking about when he told me Dr Beale was taking me away from Houston. It's why they took their time to let me settle in. I'd seen her, they made sure of it. I'd spoken to Briers about her and little by little, I guess, they let it all feed in. How she used to be a nurse and everything, one of four good friends, and how she was married back then.'

He was crying. Clara could hear the tears as they climbed in his voice. She peered through the darkness trying to catch the look in his eye.

'You don't have to do this, Ishmael,' she stammered. 'You don't have to—'

'Yes, I do. Of course I do. This is for her. I'm not doing it for you.'

Outside they heard a sound like the creak of a door and Ishmael was rigid where he crouched. Picking up the shotgun, he stuffed the pistol back in his waistband and scurried to the door. Shoulder to the doorjamb he peered the length of the hall. There was no one there and, shifting his weight, he looked the other way. Briefly he flicked on the flashlight and shone it along the hall then back again to the door. No one, nothing, everything was as before. Switching the flashlight off again he remained where he was for a few moments then turned back into the room.

'So this woman,' he said, 'this pathetic creature clutching her doll, they sit her down across the table and I know this is someone who stabbed her old man three times on account of he was having an affair.' Pausing in front of Clara, he dropped to his haunches once more. 'Imagine that,' he said. 'Stabbing your husband because he had an affair. But it wasn't just any old affair. Her old man was sleeping with her best friend, another nurse working nights at the same hospital and that hospital was right here.'

His voice seemed to echo, hollow almost in his chest. 'No wonder she got so mad. I mean, your husband and your best friend fooling around behind your back, that's most of what you ever put your trust in gone in a moment, right there.' He paused for a second before he went on. 'She only found out because she was sick one day and had to go home. Peggy-Anne her name was, she drove herself home to her husband because she wasn't feeling so good and needed him to take care of her like a husband is supposed to do. But when she got home she found her best friend's car parked in the driveway and she couldn't figure why it was there.'

Clara was trembling, forced against the wall still, her hands caught above her head.

'Well, anyway,' Ishmael said. 'Peggy goes in the house and she can hear voices coming from the bedroom. When she opens the door she sees her best friend half-naked, grinding away on her old man.'

His voice had cracked; knuckles taut around the grips of the gun. 'Poor Peggy, she was so hurt, so shocked, so distraught by it all she didn't know what to do. Stumbling around in the hallway she found the bayonet her husband was supposed to have taken from a German in World War II. I guess she picked it up and then her husband comes rushing out of the bedroom to try and calm her down, but she's not about to calm down and she stabbed him with his own blade.' As he spoke he worked the barrel of the pistol into Clara's belly. 'Three times she stabbed him but he didn't die. Peggy-Anne Bowen, your best friend and Dad's wife before he divorced her so he could marry you.'

Getting to his feet he stood above her. He had the shotgun at hip height, fingers flexed around the grips. 'Attempted murder, they called it. But by then she wasn't Peggy-Anne Bowen anymore, she was this Miss Annie person who'd been living in Peggy's head. Too sick to be tried in a criminal court, she was locked away right here.'

Stretching his shoulders he worked his head around in a circular motion as if his neck was stiff. 'As far as the world was concerned that was OK I guess; only nobody knew what Miss Annie had going on. Nobody knew anything about any of it, not till it started to show.' Viciously he bent to her then. 'But that wasn't all, was it, Clara? By the time you found out she was pregnant you were carrying Dad's baby too.

'So, anyway,' he said, stepping back. 'I'm set there with Dr Beale and Briers wheels in this sick old woman clutching her doll, and they sit her down at the table and she's eyeing the deck of cards like she wants to play.' Vaguely he gestured. 'Tells me how she used to play blackjack with her husband when she was first married, a whole bunch of years ago. I don't know what to do. I don't know why I'm there and I'm not about to play a game of cards with some old loon. So I sit there and I look at her and I look at Dr Beale because I don't know what I'm supposed to say to a woman who stabbed her husband three times. Miss Annie, it seems she doesn't know what to say either. She's not talking now. She's holding that doll as if she's afraid I'm going to take it away.'

His voice stalled as tears worked onto his cheeks. 'But I know I have to say something because that's why we're there. So I'm looking at her and I say the first thing that comes in my head. I lean across the table as far as I dare and I nod to the doll she's clutching and ask Miss Annie what's her baby's name.' Shaking his head he let go an audible breath. 'You know what she told me, Clara? You know what Miss Annie said? She looked at me across that table with Dr Beale in the corner and Briers outside and Ms Gavin taping the whole thing. *My baby's name is Ishmael*, she said.'

Clara was sobbing as he worked the action on the shotgun and pointed it at her head.

'So now you know. Now you know what happened to me, and that's why I came after you. It took me a while to track you down, but I told them I would kill them all if that's what it took, and finally here we are. You betrayed her, Clara; you betrayed your best friend. You stole me from her the day I was born just like you stole my dad.'

'Ishmael,' she cried, 'nobody stole you. Nobody stole your dad. Peggy was sick, she was very ill. There was no way we could leave a newborn baby with her.'

'But why was she sick? That's the question. What was it made her that way?' His words seemed to break like ice. 'It was you, Clara, you and the old man. Doing what you did behind her back – that's enough to send anyone crazy for sure.'

Movement in the hall outside and Ishmael froze. He stood there in silence then a voice lifted through the darkness and he stared into Clara's eyes.

'Put the shotgun down, Ishmael.' Quarrie stepped from the corridor into the doorway. 'You've done enough killing. You're not killing anyone today.'

For a moment Ishmael did not move, his gaze still fixed on Clara's face. Standing tall he turned. Quarrie no more than a shadow in the moonlight, Ishmael stared at his outline with the shotgun levelled and his head cocked to one side.

'I'm a cop, Ishmael. Texas Ranger, and I need you to put that shotgun down.'

Ishmael did not say anything. He stood his ground.

'I ain't holding.' Quarrie lifted his palms. 'You can see my weapons are holstered. I don't want to shoot you. I don't want to hurt you. I want you to put that shotgun down.'

Watching him, Quarrie waited; ten seconds, fifteen. Then, through the gloom, he glimpsed the way Ishmael's shoulders started to twitch. In slow motion almost, he saw the way his arms began to climb. The barrel came up but before Ishmael could squeeze the trigger Quarrie drew a pistol and fired.

Two shots, left hand covering the hammer, the sound seemed to shatter the air. Ishmael slammed against the wall with the shotgun spilling from his grip. For a moment he hung there and then he slid down the wall. Just a pace away Clara was screaming as he buckled at the knees.

He was on his side on the floor, both palms clutching his stomach; he blinked at stick-children where they leered from the walls.

As she bent over him Clara's arms were stretched across her chest so harshly it seemed they would be sucked from the sockets where she was bound to the window bars.

'Don't you die on me,' she screamed. 'Isaac – where is he? What happened to him? Ishmael, where's your brother? What did you do?'

Thirty-four

When Quarrie finally pulled off the highway onto the dirt road late the following afternoon, he was only three miles from home. Ahead lay the low scrub hills where Nolo was nursing a few strays back towards the southern pasture. The young foreman, he was up on the ridge where the dirt road cut underneath. With the sun splitting the horizon the whole languid panorama formed a silhouette and Quarrie watched the way he sat that colt so low in the saddle with his feet almost dangling as if he didn't need the stirrups at all.

A gravel bar, a thicket of black cottonwood; a drainage breaking from the lip of the creek that meandered all the way back to the water tank they used for the stock. For some reason Quarrie was picking up on every detail of the landscape; every stand of cactus, every stump of mesquite and every pale-colored stone. He could see Clara in his mind's eye, the pain in her face; the desperation in her voice. Again he heard Ishmael's howl.

Ishmael had survived the bullets. Down but not out, between them Quarrie and Clara had patched him up enough where they could get him to a hospital and that's where he was right now. He would not go to the chair. Quarrie doubted there would be any trial, not with his problems. Like his mother before him, he'd be shut away for the rest of his life.

Pulling up outside the house, he killed the engine and by the time he had the driver's door open, James was on the stoop, his features stretched in a smile. Leaving his guns and hat on the back seat Quarrie swept the boy into his arms.

'You OK, kiddo?' he said. 'Everything good back here?'

'Everything's just fine, Dad. You look a little beat-up though. Are you OK?'

Inside the house Quarrie sat down wearily on the couch. He lifted first one boot to the coffee table and then the other. Straddling his legs, James helped him haul the boots off. Quarrie nodded to the floor where the Aurora four-lane race track was set up with two cars all ready to go. He had sent to Sears for it and it had come in time for his son's tenth birthday just a few weeks ago.

'You been waiting on me then, huh?'

'Yup,' the boy said. 'You're going to lose, Dad. You know how Pious kept beating me? Well, I been practising now.'

Leaning back with his head against the wall Quarrie closed his eyes. 'Just give me a minute here, would you? Got to tell you, bud, been a tough few days. I hate being away from you so much and I've had a belly-full of rangering right now.' Slipping an arm around his shoulders Quarrie sat up and looked his son in the eye. 'I tell you something, what we talked about, vacation time up in the mountains. I'm thinking about maybe calling up a couple of old buddies in Teton County to see if I can't get some work.'

'You want to quit the Rangers?' His son was wide-eyed. 'You can't do that, Dad. It's what you do.'

'Not quit, son, no. Fact is you don't ever quit the Rangers, but sometimes you take what they call a sabbatical. My Uncle Frank used to do that from time to time. It's a tough old job and it keeps me away from you a whole lot more than I'd like.' He winked then, mussing a palm through the young boy's hair. 'You never know, one of these days maybe the two of us will move north again and live in that house I bought with your momma instead of paying rent down here anymore.'

They played with the racecars for a while and James won as he said he would. Afterwards Quarrie took a shower and when he came out the boy was watching TV.

'Dad,' he said, 'when do you think it'll be we get color?'

Working a towel through his hair, Quarrie glanced at the screen where James T. Kirk was in discussion with his Scottish engineer.

'Television, you talking about?'

'Yes, sir. That shirt the captain's wearing is sort of mustard color,' James said. 'I know that from Tommy Morrison.'

'Tommy got color then, does he?'

'Yes, he does. Most everybody does, even Miss Munro and she told us she don't hardly ever watch TV.' Again he indicated the screen. 'Mr Spock's shirt is blue, and that guy sitting at the helm right there, his is red, I think. How long do you figure before we can get us a color TV?'

Crossing to the bunkhouse for dinner Quarrie ate rice and red beans with bits of chopped up chorizo sausage and chilli peppers in a sauce Eunice liked to make for Nolo, because for a while now she'd been carrying a torch. Quarrie wasn't sure if it burned the other way but the foreman seemed happy to flirt.

He talked to Pious about it after the meal had been cleared away. Nolo had gone over to the big corral to work a couple of colts. Mama Sox had long since retired for the night, and Eunice was over by the water tank where she could dip her toes and watch Nolo while pretending to read a magazine.

'Yeah, I seen how she is,' Pious said. 'But it ain't exactly a regular sight, a Mexican and a colored girl, especially one older than him.'

'Pious, Nolo ain't Mex and Eunice don't look her age.'

Pious made a face. 'No, she don't, but most folk round here would figure Nolo for a Mex, John Q, and he's a whole lot younger than her. The way things are right now, I don't see much future in it, do you?'

'Well, she sure looks smitten to me, bud, so try telling that to her.'

Arms folded across his chest, Pious rocked on the legs of his chair. 'I don't know why we're even talking. It don't matter what anybody thinks, Eunice'll go her own way like she always does. It's been years since she took account of Mama, leave alone a brother like me.'

Getting up from the table Quarrie found a bottle of Jim Beam and poured out a couple of shots. Then he remembered Pious hated whiskey on account of his father being drunk on corn mash and getting run over by a truck. Tipping the second glass into his, he grabbed a Falstaff from the fridge and knocked off the top. He passed the beer over and Pious indicated the double shot.

'Ain't like you to be supping on a glass that size. What's on your mind, John Q? You been preoccupied ever since you got home.'

Swallowing a mouthful of whiskey Quarrie squinted at him. 'You read your Bible anymore, do you? You know the story of Ishmael and Isaac?'

'John Q,' Pious said, 'you know I don't got no time for religion. When I was in the pen I read me a book by a feller called Darwin. God and all – it don't matter want some preacher wants to tell you – that ain't the way things are. The way I see it God didn't make man in his image so much as man made God in his.' Taking a sip from his bottle he spread a palm. 'I heard it said one time that religion is opium for the people, but the trouble with opium is how it only soothes for a little while before it starts fucking with your head.'

'Darwin, huh?' Quarrie said. 'Survival of the fittest.' Tipping the rest of the bourbon down his throat he reached for the bottle. 'Maybe you ought to read about Ishmael and Isaac – that's natural selection right there.'

In the morning he drove to Wichita Falls and the sheriff's office where he had his part-time desk. He had to go past the hospital and, on a whim, he pulled up outside the back doors where the coroner's ambulance was parked. Making his way past the mortuary assistant he nodded to a nurse as she came out through the examination-room doors.

The red bulb on the ceiling was alight which meant Tom Dakin, the medical examiner, was making a tape. When he saw Quarrie he switched it off and stripped the microphone from where it hung around his neck. Before him was a waxy-looking cadaver on one of the porcelain tables with a stainless-steel sluice at the base.

'John Q,' Dakin said. 'I haven't seen you in here since you took down that long hair with a double-tap.'

'Wiley,' Quarrie said. 'His name was Wiley, Tom: I never killed anybody I don't know the name of, except in Korea perhaps. If that guy had listened to the advice being given him he'd be tucked up in Huntsville now.'

His tone was grim, his features equally so, and Dakin seemed to pick up on it. 'So what's up?' he said. 'I can see something's chewing at you, so what is it? What's going on?'

Hunching his shoulders Quarrie worked them into his neck. 'Can't tell you, Tom. Fact is I can't put a finger on it myself.'

'Well, I heard how you've been busy shooting somebody else.'

'I shot him all right. Over in Panola County, but I made sure he didn't die.' Quarrie glanced at the corpse on the table and then at Dakin again. 'Weirdest thing,' he said. 'Sumbitch took down a whole bunch of people yet I kind of feel sorry for him.'

'Yeah, well, some things just get to you, don't they? We're all human, Johnny. It even applies to you.'

'So anyway,' Quarrie stood straighter now. 'These bones we found up on the Red, that old train wreck from way back when. My boy's writing up about what happened. Did you hear anything about that?'

'A project for school – Sheriff Dayton told me, yes.' Dakin still had his arms folded across his chest. 'Those bones though: that skull and the clavicle, the little bit of vertebrae they brought in.' He shook his head. 'They're not sixty years in the water. At the most I'd say fifteen.'

Thirty-five

Squatting on a rock among the cottonwood trees Quarrie wiped sweat where it gathered on his brow. Mid-afternoon and the sun was a molten ball. A week had passed since his son's school project had been completed and James was still basking in the fact that his teacher had been so pleased with what he had done she had exhibited the whole thing.

Quarrie watched James where he swam between the wrecked railroad cars. Pious was down there with him, and the way the boy's straw-colored head seemed to bob against the surface of the water reminded Quarrie of days gone by with his wife. A moment of reverie, it was broken by the sound of approaching vehicles and he got to his feet, wearing a pair of sand-colored pants and a short-sleeved shirt. He wore his pale gray hat.

Climbing to the top of the bank he spotted an Oklahoma state police car driving the dirt road, followed by a panel van with three people up front and one man in the back. The van was tailed by a second cruiser, from Louisiana.

Quarrie waited for the cortege to arrive with his arms across his chest, watching dust shimmer as the vehicles came to a halt. Sitting in the passenger seat of the first car Clara Symonds smiled a little nervously at him through the windshield. They had spoken on the phone a couple of times since the night in Miss Annie's old room, and when Quarrie told her what he'd discovered and what he was proposing because of it, Clara jumped at the chance.

All the vehicles had stopped now and Quarrie noticed that the driver of the Louisiana cruiser was the same trooper from that day by the railroad tracks. Climbing from the car he nodded Quarrie's way then fixed the strap at the back of his hat. A Colt holstered at his side, he carried a pump-action Winchester shotgun, as did the driver of the Oklahoma car. When all three troopers were ready the driver of the van got out. He was dressed in the black uniform worn by the guards at Bellevue Hospital and he was accompanied by an orderly and a nurse. Nancy McClain, she glanced at Quarrie briefly before her attention returned to the van.

The guard looking on and the state troopers with shotguns across their chests, the orderly opened the back door. One man shackled to his seat, his hair slicked back, he wore a pair of cotton trousers and a white shirt. He climbed down awkwardly, his man-acled hands fixed by a chain to the irons that hobbled his legs, and the orderly supporting his arm. Taking a moment to consider his surroundings, his gaze settled where Quarrie stood.

'John Q,' he said. 'They never said I was coming to meet you. Been some kind of crazy mix-up, maybe you can help straighten it out. Fact is they got me locked up at Bellevue right now for some reason I can't understand – and me wounded and everything.' He indicated his torso. 'You remember Bellevue, the hospital where we visited that time?'

'Sure,' Quarrie replied.

'I'll get the situation squared away eventually, though it's taking longer than I thought. I imagine they think I'm suffering from shell shock or something, post-traumatic stress or whatever it is they want to call it. Only to be expected I reckon, after three full tours.'

With a glance at the state troopers he shuffled towards Quarrie, picking his way through the scrub and saltgrass with one eye peeled for snakes.

'This your idea to have them bring me out here? Sure is good to have a little fresh air. They let me out in the grounds every once in a while, but you know how that is with all those basket cases sitting out.' Looking over his shoulder he arched a brow. 'I can't seem to get it across to them that it's not me with the problems, but they've clean forgotten about Ish.'

Taking him by the arm Quarrie led him across the lip of the bank into the stand of cottonwoods where there was a little shade. Behind them Nancy followed along with Clara and the troopers carrying their guns.

Quarrie helped him down so he could sit on the rock where he himself had been squatting a few minutes before. It took some doing because of the manacles and chains that rattled like he was Marley's ghost. It was cooler there though, and between the pale trunks they could see the waters of the river and the hunks of rusting metal where the railroad cars had wrecked.

'Did they tell you I caught up with Ishmael?' Quarrie took a pack of cigarettes from the pocket of his shirt. 'Found out what was wrong with him finally. You know those problems you told me about?'

One eyebrow hooked, Isaac squinted at him now.

'Something Dr Beale was working on. It was why he wanted Ish brought down there to Trinity when he did.' Shaking a smoke from the pack Quarrie tamped it against the base of his thumb. 'You remember how we couldn't figure that out, the two of us, what it was he had going on?'

Isaac did not answer. His gaze was not on Quarrie but the clay-colored water below.

'Fact is Dr Beale was ahead of his time,' Quarrie told him. 'He was on to something Nurse McClain says most shrinks don't believe exists.' He glanced to the edge of the little glade where Clara and Nancy were listening intently. Isaac was staring at the river still, concentrating not on Pious so much as James.

'Did you hear me?' Quarrie said. 'What he was working on – something he called *Dissociative Identity Disorder*. It's a condition most psychiatrists figure is just a bunch of symptoms that some folk like to create on account of the attention it brings.'

'What kind of symptoms?' Isaac was still watching James.

'Miss Annie's kind: I guess you heard how she used to be Peggy-Anne Bowen when she was married to Ike.'

'Ishmael's mother, I know.'

'How do you know?' Quarrie said.

As if it was hard to drag his attention away from the two figures in the river, Isaac looked back to where Clara was watching with her features stiff. 'You OK there, Mom?' he said.

She gave a half-smile. She did not reply.

'How did you know?' Quarrie asked him again.

Isaac was still looking at Clara. 'I found his birth certificate in a banker's box. The key was in the first aid kit in the storm shelter, and that's just the kind of weird place the old man would've hidden it, I guess. I knew it had to fit something important but I couldn't figure out what it was. We had to go to Shreveport, remember, so I left the key on the shelf.' He looked back at Quarrie then. 'When I got home it wasn't where I put it, so I looked everywhere and eventually found it back where it'd been before. Ish must've done that because I found the banker's box in Dad's closet under a sweater and it wasn't there when I looked before.'

Pumping air from his cheeks he shook his head. 'I had no idea. As far as me and Ish were concerned there was fifteen minutes between us, and there I am reading his birth certificate where his mom isn't my mom and he was born three months before.'

'And that was the first time you knew about it,' Quarrie asked. 'You had no notion up until then?'

Again Isaac shook his head. 'So anyway,' he said. 'This condition – what is it? Dad never said anything to me.'

Silent for a moment, Quarrie looked squarely at him. 'It's complicated. I guess if you want to whittle it down it means that for fifteen years now Ishmael's had Isaac living in his head.'

Lifting a manacled hand, Isaac tried to shade his eyes from the sun.

'Kind of weird to think about,' Quarrie went on. 'All these years walking around with a whole other personality inside your head. That's what it is though, this disorder Dr Beale was trying to prove exists: at least two personalities at the same time and neither one knowing the other is there. They have different ways of talking, they dress in different clothes, and neither knows about the other at all. I guess Beale saw that kind of thing in Miss Annie when he took over at Trinity, and then he heard about you.'

'I don't get it,' Isaac said. 'I don't understand what you're talking about. How can Ish have me inside his head? I'm right here. So we're not twins anymore like I thought, but that doesn't change who I am.'

'Sure it does,' Quarrie said. 'You're not Isaac. You're Ishmael. Isaac is dead.'

Mouth open Isaac stared. 'Dead?' he said. 'What d'you mean? I'm Isaac. I'm not dead. How can I be dead?'

Quarrie held his gaze. 'You might think you're Isaac. You might think it's Isaac I'm talking to right now, but you're Ishmael, you just got Isaac doing the talking instead. It's why his mother left out when she did. It's what drove her away, her missing son right there before her, manifested in her stepson's head.'

Isaac was staring still. 'I don't understand. I don't get you. What're you talking about?'

'I'm talking about Clara being your stepmother, not your mother. I'm talking about how she wasn't able to cope with the fact that her son went missing fifteen years ago and you started to act like him.'

Isaac looked from him to Clara and back.

'Miss Annie's your mother, remember? When they introduced you to her that night at Trinity they were hoping it would spark you into remembering what happened to your brother, but all it did was push you over the edge.'

'Miss Annie?' Isaac knit his brows. 'I don't understand.'

'Sure you do – the woman who used to be Peggy-Anne Bowen.

She was married to your dad before he divorced her and married Clara instead. Your mother, Ish: Peggy-Anne. She was much sicker than anybody knew. She had a whole other personality called Miss Annie inside her head and she used to show up from time to time until one day she never left.'

'On account of her kid,' Isaac was nodding now. 'On account of how they took him away from her the day he was born.'

Quarrie looked closely at him again. 'Yes, that's right. But how did you know about that?'

Isaac shrugged. 'Ishmael told me, I guess.'

'When did he tell you?'

With another shrug he shook his head.

'It was Miss Annie that stabbed your dad,' Quarrie went on. 'That wasn't some German soldier, it was Ike's first wife, only not Peggy, but the other personality she had living in her head. After that Peggy came back for a while, but then they took her baby away and that's when Peggy disappeared altogether and nobody has seen her since.'

'And Ishmael? What happened to him?'

Quarrie lifted his palms. 'You tell me, bud. We don't know what happened, but the way we figure it something went down back when you were a kid. Something with Isaac because the two of you went out one day but only you came back. Dr Beale believed that's when this all started. Your brother's disappearance – you knew more about it than you were telling anyone, and that set you off on this path you been walking ever since. The whole point of that meeting with Miss Annie was to shock you, Ishmael; show you the truth of who you are and hope it would bring you back to reality so you could face up to whatever it was you did.'

Isaac looked quizzical again. 'Wait a minute, wait a minute. You just said the path I've been walking. You mean the path Ishmael was walking, right?'

'There is only Ishmael: that's the point.' Quarrie indicated the river. 'Isaac went missing fifteen years ago, and there was no trace of him till my buddy down there found a skull under those railroad cars that belonged to a ten-year-old kid.'

'No, that's wrong. That's all wrong.' Isaac was gesturing under the weight of the chains. 'I'm Isaac, not Ishmael. These irons, the damn hospital – that's all because of Vietnam.'

Quarrie shook his head. 'I listened to Dr Beale's tapes and he was convinced that the only way you could come to terms with this was if you were shocked into remembering what it was you did.'

Isaac opened his mouth to speak again but Quarrie gripped him by the arm. 'What was that, Ish? Was it Miss Annie? Did you know about her somehow, all those years ago?'

Isaac did not answer. His gaze was slack. He was no longer looking at Quarrie. He was concentrating on the river instead.

'This is bullshit,' he said. 'I thought we were buddies, but Jesus – you're as bad as them. I was a soldier. I lost friends, John Q. I was fighting in Vietnam.'

'No, you weren't,' Quarrie said. 'You never went to Vietnam. You never even joined the service. You weren't in any last firefight and none of your buddies are dead.'

'Thirty-one,' Isaac murmured. 'Thirty-one dead and one hundred and twenty-three wounded ...'

'You weren't there,' Quarrie said. 'You heard that report on the radio same as me. That's why your father never wrote. The letters you sent weren't about real missions and they weren't from Vietnam. I found one in its envelope in that banker's box you talked about and the postmark was Houston, not Saigon. You didn't join the army like your dad. That uniform you insisted on wearing – you bought that from the Army/Navy store in Marshall, Texas, when you left the salesman's car. From there you hitched a ride to Trinity, a vet just home from the war. Then you took a train to Shreveport, Louisiana, and spoke to Dr Beale. His mistake was not keeping you there like he should. But he didn't know you'd started the fire. He didn't know you'd killed Mary-Beth and he didn't know about your dad. According to a tape he made over in Fannin County, he felt he had to take the opportunity of observing his subject under conditions he didn't control.

'Ishmael to Isaac, Isaac to Ishmael; both of you at Trinity and both at your father's house. You passed each other at the grocery store. You told me how you thought you'd seen Ish at the H-E-B, remember? Well, I spoke to a mechanic who said how he'd given you a ride out to an Oldsmobile that had run out of gas. That car was the one you stole from the newspaper seller in Shreveport, remember? The guy you clubbed over the head.'

Isaac turned to look at him briefly before his gaze shifted back to the river. 'What're those guys doing?'

'Pious, you mean, and that ten-year-old kid?'

Isaac looked sharply at him then.

'That's my son, Ishmael. He's ten years old, which is exactly how old your brother was the day he went missing, right? Fifteen years ago in Lawton, Oklahoma. Remember? That's barely forty miles north.'

'Yeah, but what're they doing?'

'They're noodling, hand-fishing; they're grabbling for catfish and I think you know how that is. The day Isaac was lost you told everyone the two of you only went as far as a cornfield a few hundred yards from the house. You told them you were playing hide-and-seek and you were the one doing the counting. You told them Isaac went off and you went to look for him but you couldn't find him no matter where you looked. Nobody could find him. The search was concentrated on that area but nothing was ever found. In the end the only conclusion anybody could come to was that Isaac had been abducted and he was never seen again.

'Clara.' He pointed to her now. 'Isaac's mother, her boy missing and within a few months you were talking like him and taking on his mannerisms, acting as if you were him. She could not deal with

271

that. She knew there was something you weren't telling anybody but there was nothing she could do, and in the end she couldn't stand it anymore so she left. Later, she heard how you'd gotten worse and worse and she ended up so worried about what might happen your dad advised her to change her name.'

Isaac did not seem to be listening: still he stared at the wrecked cars in the river with sweat beginning to soak his hair.

'You've been here before,' Quarrie told him. 'This spot right here where a train crashed in nineteen hundred and three. You see my boy in the water and he looks just like Isaac, doesn't he? The same age, swimming among the same railroad cars. What happened to him, Ish? You were here. I know you were. What happened down there at the wreck?'

Head bent, Isaac stared at the water. He stared for a full minute, not speaking, barely moving his head. Then he wrenched at his chains. When he looked up he wasn't Isaac anymore, he was Ishmael: gaze dull, he looked Quarrie hard in the eye.

'You're the cop that shot me. You could've killed me. Why didn't you? It would've been a whole lot better if you did.'

'Not for her it wouldn't.' Quarrie indicated where Clara was looking on, her face very pale and pinched. 'She needs to know what happened to Isaac and that's the only reason you ain't dead.'

Ishmael followed his gaze. 'You think I give a shit about her? She's the one took me away. First she took my father from my mother and then she took me. The two of them trying to pretend how nothing had happened, telling me I was fifteen minutes older than my brother when it was three fucking months at least.

'We're not talking about her, we're talking about you. We're talking about how you knew about that back when you were a kid.' Quarrie was studying him now. 'Not at first maybe, not till that vacation perhaps, but you knew who you were long before you met Miss Annie. All that meeting did was confirm what deep down somewhere you already knew.'

Ishmael's stare was suddenly less certain. Briefly he considered Clara and Nancy, then he swivelled where he sat on the rock.

'My son,' Quarrie said, following his gaze. 'He's the same age Isaac was. You've been here before, Ishmael. This very spot: this is where he was lost.'

Ishmael peered at him then he looked down to the water again where James was looking up. He sat there, shoulders hunched, then his face just seemed to crumple and a shiver worked from his head to his toes.

'Time you got it off your chest,' Quarrie said, more gently.

Ishmael looked back at him. He opened his mouth and closed it again.

'Come on,' Quarrie prompted. 'I know you remember. Talk to me. You have to. It's been way too long.'

Trembling slightly, Ishmael returned his attention to the river. 'The long count,' he uttered finally. 'That's what Isaac called it. Said he'd overheard the old man talking about how it was back in the day with Sergeant Morley. Memorial weekend, they sat up drinking whiskey and telling war stories, and Isaac heard them talking about when they were training in Georgia, how they'd grabble for catfish and the locals told them there was the short count as well as the long.' He tried to gesture but with the chains on his wrists he could not. 'All depended on what was going on underwater and how long someone could hold their breath. Isaac told me the old man was slurring his speech he was so drunk, but he could still work out what he said.'

Glancing beyond him to the river Quarrie considered where James was swimming still.

'That's not all he told you though, is it?'

Ishmael's lip was trembling. His eyes were not dull anymore, they were moist.

'He told me he heard Dad say how the wounds he'd told us he'd gotten in Africa were stab wounds given him by his wife. Not our mom but another woman, one he was married to before, someone we'd never met. Isaac heard him tell Mr Morley how she took his blade one day and gutted him like a pig. We were supposed to be sleeping but they were right there under the window of our room and Isaac was awake. He heard the old man talk about being married before. He said how he always meant to leave her because she was nuts already, but then she caught him and Clara in bed together and it saved him the bother.' The tears in his eyes spilled onto his cheeks. 'Nobody knew she was carrying me though, and, by the time they found out, Clara was pregnant too.'

Quarrie looked over at Clara who was watching them intently. 'Isaac heard your dad say all this to Sergeant Morley?'

Ishmael nodded. 'By the time I woke up my life had changed completely. Me and Isaac, we weren't twins anymore; we weren't even full-blood brothers. That's why they named us like they did. Ishmael and Isaac, half-brothers like in the Bible. The way he said it, the way Isaac told it to me that morning, he was goading me with how he was the one with family and I was the son of a fucked-up bitch who tried to murder our dad.'

Tears rolling he looked again to the river. 'You should've seen him. You should've heard him – Isaac, I'm talking about. Up at dawn he'd dug out this old newspaper cutting about the train wreck from someplace so we hit the highway with our thumbs out and that's when he starts in.' He shook his head. 'Not talking, it wasn't talking, it was taunting is what it was. Oh, he was having the time of his life. He could be like that sometimes, though to hear Clara talk he was such an angel, butter wouldn't melt in his mouth.'

Dragging his chains he scraped both hands across his face. 'Anyway, you're right. We never went near any cornfield. What we did was hit the blacktop and hitch a ride in a truck with this old Mex who pulled over and we hopped in. Didn't seem to matter to him how we were so young and all, I guess things were different back then.' Falling silent he buckled his little finger so it looked as though half of it was gone. 'He told us he was headed south, said he'd take us as far as we wanted to go and we jumped out a couple of miles from this spot. We hiked the rest of the way, and when the cops were looking for Isaac later nobody heard from the Mex, so they never knew this is where we'd gone.'

'Pablo,' Quarrie said. 'That truck driver's name was Pablo. The caretaker at Trinity, right?'

Ishmael nodded. 'When they brought me down there I saw his missing finger and I knew I remembered him.'

He shifted his weight on the rock, gazing down at the railroad cars once again. 'All that day he would not let up – Isaac, I'm talking about. All he did was laugh at me, keep on with the jibes and piss me off. He went on and on, making out he was superior on account of everything our daddy had said. I wasn't kin to him anymore, not properly anyhow. I wasn't blood kin to our mother at all, and Isaac just loved the fact that the old man had one cold eye on me to see if I was going to turn out like his first wife.'

His gaze clear suddenly, he looked from the river to where Clara had moved closer so she could hear everything he said.

'I'm sorry I did what I did. Down at the hospital, I'm sorry I hurt you, and I'm sorry I shot my dad. I never meant to do any of it. I never meant to hurt anybody because I never believed what Isaac said.' His voice was breaking. 'But they took me away from Houston. They took me down to Trinity and I saw that old caretaker, then they sat me down with Miss Annie and she told me her baby's name. After that I knew it was true. I knew her baby was the one Isaac had been talking about all those years ago.'

He turned from Clara to Quarrie again. 'That day down here I told him he was full of shit and I didn't believe a word he said. I told him I was nobody's half-brother and his mother was the same as mine. I told him he was making it up and his jokes had always been sick. I said to him how he would pay for it if he didn't let up because I was stronger than him.'

'What happened?' Clara spoke now, her voice shaking. 'Ishmael, please, it's been fifteen years. You have to tell us what you did.'

Head bowed Ishmael did not answer. 'I didn't mean for it to turn out like it did. I didn't mean to be killing people, not Ms Gavin or Briers, and especially that girl at the mission house. I figured God wouldn't damn me for what I did to my dad, because he was first-class sonofabitch.' Lips pursed he shook his head. 'It don't matter how much I plead with him now though, he ain't going to forgive me for shooting that kid.'

'Ishmael,' Clara said. 'You have to tell us what happened. This river, those railroad cars – you have to tell us what you did.'

Looking up at her he shook his head. 'I didn't do anything. That's the point. I didn't do a thing. Catfish . . .' Lifting both chained hands he tried to point to the water. 'A catfish is what it was. Down there among that wreck we felt the vibration of a fish thumping its tail. Isaac said that had to be a flathead so he went down to try and see where it was burrowed up.'

'And what did you do?' Quarrie said.

Ishmael looked at him. 'I started counting. Isaac said he could hold his breath for a while but he didn't know what was going on down there so I had to make a count and it couldn't be long.' Eyes closed, his voice was shaking. 'But all of what he'd told me was in my head. Filling up all the space, there was no room in there and I couldn't think straight to be counting, what with worrying about what he said.

'So I lost the count and started again. And then the same thing happened – all of what he'd told me bubbling up to confuse me again. I didn't believe it. I couldn't believe it. So I lost the count and started again.'

Sobbing like a child he hung his head. 'By then Isaac was stuck and I was so absorbed in my thoughts I didn't even notice the way the water was boiling up. Soon as I did I dove down but I couldn't save him. His foot was trapped between a tree root and a piece of wreckage and I couldn't get him clear no matter what I did.' Breaking off for a second he wiped his eyes. 'Isaac, he was thrashing around like a fish. Trying to shout to me, he was trying to shout with bubbles coming out of his mouth. He was sucking in river water. He looked at me and he was sucking in river water, had a hold of my shoulder, fingers digging into my skin. I tried to get his foot free but I had no breath so I come to the surface to gulp some air and I dove back down again. He wasn't thrashing anymore, he wasn't sucking in water; he was swaying back and forth like the wind was blowing him. His eyes were open and his hands reaching out like he wanted to grab me but he was gone already. My brother was dead.'

The sobs overtook him completely. For a moment Quarrie looked on, then he laid a hand on his shoulder.

'I couldn't get him out,' Ishmael said. 'I couldn't bring him up and what was I going to say even if I did? There was nothing I could say. I'd let him drown on account of what he said to me fixing in my head.' Helplessly he gestured. 'I swam back to the bank and lay there thinking how there was nothing I could do. I don't know how long I stayed there but in the end I got a ride back the way we'd come. I didn't hitchhike, I stowed away in a farm truck that pulled over so the driver could take a leak. He never knew I was there. He just took off into the brush and when he climbed back in the cab I was already hiding in the bed.'

He got to his feet, almost stumbled with the chains and Quarrie had to take his arm to stop him toppling all the way down the bank.

Looking up at him Clara was crying, tears working her cheeks. 'There was no cornfield, no game of hide-and-seek?'

Ishmael stared at the railroad cars once again. 'No,' he said. 'There was just me and my brother, that river right there, and a count that went on too long.'

*

Isaac's remains were buried with his father in a grave Clara commissioned back in Fannin County. She was there for the service along with Nancy McClain and Mr Palmer, as well as Quarrie, Pious and James. Ishmael was granted special dispensation and he was brought over by armed guards from the hospital at Bellevue.

When the service was over and the coffin in the ground, Ishmael tossed a handful of dirt. Quarrie tossed a handful, as did his son. Afterwards Quarrie took a moment to speak to Nancy.

'How is he?' he said, looking on as the guard walked Ishmael back to the hospital van.

'He's OK,' Nancy said. 'He's Ishmael at least, and that's a good thing. Ever since that day we brought him to the Red River we've seen no sign of Isaac, and the Ishmael you saw today is exactly how he's been. He's quiet, John Q; he's not aggressive anymore, he's contemplative and keeps himself to himself.'

'No relapses?' Quarrie said.

'Not so far. It doesn't mean there won't be any, of course, but the therapy is getting better all the time. We've a new doctor at Bellevue who accepts the theory of Dissociative Identity Disorder and that's reflected in the treatment Ishmael is getting. We're not in the 1940s anymore, thank God. We've moved on, and what they thought back then about Miss Annie is not what they think now. If Ishmael does have a relapse we can walk him back to that day on the river as many times as we need to until he realizes that Isaac is dead and he kept him alive because he just can't deal with the guilt.'

Quarrie watched Ishmael climb into the van. 'That's good,' he said. 'I'm glad he's doing OK, if only for Clara's sake.' He turned to Nancy again. 'What about Miss Annie though? How's she getting along?' In his mind's eye he could see her in that cell once more, surrounded by stick-like kids.

'She's doing pretty well,' Nancy said. 'She sees Ishmael from time to time. It's part of her therapy and it's also part of his. They know who each other is of course – that much at least was accomplished

278

by Dr Beale the night it all kicked off. The new doctor allows them to play cards together once a week because that's what Miss Annie likes, and Ishmael seems to look forward to it as well.'

She glanced to where the driver of the van was waiting. 'The truth is Miss Annie is better than she's ever been. Now and again I catch a glimpse of the old Peggy I used to know and I've not seen her in twenty-five years. She's still not allowed to mix with the other women and she's on heavy medication, of course. But her room's been painted and she's finally given up that doll.'

Taking Quarrie's hand she gave it a gentle squeeze. 'She keeps asking me when you're going to come and visit though, and I've been meaning to call.'

'Visit? You mean she remembers me?'

'John Q, Miss Annie never forgets a thing. You told her your name and that you were a Texas Ranger and how you were there to protect her. She's always asking about you.'

Quarrie looked beyond her to where Pious had his arm around James's shoulders, the two of them leaning against the door of his car.

'Is that a fact?' he said, squaring his hat and tracing a finger across the brim. 'Well, if she's waiting on me to visit with her then I guess it's time I did.'